CLUES, CASH, PIECES OF MURDER

D.B. ELROGG

A MILO RATHKEY MYSTERY

Clues, Cash, Pieces of Murder
A Milo Rathkey Mystery

ISBN 979-8-9856252-4-0 (Paperback)
ISBN 979-8-9856252-5-7 (eBook)
ISBN 979-8-9856252-6-4 (Hardcover)

If you wish to contact the authors, you may email them at: authors@dbelrogg.com

Cover Art by John Edgar Harris

Dedicated to The Real Morrie Wolf—You Know Who You Are

SPECIAL THANKS TO

STAN JOHNSON
JODY EVANS
DR. ELENA CABB
DOUG OSELL
NICK GOLDBERG
PIPER GOLDBERG
ROB RAINEY
ROBERT FRASER

1

Duncan 'Chip' Campbell IV, patriarch of the Campbell family, stared out the huge wall size window framing his beloved Island Lake. The minister droned on in the family's generations-old hunting lodge turned makeshift chapel. Chip longed to be hunting or fishing on this crisp, sunny spring day. Instead, he was trapped, listening to a eulogy of someone not considered family. To Chip's mind, not being family was tantamount to being disposable.

"Our dear friend, Lewis Rutledge, loving husband to Blair—who, as you all remember, was taken from us far too soon." The minister stopped, sighed, and affected a downward gaze, all practiced to perfection. "Lewis was also a caring father to Mazy, who is devastated at his passing." The minister's gaze lifted and nodded to the young black-haired woman whose downcast eyes were focused on her husband's tapping foot. "And let us remember he was…" the minister continued.

The family gopher! Clayton Campbell thought to himself while cleaning his nails, head bowed. Clayton, whom the family called Clay, was Chip's younger brother. He also wanted to be gone from this place, but it was the golf course—where he made many of the family's business deals—that called to Clay.

Mazy Campbell Rutledge Mason reached out her hand to halt her husband's nervous heel tapping, neck cracking, and ceiling gazing. "Michael, stop! We're at daddy's funeral for God's sake!" she whispered. Mazy was mourning twice. Not only had her father died suddenly, but the family had denied her request to place his ashes next to her mother's in the inner circle of the family vault. "Family members only," Chip had said. "No outsiders."

Michael, sitting at the end of the family semicircle of chairs, bristled at Mazy's admonishment. His placement at the gathering did not escape him. His father-in-law also spent his whole married life on the outside edge of the family circle.

Michael looked around the large, almost empty room, surveying the sparse funereal gathering. A few invited outsiders sat behind the family. *Probably Lewis' radio station employees,* Michael thought.

An imposing man in a dress green military uniform sat to the left of the minister, rather like a bishop or visiting dignitary. From his perch, he had a clear view of everyone and everything in the hall.

For the seven years Michael had been married to Mazy, he knew the man as Major Peters, the guy in charge of compound security. He thought the man to be a fraud.

The droning platitudes had ended with the announcement that the family would like everyone to join them in the solarium for refreshments. People began shuffling in that direction. The officious Peters rose, stepping behind the non-family members, herding them, per the minister's direction, to the solarium.

§

Milo Rathkey, the curly, brown-haired, scruffy PI, stood with his hands shoved into the pockets of his new spring windbreaker. His eyes began roaming over the Bingham Hardware wall of batteries. He needed four double-A batteries for his camera drone, but his need proved to be too simple. His choices were packs of sixteen, sixty-four, or masses of batteries in a giant, yellow plastic container called a battery caddy. Every battery Milo could ever need all in a convenient container, or so the label advertised.

Milo reached for the outlandish caddy and just as quickly snatched his hand back. *What the hell am I doing?* He chided himself. *I don't need two hundred batteries!* He jerked the sixteen pack off the spindle, blamed his momentary loss of perspective on having inherited too much money. Having made his selection, he found his way to the checkout counter.

Bingham Hardware's interior was a dark and dusty landmark destination for hardware buffs—no appliances or flooring. Otherwise, it had everything in the way of hardware, absolutely everything anyone would want or need across its aisles of merchandise from the tiniest screw to an obsolete buggy whip holder.

Bingham was not weekend crowded, but Milo thought too crowded for a Monday. Springtime do-it-yourselfers were intent on sprucing up their yards for the outdoor season. Milo stood in line behind a short, stocky man gripping seven ear flapped, brown plaid winter hats as if they could run away. Milo absently wondered why anyone would buy seven winter hats at all, but especially in May. *Maybe they're on sale.*

"You must be getting a good deal on those hats?" he mentioned to the man, making what he thought was friendly conversation.

"None of your business," the man mumbled. His grip on the hats tightened as if Milo were threatening to rip them out of his hands.

Clearly, the hat man was not in the mood to shoot the breeze, so Milo's attention drifted to a box of motorcycle-racing fliers on a rack near the checkout. He recognized the track, Brainerd Speedway. Milo had worked security there forever ago. Picking up the flier, he marveled at how the track had changed. Either it was a trick of the photography, or the facility had been seriously updated.

Hat guy bellied up to the counter and dropped his trea-sured hats on the counter, keeping his hands encircling the pile, making sure no one could snatch one away. As the clerk rang them up, one caused the cash register to chirp.

"Sir," the clerk said, "it seems this hat has already been purchased."

"No, it wasn't. I'm doing it now! I want it!" the man shouted.

"I can't ring it up. The register won't let me!"

With fingers splayed on the counter, the man leaned into the clerk and growled. "I need all the hats!"

Milo wondered if the situation would escalate, but the clerk put the hat in the bag. "No problem, sir. Since we already sold this hat, I'll just give it to you."

The man was silent as he watched the rest of the transaction. He paid in cash, grabbed his bag of hats, counting all seven one more time, then left the store.

Milo tossed his pack of sixteen batteries on the counter. "There goes a man who loves brown plaid hats," he said to the clerk, who laughed.

"We've had those ugly hats since I started working here two years ago," the clerk said. "Good riddance."

Milo looked around the store. "Maybe you'll sell that buggy whip holder in the back today."

"You laugh. We sold two last year. That's the only one left."

Milo took his batteries, stuffed the racetrack flier in his pocket, and exited into the bright sunshine.

§

Michael Mason, drink in hand, approached Larry Latto, the manager of KDDW, his late father-in-law's radio station. "The family is eager to end this stupid puzzle contest."

Latto's nearly bald head sported wisps of stringy blond hair. He squinted at this stranger and dabbed his handkerchief on his forehead. "I'm sorry. Who are you?"

Chip Campbell, overhearing the exchange, quickly interceded. Holding out his hand, he thanked Latto for coming. "We all miss Lewis. His death is such a loss to us all."

"It is. We enjoyed his visits to the station. He was fun and cared about the station and all of us," Latto said.

"Yes, he did. I remember him talking often about how proud he was of all of you and shared wonderful stories. Have you gotten a drink yet?" Chip asked, pointing to the bar. "Lewis wouldn't want any of his friends to be without some of his fine Scotch Whiskey."

As Latto moved away toward the bar, Chip stepped in front of Michael, stopping him from pursuing Latto. "Why would you take it upon yourself to discuss anything family related with an employee?"

"I…I know the family wants this contest to stop. I was helping."

"The family doesn't need your help. You should have stopped Lewis from doing this irritating contest to begin with, but you were too busy playing with your motorcycles."

Save me from the hobbies of outsiders! Chip thought.

§

Police Lt. Ernie Gramm leaned back with his hands behind his head looking over the finished paperwork on the Warren murder, a shooting during a particularly divisive card game. He presented a rare smile at the ease with which he and Sgt. Robin White had closed this case. The perp had shot the deceased in front of three other people. It was the sort of case Duluth's other homicide detective, Doug O'Dell, usually caught. He hoped maybe some of O'Dell's karma was rubbing off.

White finished securing her long, dark ponytail as she poked her head into his office. "Early lunch?"

Gramm nodded and gestured for her to come in and sit down. "Strange goings on. We have to keep busy, or at least look busy."

"Why?"

"The deputy chief said that there's some radio contest that's gotten out of hand. People are coming from all over, vandalizing, digging up lawns, and sleeping in parks, trying to find some silly puzzle pieces. Anyone of us just sitting around could end up on what he calls contest duty."

"Who listens to the radio?"

"Me! But apparently, this contest has spread on social media, so it's reaching beyond Duluth radio listeners. The deputy chief showed us three or four blogs about it in the morning meeting. These nut bags aren't our normal tourists. They don't care about the lake or the Aerial Lift Bridge. Like I said, they just want to find some hidden treasure. Have you heard of a Lewis Rutledge?"

"No. Why?"

"He owns KDDW and KPIR-FM. He's the one who came up with this cockamamie contest. Both the chief and the sheriff asked him to stop it, but he refused."

"I like treasure hunting. How does this one work?" White asked.

"I didn't get the whole thing. He hides money, gives clues. If you find the money, you also find a puzzle piece that leads to a bigger payday."

"How many puzzle pieces?"

"I don't know, and I don't want to know. Just look busy."

"But first lunch?"

"Definitely."

§

Exhausted after his battery errand, Milo relaxed on the back terrace of Lakesong, the Jacobean style estate he co-owned with his benefactor's son, Sutherland McKnight, and Sutherland's wife, Agnes. Agnes had been Lakesong's house manager, then morphed into Milo's personal assistant after she and Sutherland began *keeping company*. Now she was Sutherland's wife and co-owner of Lakesong. Her current status had Milo confused.

Agnes also decided to take her coffee break on the back terrace. Surprised to see Milo, she joined him, settling in to one of the terrace's padded wrought-iron chairs. Looking over the expansive back lawn, she sighed as she watched and listened to Lake Superior's waves lapping up on the gravel shore. Agnes marveled at the blue water, which stretched for miles beyond the horizon. "I never tire of the lake—so soothing," she said to Milo. "It's a friend."

Milo nodded. He never thought of the lake as his friend, but he wasn't opposed to it.

"Sutherland's aunt is arriving Wednesday. We are putting her up in the yellow guest suite," Agnes informed Milo.

"Has Sutherland gotten over the shock yet?" Milo asked.

Agnes glanced at him. "Have you?"

"I don't know."

"It's strange what families don't share with children. Sutherland didn't know his mother was a twin."

"An identical twin," Milo added. "Looking at a picture of Lana Freskin is like looking at an older Laura McKnight."

A deer family came out of the woods to drink at the water's edge. This Disney scene was a Lakesong normal.

"How's the remodeling coming?" Milo asked, referring to the work on the second and third floor on the north side of the house.

"We have talked over some ideas and have contacted an architect. I would like to get going soon so I can stop using the green guest suite just to take a bath and store my clothes."

As the deer moved into the cover of the trees, Milo asked, "Are you still my personal assistant?"

Agnes sighed. "I don't know about that either. You haven't fired me yet, have you?"

§

Ham Gilbert paused in the doorway of the Rasa Bar, waiting for his eyes to adjust to the dark interior. His partner, Shane Bell, standing at the bar, was downing a shot of whiskey with a beer chaser. Benny, the Rasa's bartender and part-time muscle for gangster Morrie Wolf, collected the empty beer glasses and asked Bell if he wanted another boilermaker.

Shane nodded as Gilbert stepped up onto the bar stool, centered himself, and ordered a beer.

Benny delivered the requested beverages and moved on to other customers. Shane tried to down the shot, spilling some of the whiskey. "Damn it!" He grabbed his wrist, lowered his head to the shot glass, lifting it up just enough to pour the brown liquid down his throat.

"Geezus, Shane. What's wrong with you?" Ham asked. "Maybe you should quit drinkin' for a while."

Shane turned to him with a malevolent stare. "Maybe you should mind your own business. Tell me about those hats."

"There weren't anything," Ham Gilbert lied.

Bell's left arm shot out, grabbing Gilbert by the back of the neck. "If you're lying to me, I'll kill you!" Bell hissed.

"I ain't lyin' Shane. I've got 'em in my truck. Rip 'em apart yourself. There was nothing!"

The ruckus caught Bennie's attention. He walked over to the two strangers. "If you two have a problem, take it outside."

Shane let go of Ham's neck. "No problem."

"Good. Keep it that way," Benny advised.

Ham rubbed his neck while looking sideways at Shane in case another attack was coming. "We was wrong, Shane. Or someone beat us to it. One hat had a rip in it already."

Shane took a gulp of his beer.

"Besides," Ham continued his lie, "Duluth's a big place. Maybe the clue is for somewhere else, some other store. We can keep tryin' between jobs."

Shane swayed, caught himself from slamming into Ham. "Duluth is stupid. You're stupid. You look like a ham." Shane drained his beer and banged the glass on the bar. "Stupid name! Stupid Ratface!"

"Why call me Ratface?"

"No. You're a ham. He's a Ratface! I…Ratface! The Navy. I really hated that…"

"The Navy? Don't go into all that again. Shane gave him another angry stare. Benny gave Shane him another beer. "Milo Ratface. No pension. Milo friggin Ratface, no money. I could be sittin' on my ass."

Benny left the bar and walked over to his employer, Morrie Wolf, who was looking over last night's betting sheets in his usual corner booth. Morrie, dressed in his customary striped sports coat and skinny tie, didn't look up. "Benny?"

"Two guys at the end of the bar are talking about that radio contest and one of them mentioned the name Milo—called him Ratface. How many Milo Ratfaces can there be in this town?"

Morrie almost smiled. "Find out more." He motioned toward the bar.

Benny headed back to the bar just as Shane was trying to leave. Benny poured them both another beer. "Sit down. On the house, gents."

2

"Yesterday morning I saw a man who bought seven hats at the hardware store," Milo said as Sutherland and Agnes sat down to breakfast in Lakesong's morning room with its floor to ceiling windows. "They were winter hats—ugly winter hats—bad winter hats. I need to know why."

"I need a cup of coffee," Agnes said, moving over to the ever-present coffee urn.

"Didn't you ask him?" Sutherland questioned.

"He said it wasn't any of my business. He wasn't pleasant about it."

"Was it?" Agnes asked, returning to the table with her coffee.

"Was it what?"

"Any of your business?"

"Well, no, but if it's May and you're going to buy seven winter hats from a hardware store in plain sight of other customers, you should expect to be questioned."

"I have a question," Agnes stated. "What am I?"

"You're a girl?" Sutherland offered.

"That is so wrong on so many levels, but thank you for noticing." Agnes grinned at her smiling husband. "Milo and I were talking yesterday, and he asked if I was still his personal assistant. Remember, I started out as the house manager working for both of you, but Sutherland, you thought it would be *untoward* to work for you while we were dating, so..."

"I always wondered," Milo interrupted, "*untoward* to whom? The cats?"

Annie, the cat who was waiting for her bacon, meowed. Jet blinked and flipped over on his back, waiting for someone to rub his belly.

"This cat is really concerned with *untoward*," Milo said, doing the belly rub duty. Jet purred and grabbed Milo's hand—claws in.

"Despite evidence to the contrary," said Sutherland, defending his decision, "the cats are very proper and did not approve of my dating an employee."

Martha, the Lakesong chef-in-residence, entered the morning room with Milo's eggs, hash browns, bacon, and toast, plus Sutherland's green vegetable smoothie.

Agnes, being the only one whose breakfast order varied, decided on vanilla yogurt with whatever fruit Martha had in the kitchen.

"I have bananas."

"Perfect. Today is my running day."

"Are you going to be a running personal assistant, a running house manager, or a running co-owner?" Milo asked.

"That's what I'm wondering."

"Which one is cheaper?" Milo asked.

"I don't know. So muddy. I want to know my title, so I can properly pay myself. I think I'll give myself a raise."

"Why? Are you going to buy seven hats?" Milo asked.

§

The early morning fog had burned off the St. Louis River. Ollie Luthinen and his buddy Red Maki had been fishing under the Oliver Bridge since dawn. They already had a walleye and a couple of crappies when Red got a big one on the line. "Be careful, Red, it's gonna get away."

"I know how to reel it in, Ollie. Get the net!" Red fought the fish—reeling in the line, pulling up the rod repeatedly.

Ollie steadied himself as he leaned over the boat, ready with the net. Red grunted as he worked the fish. "It looks like a sturgeon, Red," Ollie yelled.

"Uff da." Red was disappointed. "Too bad we gotta throw it back."

Ollie agreed. "Yeah, still catch and release 'til the popula-tion grows. Nice of 'em to restock the sturgeon, though." He netted the fish and showed Red, remarking at how ugly it was.

"Careful to avoid those sharp teeth, Ollie. I think it's prehistoric," Red remarked.

Ollie removed the hook and threw the fish back in.

"Hate to see it go back, but you can't get caught takin' one home," Red lamented as he rebated his hook.

The two old friends had been fishing together since childhood and now that both were retired, they spent as many mornings as they could on the water—Red in his checked shirts, Ollie in his tan, multi-pocketed fishing vest. "Maybe we should pack it in, doncha think?" Red said. "We can't eat too many fish from the river, you know mercury."

"They're cleaning it up, though."

Red was silent.

"I said they're cleaning it up, Red."

More silence.

"You havin' the big one over there, Red?"

Red had been staring at the water between their boat and the shore. "No catch and release on that, Ollie."

"Whaddaya sayin'?"

"Look!" Red pointed.

Ollie squinted, trying to find what Red was pointing at "What's that?"

"Looks like a body," Red said simply.

"Oh gosh. It sure is. We should call someone."

Red already had his phone out and dialed 911.

"911, what's your emergency?" The female operator asked.

"This is Red Maki. I got that place down on highway double A."

"Yeah, Red, I know, the one with the metal roof. What's going on?"

"Ollie Luthinen and I are fishing under the Oliver Bridge, and I just caught a heck of a sturgeon."

"Gotta throw that back, Red."

"I know, we done that, but then I says to Ollie, can't throw that back."

"What's that?"

"A body. It's floating about twenty yards away. I think it's caught on a log."

"A body, you say? A feller or a gal?"

"Head down, can't say. We can track it. You may want to tell the sheriff."

"He's out in South Range. I'll tell the deputy."

"Which one?"

"Pokema."

"Oh yeah, good guy. We'll wait for him."

"Say Red…what side of the river is he on?"

"Don't know if it's a he, but now that you mention it, I think he's on the Minnesota side. Headin' towards Mud Lake."

"That's Duluth. I'll call Duluth PD."

"Oh, okay."

Ollie reached in his bait box. "Might as well keep fishin' 'til they get here."

Red agreed.

§

"Creedence, I almost bought a box of batteries yesterday," Milo blurted at his financial advisor, Creedence Durant.

Creedence looked at his phone as if the phone were crazy.

"It was a big, yellow, plastic box with more than a hundred batteries that I would never use. I only needed four!"

"So, only buy four."

"I can't find just four, but that's not the point. I bought sixteen, but that isn't the point either."

"Let's get to that point, Milo." Creedence leaned back in his chair and stared out his Palladian window.

"I reached for that box of batteries and almost picked it up and bought it! I blame you."

"Are you going to leave me a bad review? *Durant makes money for his clients, but he can't stop them from buying a boat load of batteries.* That could ruin me."

"So, you admit it."

"Guilty. I didn't stop you from buying batteries."

"No, you just admitted you made me money."

Creedence leaned forward and put Milo on speaker. Milo's infrequent calls were an entertaining break in his day. "Yes. I'm so deeply sorry. Milo. Did you eat breakfast this morning?"

"Yes, but I just looked at all this tax stuff you sent me. I have more money this year than last year."

"It's May, Milo. I filed your taxes in April."

"Your point?"

"I sent the taxes to you back in February."

"Yeah, I was a little busy back then—murders and stuff like that. I just got around to reading them. The point is, I have more money now than I did last year."

"And?"

"That's why I picked up those batteries. I have all this money. I can just go buy things I don't need. It's disturbing."

Creedence folded his hands together and placed them on his rotund belly. "This is the way it works, Milo. John McKnight left you fifteen million dollars. The fifteen million collects interest and dividends. You make money, and you spend almost nothing."

"I bought a car! That's something."

"Good for you! If it were a Bugatti Veyron that would have dipped a little into your cash, but you bought a 1987 Mercedes 560SL. You even got a friend and family discount. If you want to keep your money from growing too quickly, give some to charity."

"I did. I gave some to the ovarian cancer people in memory of Laura McKnight."

"Lots more Milo. You have to give lots more."

"I'll keep that mind. What do I do about the battery thing?"

"I'll check and see if there are any support groups for people who buy too many batteries."

"I didn't buy them. I almost bought them."

"The first step to recovery. Look, Milo, I always enjoy our chat, but I have to go. Some of my saner clients are calling."

§

Sgt. White poked her head into Lt. Gramm's office. "Morning, having a good Tuesday?"

Gramm raised his bushy eyebrows. "What makes me think I'm not?"

"We have a floater."

"Where?"

"St. Louis River across from the Oliver, Wisconsin bridge. Before you ask, the body is firmly stuck on the Minnesota side. Forensics says it looks suspicious."

"It's forensics. They say everything looks suspicious. That river is as much in Wisconsin as it is in Minnesota. If this is murder, it could have happened in the Cheesehead state."

"Both Douglas County and St. Louis County Sheriff's departments are looking for a car. Doc Smith said he thinks the body went in upstream, maybe Jay Cooke."

Gramm smiled. "That would be St. Louis County, not the city of Duluth."

"But for now, the body is in Duluth. It's ours. So much for a dull Tuesday."

3

Chip Campbell was sitting on his back patio at the family compound, holding a piece of paper up to the sun. He did the same with the white envelope it came in. The envelope was bare, no address, no watermark, nothing. He found it this morning tacked to his porch support.

"What's so urgent?" his brother Clay called, hiking the two hundred yards from his own house.

"This!" Chip shouted, waving the envelope and paper. "This morning!"

Clay sat down, trying not to spill his coffee on his baby blue golfing pullover. "What is it?"

"It says, *Sins of the fathers are to be laid upon the children.*"

"It's a little early for the Old Testament, isn't it, brother? Someone is pushing your big, red paranoid button."

Chip turned to his brother. "Someone?" Chip snapped. "Who might *someone* be? It wasn't mailed: it was tacked to my porch post. We are in a gated compound. How would anyone get in without being seen? This," Chip waved the paper at Clay, "is an inside prank. Is it you pushing my big red paranoid button?"

Clay sneered and took a sip of coffee. "Oh, take a pill."

"If it wasn't you, who posted it? Where is the breech?"

Clay grabbed the envelope and inspected it. "Inside job, unless someone got by your resident bloodhound."

"No one gets past Peters. Who did this?"

"Calm down. It doesn't have to be family. We have groundskeepers, maids, cooks—a host of people who could have nailed this to your porch. Besides, there is no specific threat."

"I'm going to show it to Peters," Chip said.

Clay laughed, thinking of Major Peters—the Campbell family head of security—who spent much of the time riding his golf cart around the compound in full military uniform. "What's that pompous bastard supposed to do about it?"

"He has skills." Chip defended the man.

"Yeah, he can out drink the entire family. How do you know Peters didn't place that note?"

Chip set his jaw. "He's loyal, maybe the only one that is."

"How can you be so sure? What do you know about him? I don't even know his first name. Is Major his rank or his name?" Clay laughed.

Chip rose. "He's loyal and important to me. One day soon, you will thank me for keeping Peters around."

§

Lt. Gramm, never a watercraft person unless he was fishing, wished he had a place to sit down on the rocking police boat. Despite the sunshine, a chilly wind rushed down the St. Louis River, adding to Gramm's discomfort. Sgt. White didn't seem to notice the cold. Her gaze fixed on the forensics people and the medical examiner on their own boat ten yards ahead of them. Two technicians with long grappling hooked poles were pulling the body toward them, trying not to disturb any evidence—a difficult job on a bloated floater. One diver was in the water, removing any branches and debris that would stop the poles from forward motion.

"If that body comes apart, you're on your own," White said to Gramm.

"If that body comes apart, Doc Smith is on his own," Gramm countered.

Doc Smith had the same worry. "Easy, people." He admonished loud enough for Gramm and White to hear.

The diver submerged.

"Where's he going?" White whispered.

"Looking for anything that might have dropped, keys, knives, a nose."

"Ew!"

Finally freed, the body was being guided alongside the forensics boat. The diver reappeared in time to catch a stretcher-like device being lowered from a winch. He placed it under the body and gave a thumbs up. The winch motor whined as it lifted the branch ladened, dripping wet body up, swinging and lowering it onto the boat.

Doc Smith bent down out of sight of Gramm and White.

"Come on Doc, it's a drowning. I'm cold and tired," Gramm mumbled to himself. "Let's move this along."

When Doc Smith reemerged, he gave the signal for the forensics boat to move. As it turned and pulled alongside the police boat, he said. "Our floater is male, and I would guess a murder victim."

Gramm's bushy eyebrows lifted in surprise.

"He's got an ID—Harold Gilbert from Fortuna, North Dakota," Doc Smith advised.

"Why do people come to Duluth to die?" White asked, remembering a realtor from Minneapolis who died last summer.

"Isn't that my line?" Gramm asked.

Doc Smith held up the dead man's wallet to show that there was money inside. "It's wet, and everything is sticking together. I'll get you the exact amount. No robbery. However, no keys either."

"They could have floated out," Gramm said.

Smith shook his head. "I doubt it. He's a chubbo. Pants are tight. I had to cut the wallet out for an ID."

"Chubbo?" White questioned.

"It's a medical term," Gramm quipped.

§

Mazy Mason walked toward the family board room in the same lodge that yesterday hosted her father's funeral. The funeral props—chairs, podium, flowers—had been cleared as though it had never happened.

Standing outside the Campbell family boardroom, she closed her eyes and took in a large, cleansing breath. Grabbing the handle to one of the double doors, Mazy yanked it open and took her usual seat at the table. She pulled back her long, black hair, putting it up in a soft bun, which accentuated her thin, hawk-like features, a family trait.

Uncle Chip, lips drawn tight, eyes fixed on the table, was tapping his right hand as Mazy entered. Her other uncle, Clay, was filling his plate from the lunch buffet. Clay greeted her, made some passing remarks about the food—the specifics of which Mazy didn't hear and didn't care.

He brought his plate to the table and placed it next to his Bloody Mary sweating on the cocktail napkin. Placing the cloth napkin in his collar to protect his Caribbean blue golf sweater, Clay sat down to join the family.

Mazy's Great Aunt Greer sat in her usual chair, sipping her usual lemonade. She was staring at Chip and did not greet Mazy.

Mazy declined lunch and kept her eyes down on her folded hands, concentrating on her breathing, keeping her anger in check. All morning she had vacillated between sadness and the anger. A polite amount of sadness would be accepted. Her anger would not.

Chip called the meeting to order. Greer flipped open her notepad. Mazy always admired the glamor of her great aunt, who hid hair loss in dramatic silk hair wraps. Today's wrap was pink and gray to complement her long gray dress. It was the perfect foil for the diamond earrings and the four-strand diamond bracelet on the outside of the gray dress sleeve. Only Greer could pull this off without being gaudy.

Chip was about to speak when Greer interrupted, indicating there was new business that needed to be dealt with. Chip pursed his lips, not liking to have his agenda thwarted, but nodded for her to continue.

"I have received notice of a new LaPointe lawsuit against the Campbell family. The notice states the suit will be filed in the near future."

"What? Why would you get that letter?" Chip demanded. "That's important."

Greer stared at Chip, unfazed. "I handle all correspondence, Chip, even that which you consider too important for me." With that, she picked up her pen and waited to take the minutes.

Mazy cringed at the subservient position Greer had in the family dynamic. She was the oldest. She should be running the meeting, not taking notes and being told she was unimportant.

"I have a question," Mazy said, surprising herself at how calm she sounded.

Chip gave her a half condescending smile. "Mazy, I haven't officially started the meeting yet."

"This is a before-the-meeting question. No need for notes, Aunt Greer."

Clay put down his sandwich.

Aunt Greer closed her book.

"I was wondering why none of my cousins, your children, Chip and Clay, attended my father's funeral."

Chip lowered his head, peering sideways at Mazy—his habit when annoyed. "I can't speak for Clay, but the funeral was on a Monday. My children were at school."

"Same here," Clay said. "I think it's finals week."

"Yet, they all managed to be here for my mother's funeral, which was the same time last year," Mazy said, still under control.

Chip began biting his lip. "You're upset, but, simply put, your mother was a Campbell. When a family member dies, we are *all* obligated to pay our respects."

"And *we* clearly were not obligated to pay respects to my father." Mazy could feel her ire rising. She fought to keep it down.

"Mazy," Clay interrupted, "the family was more than well represented, especially since Lewis has caused us problems as of late."

"Problems is an understatement," Chip agreed. "Look Mazy, assuming you own that radio station now, it's time you put a stop to that deplorable contest your father started. We all know where it is leading. I don't want all those people digging around that old mine."

"People hunt and fish on that land all the time. What's the difference?" Mazy asked.

"None of those people are digging for treasure. We have allowed access to the land for generations, so none of the locals are curious about it," Chip said. "Mazy, stop that contest!"

Mazy wanted to scream but delivered her best Campbell business tone. "It's not that simple. This contest has been spread on blogs. People are showing up in Duluth from all over the country. My father's twelve clues have already aired. They're gone. They're out. No pulling them back."

"Twelve clues? It's a twelve-piece puzzle? Twelve people poking into our family business?"

"Twelve pieces is more than we knew before, Chip," Clay said.

"All you had to do was ask," Mazy challenged.

"We asked Lewis," Chip snapped. "He refused to tell us." Chip threw two puzzle pieces on the table. "We have spent thousands buying these two pieces from your father's damn treasure hunters, and we will be forced to spend more to stop this invasion of our privacy!"

Mazy laughed.

"What's so funny?" Chip barked.

"Daddy said you would."

§

Having spent the morning in a police boat on the St. Louis River, Lt. Gramm and Sgt. White were now following the medical examiner's boat to shore. Gramm was pleased to see a strong signal on his cell phone. He called Milo's number.

"Late lunch?" Milo asked hopefully.

"No!" Gramm snapped. "If you're not too busy being rich and famous, we need you down at Boy Scout Landing. It's off of Commonwealth…"

"I know where it is."

"We have a floater and are coming ashore there."

"Accident? Suicide?"

"Yeah, because I love to spend my day on the river investigating accidents."

"Why would someone buy seven bad winter hats?" Milo asked, as if that question followed the conversation.

"What?"

"Seven winter hats. Some guy bought them yesterday in Bingham Hardware. I wonder why."

"His head was cold. Mine is! Get down here! Now! This guy's head was caved in. No hat."

"On my way."

§

Morrie sipped his coffee. He rarely drank alcohol. Motioning for Milosh to join him, he said, "There are more strangers in the bar today. Benny says they're all talking about puzzle pieces, like those two guys yesterday. Where's Leroy?" Morrie asked, referring to Leroy Thompson, one of his minor employees.

"I haven't seen him in three days. He says he's sick."

"Bring him flowers and find out."

Milosh knew the flowers would not be necessary. If Leroy wasn't laid up, he was going to be. "Anything else, boss?"

"Invite Milo in for a little chat."

"A friendly invite, or the other way?" Milosh asked.

"I think you can extend a friendly invite."

"Which one first?"

"Leroy. I don't do sick leave."

§

When Milo arrived at the Boy Scouts Landing, Gramm, White, and the Medical Examiner, Doctor Cyril Smith, were standing by the dock. The covered body was on a gurney awaiting transport.

"Nice of you to join us, Mr. Consultant," Gramm said.

"Have you solved my hat mystery yet?" Milo asked.

White looked at Gramm for an explanation.

"Milo doesn't have enough to do, and somebody let him go to the hardware store by himself."

White dismissed it all as a Gramm-Milo moment, not worth wasting her time.

"So, what do we have?" Milo asked.

Doc Smith pulled the sheet down so the cops could see the face. White—not a fan of floaters—turned away. "Bashed in the back of the head and dumped in the river, Milo. I have to get him back to the table to see if he was alive or dead when he went into the water."

"I've already asked if he could have fallen and hit his head," Gramm said.

"Not unless he fell several times, hitting his head each time and then rolled himself into the water," Doc Smith said. "For the Lieutenant's sake, I won't rule it out here."

"Why is this our case?" Milo asked.

Gramm sighed. "The body was on our side of the river. It probably went in upstream, but according to the deputy chief, St. Louis County is strapped for people, and we owe them a favor. We'll take the lead. They will assist."

Milo walked over to look closer at the ashen, wrinkled, swollen face.

"We need to know how long the body's been in the water," Gramm said to Doc Smith.

"Really? I wouldn't have guessed that. I learn something new every day," Smith sneered.

"So, getting back to my problem," Milo said, squatting down by the body. "I went to the hardware store yesterday. Some guy bought seven winter hats, wouldn't tell me why."

"Again, with the hats," Gramm said. "Why are you telling us that?"

"Because I'm looking at my hat man."

White and Gramm stared at Milo.

"Of course," White said.

"Let's go back to the office," Gramm said, "and leave the dead to the Doc."

"Harold," Smith said.

"What?" Gramm asked.

"Harold. The dead guy's name is Harold."

"Right, Harold. Let's go to the office and leave *Harold* to Doc Smith."

On the way to the cop shop, Milo's phone came to life with "A Boy Named Sue," Sutherland's ringtone. Milo answered with a question. "Remember Hat Man?"

"I thought I called you," Sutherland objected, "but I'll play along. Yes, I remember you talking about Hat Man."

"They just fished him out of the river."

"As in dead?"

"Face down."

"Because he bought six hats?"

"Seven."

"So, I take it he is your new murder case."

"I suggested he slipped several times, crushing his skull each time, but that theory was rejected in favor of his being beaten with a blunt object."

"Rather graphic for a pleasant Tuesday afternoon, Milo. For my part, I sold that commercial property on First Street to a guy with no hat."

"And I need to know that, why?"

"I thought we were sharing what we did today. You're doing some mundane murder thing while I was again leading the exciting life of a realtor."

"Okay, I'll shut up. You called me."

"Yes, I did. Aunt Lana is arriving tomorrow. She confirmed it this morning. I thought you'd like to know."

"Your Aunt Lana, identical twin to your mother that I found several weeks ago. It took one Google search and a phone call. It was a tough case. I think the payment is horribly overdue."

"That's the one. Because you knew my mother before I did, I thought you would like to be there."

"Sutherland, I live in Lakesong. I'll be there."

"You're right. You're right. Good."

"You're nervous, aren't you?"

"It's the pictures—she looks like my mother. It's freaky."

"Are you going to pick her up from the airport?"

"Agnes offered to do that."

"House manager Agnes? My personal assistant Agnes? Or your wife Agnes?"

Sutherland sighed. "I don't know. Do you think it matters?"

"Pet a cat."

"Pet a cat?"

"Works for me. I've just arrived at the cop shop. I've got to go talk wrinkled, waterlogged floaters."

"Oh, please don't share any more. I may need to adopt an office cat who won't like me either."

Milo clicked off, figuring Sutherland would be just fine.

Gramm and White were already ensconced in Gramm's office when Milo walked in. "What took you so long?" Gramm asked, stretching his back.

"Sutherland is upset."

"Does he know the dead guy?" White asked from her usual chair in front of Gramm's desk.

"No. His Aunt is coming to visit."

Gramm looked at White. "Have you ever noticed that much of what Milo says has no point?"

"Except when it does."

"His Aunt is an identical twin to his late mother. He's never seen her before except she looks like his mother. So, he has seen her, but not really."

"Good to know," Gramm said. "Now then, as to your hat man…"

"If I knew he was going to be murdered, I would have pressed him about the hats."

"Tell us again what happened."

Milo leaned back in the chair, about to speak, when Officer Kate Preston, the fourth member of Gramm's team, came in wheeling her own chair. "I understand we have a floater."

"Milo's hat man," Gramm said.

Preston sat down. "I'll just sit here and take notes, even if none of this makes sense."

Gramm sighed. "She's not afraid of us anymore."

"Milo, you were about to tell us about your encounter with Hat Man," White said, trying to keep the team on track.

"I was picking up four batteries at the hardware store when I discovered they don't sell four batteries in a pack anymore. You have to buy at least…"

"Milo, if you keep babbling, I'm going to shoot you in the knee," Gramm threatened.

"As I was saying before I was so rudely interrupted, I picked up a sixteen pack of double-A's and went to the check-out counter. The guy ahead of me was buying seven ugly, brown, plaid, winter hats."

"It's spring!" Preston said.

"Exactly. I asked him why, and he told me to shove off."

"So, this morning two fishermen find Hat Man floating face down in the St. Louis River," Gramm said. "Milo is a suspect."

"Were they using jiggers?" Milo asked.

Preston started to laugh, remembering being with Milo when he learned about jiggers from two fishermen in a bait shop and archery range.

"Milo, you are particularly random today," White said.

"I'm nervous."

"Why?" Preston asked.

"Sutherland's aunt is coming to visit."

"Why are *you* nervous?"

"She is Sutherland's mother's identical twin. I knew Sutherland's mother before Sutherland was born. I grew up in Lakesong. Remember, my mother was the cook. I agree with Sutherland. It's going to be freaky."

"Would shooting you in both knees help?" Gramm asked.

"I doubt it," Milo said.

"Pity. Preston, we need background information on Harold Gilbert from Fortuna, North Dakota. Why is he in Duluth? Does he have a car, and where is it now?"

"On it," Preston said, wheeling her chair back out into the bullpen area.

"See Milo, that's how it's done. No nonsense about jiggers."

Milo stood. "I have to go home and pet a cat."

Gramm sighed, "Go!"

"I alerted Ralph at the Coast Guard. We will need his expertise to figure out where the body went into the water," White said.

"Good. Doc Smith has to tell us how long the body was in the water first," Gramm added.

"You know those two guys who found the body had several pretty good-looking walleyes," White said. "I wonder if they *were* using..."

"If you say jiggers, I'm shipping you to traffic."

"We should have asked."

4

Leroy Thompson, dressed in his signature white suit and purple shirt, tried to look important as Milosh ushered him into the Rasa Bar. Leroy's goatee had grown in since he was forced to shave it off during his recent incarceration. "Hi Boss," he said to Morrie, with more enthusiasm than he was actually feeling. Leroy's tongue kept touching his lower lip, which was cut and swelling—a little hello delivered by Milosh.

Morrie was reading the morning paper and did not look up as Milosh pushed Leroy unceremoniously into Wolf's customary booth at the back of the Rasa Bar.

"Leroy, you disappoint me."

"I'm sorry, Boss. I was looking to make us some extra cash."

"Leroy, when you make *us* money, it somehow doesn't include me."

"That's in the past, Boss. That's all in the past. We're a team now. I'm paying off my debt. I learned my lesson. We're a team now."

Morrie looked up. Leroy flinched. "Leroy, if you keep screwing around, you're gonna get cut from the team. Get it?"

Leroy swallowed. "Loud and clear, Boss."

"Explain how you were going to make *us* money?"

"There's this radio station contest, puzzle pieces. I was figurin' the clues. You know, to see if there's anything in it for us."

"And?"

"Outside people are paying big money for these pieces. To begin with, I figured on finding a few and selling 'em to these outsiders—cutting you in, of course."

Morrie went back to his newspaper. "Do you have any of these puzzle pieces?"

"No, the clues are hard, but the suckers payin' big bucks don't know that. I figure I can buy a puzzle and use some of those pieces. They won't know the difference."

Morrie looked up again. "Leroy, I swear you get dumber every day. Have you seen any of these pieces? Do you know what they look like?"

Leroy thought for a minute. "Not exactly."

"But you plan to sell them to people who have purchased puzzle pieces and know what they look like."

"I'll tell them they bought scam puzzle pieces. My puzzle pieces are real. I got a touch, Boss. I can talk people into things."

"If this is an example, don't bother. This is over. Get to work!"

§

Milo walked out into the cop shop parking lot and stopped cold. A familiar black Lincoln was parked next to his old Honda. Milosh, Morrie Wolf's bodyguard, was standing with his arms folded over his massive chest. Milo noticed that Benny, the Rasa bartender, was sitting in the Lincoln's front passenger seat. Milo's heart beat a tad faster as he continued toward the Honda.

"You know, Milo, you need to get rid of this piece of junk. I'm told you're a rich guy. Buy something classy."

"On a chilly afternoon, you suddenly felt the need to come into the police parking lot to insult my car?" Milo asked.

Milosh smiled. A good sign. "Mr. Wolf would like to speak with you. You could follow us to the Rasa, or we could go old school."

"Throw a bag over my head and dump me in the backseat?"

"Your choice."

"I got an idea. Why don't I follow you?"

Milosh got back in the Lincoln and peeled out. Milo jumped in the Honda and followed with far less urgency. He knew how to find the Rasa.

As was his custom, Morrie didn't look up when Milo entered the bar. Milo stood by the front door looking over the clientele. The usual unsavory customers were at the bar getting an early start to the evening. To his left, he noticed that three of the people in the front booth were wearing trendy hiking outfits looking as though they had wandered into the wrong bar.

In the mornings, Morrie's attention was on last night's betting sheets or the morning paper. This afternoon, he was reading a book—Ron Bello's book, *The Life and Death and Death Again of Harper Gain,* in which Milo played a significant role.

"I can autograph that for you," Milo offered as he slid into the back booth.

Morrie looked up. "Why? You didn't write it."

Milo wondered why only Morrie seemed to grasp that point. "Why are you reading it?"

"I like to keep up on what goes on in my town." Morrie took a Duluth Public Library bookmark, placed it between the pages, and closed the book. "Do you think I don't read?"

"I would never think that." *Duluth Public Library?* "Why am I here?"

"You see those three people in the first booth by the window?"

Milo didn't need to turn around. "Two men, trendy hiking clothes, lite beers. A woman sipping wine. I noticed them."

"Is that odd to you?"

"Yeah, I didn't know you sold lite beer," Milo said, surprised at himself for being so flip with Morrie. *Stop it, Milo!* he chided himself.

Morrie didn't react. "I don't know them. Strangers have been coming in here all week. Why?"

"I have no idea," Milo said.

"One of them mentioned your name. He called you Milo Ratface. Not totally wrong." Morrie almost smiled.

Milo was about to speak but stopped.

"Sound familiar, Milo?"

"Got a description?"

Morrie motioned to Benny to come over.

"Yeah, Boss?"

"Tell Milo about the guy who mentioned Ratface."

"How old was he?" Milo asked.

"I don't know. Maybe forty, forty-five. His name was Shane. He had cheap tattoos—anchors on his arms and neck. He didn't like Milo Ratface much. The guy was drunk."

"Anchors? Probably some guy from the Navy. I could have arrested him."

"See, Milo, that's your problem," Morrie said. "You go around arresting people, and they get a bad opinion about you."

Milo had a smart-ass answer but figured he had already pressed his luck. "Was he alone?"

"No. He had a buddy—younger, quiet, not drunk. Didn't seem to know you. This Shane guy called him Ham. He looked like a ham, short and wide."

"What's your interest?" Milo asked Morrie.

"Like I said, I got strangers in the bar. It's distracting some of the help." Morrie looked in the direction of Leroy, who was restocking the bar.

Milo could see Leroy's swollen lip. "Leroy looks like he's had some interpersonal problems. Has Leroy been distracted?"

"I don't discuss personnel matters, Milo. You're here to discuss the guy who called you Ratface."

"Shane, a guy who might have known me in the Navy, who doesn't like me."

Morrie nodded.

"That was twenty years ago. I don't remember any Shane. As for his friend, they fished a short, wide guy out of the St. Louis River this morning."

Morrie didn't react. "Nice of you to stop by Milo. If you learn more, I would appreciate you keeping me up to date."

Taking his cue to leave, Milo stood up. "My pleasure."

Morrie watched Milo leave for a few seconds before calling Milosh over. "Someone might have offed this Ham guy—dumped him in the St. Louis River. Make sure our boy Leroy wasn't freelancing."

§

"Ashley—you know, my PT person—says I'm officially finished with the therapy on my shoulder," Sutherland said to Agnes as they enjoyed a predinner drink in the family room which had become Lakesong's informal dining room. "I'm back to my old vibrant self."

"At least until I knock you off your bike again," Agnes said, making light of her necessary action several months ago that saved Sutherland's life.

Sutherland rotated his shoulder. "Try not to do it again. When Ashley first started working on me, it hurt!"

"Aw, poor baby." Agnes leaned her head against his shoulder just as Milo came in from parking his Honda in the garage.

"Morrie Wolf reads books," he blurted.

Both Agnes and Sutherland stared at him.

"He was reading Ron's book today. Not only that, there is also a chance it came from the library. Morrie Wolf may have a library card!"

"Have a drink, Milo," Sutherland said. "Yesterday you were obsessed by a man with hats. Today you're hallucinating about a gangster at the library."

Milo nodded and began making himself a vodka gimlet at the family room bar. "It wasn't a hallucination. Morrie reads library books, and, like I told you, Hat Man is dead. Fished him out of the St. Louis River."

Sutherland blanched. "Did Morrie kill him?"

Milo stopped the drink halfway to his mouth. "No! Where would you get that idea?"

Sutherland turned to Agnes. "Where would I get that idea?"

Agnes shook her head. "I'm enjoying the extra olive in my Extra Dirty Martini and staying out of whatever this is."

Martha arrived with the evening salads. Asparagus and snow peas on a bed of romaine lettuce dotted with goat cheese and a fresh lemon dressing for Sutherland and Agnes. Milo received his usual wedge of iceberg lettuce, blue cheese chunks, complemented by blue cheese dressing.

Sutherland mentioned the absence of a salad knife by Milo's place setting. "Have you given up, Martha?"

"I have surrendered," she said, returning to the kitchen.

Milo began to cut the lettuce with the side of his fork.

"Why would you visit Morrie Wolf?" Sutherland asked.

"He summoned me."

"To show you his latest library book?" Agnes mocked. "Perhaps to begin a book club."

Sutherland smiled at her. "I think Milo is a bad influence on you."

Agnes smiled back.

"Strangers are showing up in his bar, not his usual unsavory types. He was wondering why."

43

"Why would he think you would know?" Sutherland asked.

"One of them mentioned my name in a drunken rant. Some guy that might have known me in the Navy. He was in the Rasa along with what could be the late Hat Man."

"This Navy guy, a buddy?" Sutherland asked.

Milo shook his head. "I don't think so."

Martha picked up the empty salad plates and returned with rhubarb and ginger jam lamb chops complemented by roasted potatoes and beets. "I hope you don't mind, Mr. McKnight, but I thought one of your Chateau Haut-Brion 2014 would be perfect with the lamb."

"Mind? Why would I mind?" Sutherland said. "I was waiting for one of these to come up from the wine cellar."

"I didn't sleep nights, wondering why we weren't drinking the Chateau of Harry Byrons," Milo said.

Having received Sutherland's approval of her wine choice, Martha poured Sutherland a tasting amount. He briefly held his glass up to the light, inhaled the wine's bouquet, took a sip, and closed his eyes. "Wonderful!" he proclaimed.

She then poured several ounces for Sutherland, Agnes, and Milo.

Sutherland raised his glass. "A toast to my Aunt Lana, who arrives tomorrow. If she is a nice lady, we will praise Milo for finding her. If she's not, we will blame Milo for finding her."

"Hear, hear," Agnes said, taking a sip.

"Wait," Milo protested, "you should be on my side. You're my personal assistant...I think."

"Yeah, but I'm his wife," she said, pointing at Sutherland.

"That beats personal assistant?"

Agnes nodded. "I'm pretty sure it does."

"There is no employee loyalty these days," Milo complained.

"Speaking of my dear or dastardly Aunt Lana. Her flight arrives at the airport at two. Unfortunately, I will be at the groundbreaking of the Kiner project up in Two Harbors."

"I'll pick her up," Agnes volunteered. "Do I do it as the house manager, the personal assistant, or the wife?"

"You could become the chauffer." Milo suggested. "I could buy you a hat."

"I'm having enough trouble with my many identities without adding another one. But do I take my car, the Land Rover, the Bentley, the Rolls, or Sutherland's Porsche?"

"I think the Bentley. Stately but not ostentatious," Sutherland said.

"I do like driving the Bentley!" Agnes agreed.

"You've driven the Bentley?" Sutherland questioned. "When?"

"Mr. Anderson says the cars need to be driven. I prefer the Bentley. It's newer, and its classy navy blue sets off my auburn hair."

Milo's phone punctuated Agnes' comment with the all-too-familiar *da dunk* ringtone. "Ernie Gramm," Milo said, as if the others didn't already know. "Ernie, what's up?"

"The sheriff's office found our victim's car at Jay Cooke campground. Apparently, he was living in it. Get in early tomorrow morning. We need to get on this." The phone went dead.

Agnes grabbed her phone from the table and called Milo. Sutherland looked at her, not understanding.

"Something I've always wondered," she said.

Milo's phone came to life with a funky song which Agnes recognized. "That's old, but I know it. That's Klymaxx, the all-girl band. 'Never Underestimate the Power of a Woman.' Why is that one for me?"

Milo began to explain when his phone erupted again. Sutherland was calling. He recognized his ringtone on the first note.

"Oh, come on! 'A Boy Named Sue?' Agnes gets 'Never Underestimate the Power of a Woman,' and I get 'A Boy Named Sue?'"

Agnes began laughing and couldn't stop.

"I told you when we first met that your name would have been Susan if you had been a girl. Your dad told me that. It was the perfect marriage of ringtone and reality," Milo explained.

As Martha picked up the plates, she shook her head. "Mrs. McKnight, do you need some water?"

Agnes tried to answer, but still couldn't stop laughing.

Sutherland sighed. "What's for dessert, Martha?"

§

Chip Campbell stoked the fire in the pit that he had installed last summer, at a safe distance from the woods. Returning to his Adirondack chair, he took a sip of his warm brandy. "We bought a third puzzle piece."

His brother Clay nodded. "Have you seen it?"

"No, the two we have are worrisome enough."

"You can't honestly believe the family legend about that old mine."

"Greer certainly does, and she's closer to the source in age. After the board meeting this morning, she gave me the full history she heard as a girl. She went into great detail. We can't have hundreds of people pouring over that property and going into that mine."

"Lewis made a useful gopher for the family for twenty-five years. Maybe this is his revenge," Clay said.

"Revenge for what?" Chip angrily responded. "Lewis Rutledge led a privileged life just for marrying our dear baby sister, Blair. She was able to keep her husband in line, but since her passing, Rutledge started, well, being Rutledge. Mazy said he was just having fun. Looking at the three puzzle pieces we have, and what Greer has told me, I am not amused."

"Chip, I've seen two of the three puzzle pieces. They might as well be from Mars. I don't recognize a thing. I can't tell they lead to the mine."

"Clay, I grew up hunting and fishing by the mine. I recognize the roads and portion of a lake on one of the pieces. Rutledge was sending all those puzzle collectors straight to Campbell Mine number two."

"Don't forget, we have three puzzle pieces. That's three pieces those puzzle idiots don't have. They won't be able to figure out the puzzle, and this will all go away," Clay said. "By the way, where is the third piece?"

Chip reached into his pocket and produced the third piece. "See the river, the road, the mine is right there!"

"Okay, Chip, even if that road and river mark the mine, we have that piece. No one else can figure it out. Stop buying pieces."

Chip shook his head. "We can't risk it. I'll make sure we keep buying pieces. The more we have, the better."

5

John McKnight bought the dark blue Bentley two years ago, a little before his unexpected death. Sutherland never knew why, and John didn't say. It just showed up in the garage one day. Agnes Larson McKnight had great fun driving it around the estate and, from time to time, taking it on errands when she wanted to feel fancy.

Agnes, on a whim, looked up the exact cost of the Bentley. She gasped, thinking it may not be an appropriate vehicle to pick up dry cleaning. She expressed her discomfort at driving such an expensive car.

"You're being silly," Sutherland said to her as Martha served them their breakfast smoothies.

"Good move, Chucky," Milo mocked. "It has been my experience that all women like to be told they're being silly."

Agnes continued to glare at her husband. "Listen to your friend over here, Chucky."

Sutherland shot Milo a confused look before returning his gaze to Agnes. "I want you to drive the Bentley. Just because it costs a few thousand dollars is no reason to leave it in the garage."

"A few is three or four dollars. This is easily six figures to the left of the decimal point."

Milo gave Annie the cat her morning bacon. "Does that come with the good radio? I mean, two hundred grand should get you a good radio."

"You're not helping," Sutherland said to Milo. "And by the way, oh-*not*-silly-wife of mine, Milo over here drives the Bentley."

Agnes looked at Milo for conformation.

"Occasionally, Mary Alice and I motor up to Betty's Pies in Two Harbors in the Bentley," Milo said, referring to his tennis partner and *close* personal friend, Mary Alice Bonner. "We never use the radio."

"See," Sutherland said, "Milo uses the Bentley for pie runs."

Agnes sighed. "You people are sick, but okay, I'll take the Bentley to pick up Lana Freskin. It is a nice car, and Milo, it does have the *good* radio."

"That's a load off my mind."

§

Over the years, Ernie Gramm had learned to hate the beginning of an investigation. There would be numerous suspects to interview, stories to check out, lies to navigate. Milo saying. "Everyone lies but only one lies because they are the murderer," didn't help.

"So annoying," Gramm said out loud.

"What did I do?" White asked as she walked into his office, carrying her store-bought cup of coffee.

Gramm was leaning back in his chair, eyes closed. "Not you. Milo."

"He annoys you even when he's not here?"

"Yes." Gramm said, flipping her the clear evidence bag holding a puzzle piece. "Forensics found this in our victim's car."

White looked it over. "C-o-o-k-e. Do we think this puzzle piece is from a map of Jay Cooke State Park?"

"Makes sense. That's where we found the guy's car." Gramm opened his eyes in time to see Milo make his way through the bullpen area to the office.

As Milo sat down, Preston wheeled in her chair and joined the group.

Gramm took the puzzle piece evidence bag from White, held it up, and shook it in front of Milo. "We found this puzzle piece in Harold Gilbert's car."

"I think people called him Ham," Milo said. "And by the way, Morrie Wolf reads library books,"

Gramm laid the puzzle piece on his desk. "I wonder if there's an opening in robbery?"

"I'll bite," White said. "Why do we care what Morrie Wolf reads?"

Gramm waved her off. "Wrong question. Milo, why were you talking to Morrie Wolf?"

"He invited me to the Rasa for a chat."

"And during this *chat,* what did you learn?"

"Funny you should ask. Our floater, the late *Ham* Gilbert, might have been at the Rasa Monday afternoon."

"Was he alone?"

"Not if it was Gilbert. He was with a guy named Shane who knew me from my Navy days. According to the Rasa bartender, he called me Ratface. Being a cop in the Navy, lots of people didn't like me, but this Shane guy doesn't ring a bell." Milo stopped. "Son of a bitch! Bell! Shane Bell. That was the guy's name. I arrested him a bunch. I remember typing that name over and over again. I was so happy when they discharged him, and I never had to type it again."

"Thanks for that tidbit," Gramm said. "Would Shane Bell be capable of bashing in our floater's head?"

"Absolutely."

"This might be another Lt. O'Dell good karma murder," White said, "if Shane was with Gilbert."

Gramm held up his hand. "What else did you learn?"

"Morrie sells light beer?" Milo shrugged. "Morrie doesn't give up anything. It's always a chess game. I had my two moves and was asked to leave. I thought the Shane Bell thing was pretty important. Show a picture of the dead guy to Benny, the bartender at the Rasa. He could tell you if his Ham is our Harold."

"Gilbert's been in the water. His face isn't pretty," White said.

"I could recognize him as my hat guy," Milo said. "Now tell me why I should care about that piece of a puzzle you just showed me."

Gramm picked up the puzzle piece again. "Deputy Chief Sanders says there is some radio contest going on and it has to do with puzzle pieces. It is attracting people from out of town, and it looks like this contest has led to murder."

"Where did you find that piece?" Milo asked.

"Like I said, it was in our victim's car—on the dashboard."

"If this murder was about the contest, why would the murderer leave it behind?"

"Maybe he didn't know it was there?" Preston offered.

§

Officer Young took her position on a log bench at the entrance to Jay Cooke State Park. She had a clear view of the parking lot. Tricksie, her K9 dog, sniffed the ground before picking her spot to sit down. It wasn't perfect for the queen. Tricksie stood up, sniffed some more, and settled in a slightly different spot. Much better.

A group of forensics people were scouring inside the park for any evidence Ham Gilbert or his attacker may have left behind. Another group was ten yards to the left, combing over the victim's 2011 Honda Element with a pop-up E Camper.

For Young and Tricksie, it looked like an easy day. Both were enjoying the radiant heat of the sun when two guys in a pickup with a camper pulled into the parking lot. Young rose, Tricksie jumped to attention, and the two walked over to the vehicle. Young knocked on the window.

The driver, a bulky man in his fifties wearing a Minnesota Vikings jacket, rolled down the window. "Yeah?"

"The campground is temporarily closed, sir. We are conducting an investigation."

The man smiled, revealing several missing and decaying teeth. "Yeah, that guy they fished out of the river, right?"

"How do you know about that?" Young questioned.

"Everybody knows about it," he laughed.

His partner, a younger guy with better teeth, leaned over. "You better get some help, dearie. This place is gonna be hoppin'."

Two more cars arrived at the parking lot, followed by a large RV. Young and Tricksie repositioned themselves back by the path leading to the campground, blocking anyone who wanted to progress by foot into the park.

White was still in Gramm's office when she took Young's call. "Sarge, I need backup. There are about ten cars in the parking lot now and more arriving by the minute. They're getting out of their cars. They all got shovels and pickaxes, and they want access to the campground."

"We're leaving now. I'll get a couple of patrols going your way. Hold them off as best you can." White explained the situation to Gramm who called the desk sergeant.

Gramm and White rushed away in the Police Interceptor—lights flashing, siren wailing. Preston and Milo followed in a marked car. The campground parking lot was nearly full of vehicles of all makes and descriptions, most with some sort of camping arrangement. Two cop cars were already in the lot and two more raced in behind Milo and Preston. A fifth car swerved to block the entrance to the lot. The police were looking at twenty camper type vehicles that were now unwittingly part of a murder investigation.

A crowd of people had gathered in front of Young, Tricksie, and two other officers. Young, standing on the hood of her car, was attempting to maintain order. The crowd was getting angry.

"What a mess," White said to Gramm. He was already out of the Interceptor, heading toward the crowd. White grabbed the bullhorn and followed.

Preston ran to catch up with Gramm and White. Milo emerged from the vehicle and took a more leisurely walk in the direction of the crowd. The bulky man with rotten teeth, now in the front of the rowdy crowd, bolted around Young, crashing through the bushes and trees toward the campsites. Preston gave chase as Officer Young released Tricksie, who caught the man on his thigh and pulled him to the ground. His howls of pain sobered the crowd. Preston arrived seconds later, holding the man's face down and cuffing his hands behind his back.

Gramm grabbed the bullhorn from White. "I don't know why you're here," he said to the crowd, "but this campground is off limits until we finish our investigation. By being here, you are now part of that investigation. Return to your vehicles, but do not leave the parking lot. One of our officers will come to your vehicle to interview you. The more cooperative you are, the faster this will be over."

"And what if we just charge past you?" bad teeth's passenger threatened.

"Then you can join that gentleman on the ground in handcuffs," Gramm said.

Tricksie returned to Young, who added, "If any of you choose to rush past us, Tricksie will get nervous. When Tricksie gets nervous, she bites harder."

There were grumbles, but the crowd dispersed to their cars, most standing by their vehicles. After about ten minutes, an assortment of grills had been brought out and people were cooking and chatting with each other.

"Good job!" Gramm said to Officer Young. "You held them off—not an easy task."

Preston brought her miscreant over to Gramm and White. "Mr. Pleski says he's sorry for his poor decision."

"Mr. Pleski," Gramm began, "what did you think you were doing?"

"Searching for the treasure! Just like all of them!" Pleski said, pointing to the people in the parking lot. "I figured if I could rush in the park, I could beat all these other people."

Gramm looked at the older man rubbing grass and dirt from his face. "That dog bit me!" the man said, pulling up his jacket to show his torn jeans. He went to sit down, but Gramm ordered him to keep standing.

"What makes you think there's a treasure here in Jay Cooke?" Gramm asked.

"The Duluth Puzzle Blog. Can I at least lean against the car?"

"Yeah, but keep talking."

"That blog said some guy was murdered here because he found the key piece that showed where the money was hidden. This was going to be a pretty busy place. I wanted to be first."

Officer Young told Gramm she had encountered Pleski earlier. "He was the first in the parking lot. He had a buddy, but that guy's still in the crowd."

Milo walked up to him. "Do you know exactly where the money is hidden?"

"If I do, I wouldn't tell you!"

"I'll take that as a no."

"Get his address and phone number," Gramm said to Preston, "and then let him go."

"I'm in pain. I'm bleeding," Pleski whined.

Gramm gave him his best nasty stare. "We will call the EMTs."

White had pulled up the Duluth Puzzle Blog. The headline was hardly catchy, but to the point. "Dead Man Had Key Puzzle Piece." It went on to say that the victim was looking in Jay Cooke State Park at the campground when he was murdered.

"How does this blogger know about that puzzle piece? That's not public knowledge. We need to find him," White said.

"I assume none of *you* have told anyone about the floater or the puzzle piece?" Gramm asked.

"I told Morrie Wolf that my hat man was dead. Damn! Morrie was born to blog."

"Morrie Wolf? *The* Morrie Wolf?" Preston questioned.

"We go to church together," Milo said.

White was on the phone with IT. "Find the person who does the Duluth Puzzle Blog, please. ASAP!"

§

Duluth International Airport is a tad on the small side, without direct flights from Scotland, Lana Freskin's permanent home for the last fifty years. She was arriving on a connecting flight from Minneapolis. Agnes stood, sign in hand, in the baggage claim area, trying to shield her eyes from the glare of the sun streaming through the walls of windows. Several other people were milling around, but she was the only one with a sign.

She had given some thought to what she should wear. Agnes, the house manager, would wear slacks and a sweater. A personal assistant would opt for a suit. As Sutherland's wife, she had no clue, so she decided to go as herself. Feeling springy, she chose her cocoa and white print jacketed dress with flat shoes, knowing there would be walking involved.

Agnes had asked to see pictures of Sutherland's mother so she would better recognize her twin. She didn't have to worry. Only six people disembarked from the Minneapolis flight. Five of them were men. The remaining one was, presumably, Lana Freskin, a striking, serious looking woman in her sixties. Her wavy, white-blond hair hung about her shoulders but didn't dare move.

She spied Agnes' *FRESKIN* sign, and the two moved toward each other. "Ms. Freskin?" Agnes inquired.

"I better be, or you're waiting for someone who didn't show." Lana said, looking at the other male passengers.

"I'm Agnes Larson…" Agnes stopped, not knowing if she should add McKnight. "I hope you had a comfortable flight."

Lana replied with a glance that Agnes could not interpret. The two waited in silence for the luggage to roll down the belt. Duluth was one of those regional airports with a straight-line belt, not a circular one. After ten minutes of waiting, a large, hard shelled, white suitcase came into view.

"That's it," Lana said.

Agnes wondered if she chose the suitcase to match her pearls. *Are they real?* If they were, the Bentley was a good choice.

"Well, Ms. Larson, lead the way," Lana said.

Agnes hoisted the large suitcase from the luggage belt, and they made their way outside. "If you would like to wait here, I can get the car."

"It's Duluth, honey. That car can't be far. I'll walk."

Agnes noticed Lana was wearing flats, too. As they approached the parking lot, Lana laughed. "It's that blue Bentley, isn't it?"

"Yes, it is. How do you know?" Agnes asked.

"Did you know John McKnight?"

"No, sadly, I never had that pleasure."

"Well, this car is his dream. It looks as though his son has kept it," Lana said as she slid into the front seat.

"It's a magnificent car," Agnes offered, leaving the airport, turning onto the Miller Trunk Highway.

"So, dear, who is Agnes Larson and how do you fit into Lakesong?"

Agnes smiled. "It depends. I have been the Lakesong house manager, a personal assistant to Milo Rathkey…"

"I met Mr. Rathkey once when he was a boy. Several years ago, John mentioned him to me. He was thinking of leaving half of everything to him. So how is that working out?"

"Quite well, all things considered."

"But I interrupted you. House manager, personal assistant, and?"

Agnes took a deep breath. "Wife of Sutherland McKnight."

Lana turned her head to look at her. "Really? Why wouldn't you lead with that?"

"We were only married in January. I was going in chronological order. Also, I'm still getting used to it."

"It's May. How long is it going to take?"

"I haven't taken the McKnight name, at least not officially."

"Well, I never had to make that choice. I was born a Freskin. I will die a Freskin. I preferred it that way. So, does Sutherland still wear those cute little shorts?"

Agnes laughed, thinking of Sutherland in his spandex biking shorts. "He does, but not to work."

6

Milo was the last to step into the small, cluttered KDDW studios located next to the bus terminal on Michigan Street. The long, curvy legs of the receptionist were almost as alluring as Mary Alice's in a short tennis dress—a reminder to Milo that tennis season was coming up

"This may be the only radio station I haven't been interviewed in, thanks to Ron Bello and that damn book," Milo complained.

"You're rich and famous, poor you," White said.

"I get no sympathy."

"You don't deserve any," Gramm piled on.

"Can I help you?" The receptionist asked, looking up from her cell phone.

Gramm flashed his badge. "We want to talk with Larry Latto."

The receptionist stared at the trio, pressed an intercom button, and waited for Latto to respond. "Whatcha need?" he asked in his booming, always present, radio voice.

"Three police people here to see you."

"Me?"

"Yes, you."

"Send them back."

"Down that hall, on the right, first door," the receptionist said, pointing in the general direction before going back to her cell phone.

On the way, Milo noticed a gold record on the wall. It was Gordon Lightfoot's "The Wreck of The Edmund Fitzgerald"—a tribute to a national tragedy with local loss. Milo remembered his parents talking about crew members who drowned that night when the ship sank in the storm-driven waves of Lake Superior.

Latto was rolling down the sleeves of his button-down shirt. "How can I help you?" He smiled and held out his hand at the two chairs opposite his desk. Milo stood in the doorway while Gramm did the introductions. "We want to talk to you about your contest."

"It's a winner, isn't it? Lots of publicity." His eyes carried his broadening smile. "But, before you complain, I've already talked with your deputy chief who was concerned with all the treasure hunters coming into the city vandalizing property. I assured him that was not our purpose. Apparently, social media spread word of the contest out of the city—out of our control."

"That's not why we're here. Yesterday, we fished one of your treasure hunters out of the St. Louis River. He had been bludgeoned to death."

Latto's smile faded, and he turned even whiter than his normal complexion. "Oh man! That's not good."

"Can you tell us how the contest works?" Gramm asked.

"Lewis, our late owner, was a hell of a guy. Lewis Rutledge, man, he loved radio, especially this station. He sometimes read news copy, even learned some production so he could put together ads—not a bad voice. Anyway, he produced this contest to up listenership. He hid twelve, crisp hundred-dollar bills all around town—his own money—along with puzzle pieces and urged us to hype the contest which we did."

"I understand the search for the hundred dollars. What's the purpose of the puzzle pieces?" White asked.

"The pieces form a map. The map leads to an even bigger cash treasure."

"How much?"

"Don't know. Lewis never said. He died last week."

"Why the second contest?" Milo asked. "Wouldn't the first contest, the hundred-dollar bills, be enough?"

"I thought so. I made that point to Lewis, but he said it was his money, his radio station, and he was doing it his way. He was insistent about that map leading to the grand prize. I would have liked more hundred-dollar bills scattered around town. Maybe his daughter, Mazy Mason, knows more. I think she inherits the station. That makes us all a little nervous—new owner and everything."

"In light of this death, will you continue with the contest?" Gramm asked.

Latto shrugged. "It's done. All the clues for the hundred dollars are out. Many of the pieces have been found. All we're doing now is interviewing the lucky KDDW listeners who are a hundred dollars richer and what they plan to do to find the bigger prize."

"We have reason to believe this second treasure is buried in Jay Cooke State Park. Is that true?" White asked.

Latto shrugged. "Beats me."

"I see you have a gold record." Milo inserted in one of his patented non sequiturs.

Latto nodded. "Before my time, I'm afraid. That was back in the seventies when this was a rock station. Right after that ore boat sank in Lake Superior. The gales of November and all that. I think this station alerted the record company that the song might be a hit."

On the way out the door, White asked Milo why he mentioned the gold record. "I might learn something I need to know later." Milo explained.

§

"I thought you might enjoy the yellow suite near the upstairs library," Agnes said to Lana as they walked through Lakesong's front doors.

"I've stayed there before. I assume it hasn't changed much."

"It's still yellow," Agnes laughed. "We had it cleaned and polished, however."

"If you don't mind, I'd like to sit and relax with some coffee before I go up and unpack. I'm surrounded by tea drinkers all day, every day. I want some good old-fashioned American coffee."

"I drink French Press in the afternoons. I could…"

"I'll take it," Lana said, leaving her suitcase at the bottom of the double marble staircase and walking toward the gallery. "It's still here!" she exclaimed, taking in the trees, flowers, and various seating arrangements.

Agnes followed her. "The gallery? Of course. It's amazing."

"Laura's pride and joy—other than Sutherland."

"Please feel free to wander our indoor park and choose any area you like. I'll find you." Agnes hastened to the kitchen to begin the French Press process. Martha was preparing dinner. Seeing Agnes turn over two cups, she asked, "Mrs. McKnight, what are you doing?"

Agnes jumped a little at the formal use of her name. "I thought we talked about the Mrs. McKnight thing."

Martha smiled. "We did. We agreed I would use it only if outsiders were present. You have two cups. One assumes you have a guest. If that's true, I would suggest you let the chef prepare your coffee." Martha sidled up to Agnes. "In other words, get out of my kitchen."

Agnes laughed but obeyed. She returned to the gallery, finding Lana seated on one of the sofas overlooking the lake. "This place is so beautiful!" Lana said.

"It is. Our chef, Martha, is bringing the coffee."

On cue, Martha wheeled out two cups, hot, steaming coffee, and an assortment of Ilene's best petits fours.

"Thank you, Martha," Agnes said. "Ilene's on a Wednesday. What a wonderful surprise."

"I listen at doors," Martha joked, and returned to the kitchen.

After the perfunctory chit chat about the petty annoyances of international flights, the sweetness of the petits fours, and the richness of the French press coffee, Lana stared at the tall, attractive beauty that now was family. She knew nothing about Agnes. *Who would tag a baby with such an old-fashioned name?*

"So, Agnes," Lana began. "Who are your people?"

Agnes squinted and furrowed her brow. *That phrase again.* "You're the second person to ask me that. I have no immediate people except for Sutherland. I was raised for many years in foster care."

The older woman tilted her head as if examining something foreign and strange. "So, am I to believe that Sutherland, the heir to the Freskin Shipping fortune, married an orphan?"

Agnes' heart began to pound in her ears. She felt hot. Why was she so frightened? *Was this a challenge by Sutherland's family? How do I answer?*

Peals of laughter interrupted her.

"I'm sorry dear, I'm not laughing at you. I am, in fact, quite pleased. My father would have been apoplectic. Sutherland would have been disinherited on the spot, but thankfully, my father's not here. I can only hope on some plane, he knows."

"You didn't like your father?"

"An outdated wreck of a man who lived beyond his usefulness."

Agnes' heartbeat returned to normal. Lana was not an enemy, branding Agnes as *less than* for events outside her control. The remaining visit was friendly. After about an hour, Agnes excused herself and offered to place Lana's suitcase in her room.

Lana thanked her and remained seated, watching the lake, her eyes closing from time to time.

§

"I think we should go in one car, rather than the usual parade," Gramm said to Milo and White outside the radio station.

"You just want a ride in my old Honda," Milo snarked.

Gramm shook his head. "Get in the back of the police car, Milo."

"My friends will think I've been arrested," Milo protested.

"You have no friends," Gramm countered.

White laughed.

Milo slid into the back seat of the Police Interceptor. "Why does Robin get to sit upfront?"

"Maybe we should tie that guy in the back to the roof," Gramm suggested, starting the vehicle. White found the address for the Campbell family compound and plugged it into the GPS.

"Twenty-five minutes," White said.

"How do we know Mazy Mason is home?" Milo asked.

"We don't, but we don't want to lose the element of surprise," Gramm said. "We'll take a chance on it. Besides, I'm curious about this family compound."

"Don't you think Latto called her?" Milo suggested.

"Possibly. I still want to chance it." Gramm was firm.

The GPS led them to a series of winding roads before warning them that the next left, an unnamed road, was a private drive. Gramm made the turn and traveled several hundred yards down a single lane blacktop road before stopping in front of a formidable iron gate. Gramm pushed the intercom button by the driver's side.

"Yes?" a male voice asked.

"Police Lt. Gramm and Sergeant Robin White. We are here to talk with Mazy Mason."

"Please wait." After less than a minute, the male voice returned. "She is not available."

"Maybe you didn't understand," Gramm said. "We are from the Duluth Police Department, and we need to talk with Mazy Mason about a recent homicide."

"Do you have a warrant?" the voice asked.

"We can get one, but that makes me…"

"Do that!"

The intercom went dead. Gramm pushed the call button several more times, but the voice did not return.

"Can they do that?" White asked, calling Latto for Mazy's direct number. After a brief conversation, she dialed the number given to her. After the first ring, voice mail answered. *You have reached the voicemail box of Lewis Rutledge. Please leave a message.* That was followed by *This mailbox is full.*

"I just called a dead man!" White said. "What's going on? Who are these people?" She called Latto back, who said that was the only number he had. He suggested she call Campbell Industries in Minneapolis.

As she was dialing, a St. Louis County Sheriff's car with flashing blue lights was pulling in behind Gramm's vehicle. Gramm got out and met the deputy before he could get out of the car. The deputy rolled down his window. "Gramm."

"Dennis."

"We got a call from the Campbells that someone was at their gate and refusing to leave."

"That would be me. We need to talk with Mazy Mason about a homicide, but they won't let us in."

The deputy smiled. "You don't know the Campbells. Very private, powerful family. You're gonna need lawyers."

"Just to talk to her? We're not going to arrest her."

"You'd need a warrant to deliver a newspaper to these people." The deputy's radio came to life. "Is everything okay at the Campbell's?" a female voice asked.

The deputy clicked the button on his microphone. "Yeah, it's Lt. Gramm from the Duluth PD. They're here to talk with Mazy Mason."

"I'm sure the Campbells won't let him in, and next time tell him to give us a heads up if he's going to poach on our turf."

"Sorry," Gramm said. "She has a point."

"So, is the Duluth PD going to leave?" the dispatcher asked.

"Do you have to watch us leave?" Gramm was puzzled.

"You didn't hear this from me, but these people have an in with our sheriff. Lots of money goes into his reelection campaign. If they want you gone, I gotta make sure you're gone."

Gramm nodded to the deputy and walked back to his car. "We shoulda called the county first," he said, settling into the Interceptor.

A man in a military uniform came from inside the compound, opened the gate slightly with a remote control and walked up to the police car. He tapped on the window. "Lieutenant, a word, please."

Gramm got out of the car.

"I'm Major Peters, the head of security here. State your business, please." He did not hold out his hand.

"I already did. Weren't you listening?" Gramm said, noticing that the Major's uniform did not contain a rank.

"Why do you want to talk with Mrs. Mason?"

"Police business."

"Cooperating with me may make this process easier... for you," Peters suggested.

"Cooperating with me may make your stay in jail for obstruction easier...for you." Gramm countered.

Peters spun around, marched through the gate, and headed back down the road. Gramm slid back into the police car. He waved out the window to the deputy, who began to back out.

As Gramm followed the deputy down the one lane road, White said, "I called the Campbell Industries number in Minneapolis and left a message for Mazy. I also called the District Attorney and told him we're going to need a warrant. He said we need a reason for a search."

"What are these people playing at?" Gramm questioned. "Locked gates, pretend military. What's going on here?"

§

Saul Feinberg was sitting in his office, an oversized van behind the St. Louis County Courthouse, when his phone buzzed. It was Kimberly McKenna, high-powered

Minneapolis attorney and Feinberg's preferred date at the moment.

"Kim."

"Hey Saul. I'm heading up to Duluth as soon as I pack."

"Business, or do you miss me?"

"Both."

"You can stay at Chez Feinberg."

"We've discussed that. It's not a good look, should my clients need to visit. I shouldn't mix business with pleasure."

"Dinner tonight?" Saul asked.

"Absolutely. I'm staying at the Pier B."

"I'll pick you up at eight."

§

Arriving back at the cop shop, White, Milo, and Gramm hit the vending machines. White grabbed a protein bar, Milo his two vending machine burritos, while Gramm pushed the button on the sandwich vending machine over and over again.

"You know you want a burrito," Milo said. "Stop torturing that machine and get a burrito."

"I need to take an antacid before I eat one of those, and besides, Amy thinks they're unhealthy," Gramm said, pushing the button for a tuna sandwich.

White shook her head. "I think the race is on between those burritos and the six-day-old tuna sandwich as to which one lands you in the hospital first."

The microwave buzzed. Milo removed his now nicely melted burritos, and the group made their way to Gramm's office only to be joined by Preston, who was finishing a salad from Lettuce Do Lunch, the salad place on Central Entrance.

White looked at Preston's salad, then her protein bar. "In the future, let me know when you are making a pilgrimage to the salad place."

"Sorry," Preston said. "Didn't know you were coming back."

Gramm, inhaling the fumes from Milo's twin burritos, unboxed his tuna salad sandwich. "Here's to healthy eating."

Preston looked at White and mouthed, *Healthy eating?*

White shook her head in a gesture that said, "Let it go."

Milo wiped refried beans and cheese off his shirt. "Any ID on Jimmy Pleski's blogger yet?"

"It's called the Duluth Puzzle Blog. I handed it over to IT, and they're still working on it," White said.

Gramm dropped his sandwich in favor of his phone after it began buzzing, alerting him to an incoming text. "In forty years, I've never run into this much opposition to an interview."

"What?" White asked.

"The Campbells have hired a Minneapolis lawyer."

"Really? We just want to talk to Mazy. Is she the murderer?" White asked. "It certainly makes us think that."

Milo texted Feinberg. *Is McKenna in town?*
Yeah.

"They didn't hire a lawyer," Milo said. "They have a lawyer. This is getting interesting."

"How do you know that?" Gramm asked.

"Follow along. You said the Campbells hired a lawyer, *she.* I thought immediately of Kimberly McKenna. Remember

McKenna? We dealt with her during the Harper Gain thing. When Mary Alice and I had dinner with Saul and Kim, she said all her clients kept her on retainer. She's in town. I'm taking a leap here. She's in town for the Campbells."

"Notice how he dropped Mary Alice Bonner's name?" White joked.

"And he referred to the Campbell's possible attorney as Kim." Gramm added. "Climbing up that society ladder."

"It was one dinner, and Feinberg, socialist-attorney-to-the-poor, was there too," Milo defended himself.

"*Rich* socialist-attorney-to-the-poor," Gramm countered. "I better call the District Attorney. We're gonna need our own lawyer."

"Make sure he sends a sharp one," Milo advised. "McKenna doesn't come cheap, and I think she's worth every penny."

7

Milo had forgotten that Lana Freskin would be in Lakesong when he arrived home, but there she was, sitting in the gallery, looking as if she were an older Laura McKnight. He startled for a moment.

"Yes, I look just like her," Lana said, rising to shake Milo's hand. "You, of course, are Milo Rathkey."

Milo shook her hand. "I'm glad you didn't just pop in. I might have fainted."

Lana smiled.

"I hope we have a spare bedroom for you," Milo said, sitting down across from Lana.

"Yes, you do. I believe it's called the yellow suite, and for good reason: it's very yellow."

"I'm going to make myself a gimlet. Can I get you something a bit stronger than coffee?" Milo offered.

"Perhaps a little white wine. I'd love a late harvest Riesling if you have it. Most people don't."

Milo nodded. "We have everything. Sutherland stocks the wine room. I'll be back." He hurried to the basement, past the furnaces, down a hallway to the wine rooms—once the scary indoor pool. After a year of living in Lakesong, he knew the reds were in one room, the whites in another, but that was as the extent of Milo's Lakesong wine room knowledge.

Entering the white wine room, chillier than the reds, Milo looked for wines beginning with R. He sighed. "Why are these not in alphabetical order?" he wondered out loud.

There was row upon row of white wine slots with a mixture of R's and C's and every other letter in the alphabet. Each slot held many bottles of the same wine. "This makes no sense!"

"Mr. Rathkey, what are you doing?"

Milo whirled around to see Martha standing in the white wine doorway. "I am trying to find a late harvest Riesling for Sutherland's aunt, but this wine is all jumbled up. What are you doing?"

"I am getting several bottles of wine for dinner. Does Ms. Freskin prefer German or domestic?"

Milo blinked. "White. Riesling. Late Harvest. That's all I know."

She walked down two rows before turning down and going halfway up the aisle. "Here. Take this bottle."

Martha then went to an entirely different section, pulling out a different bottle. "And take this one."

"What's the secret? Do you have a decoder ring that tells you where each wine is stored? I was never given a wine decoder ring."

Martha smiled. "The wines are stored by country and region. The first bottle was in the German section, Rhine Valley. The second was in the Washington State section, Columbia Valley."

Milo looked at his two bottles. "Rather than brush up on my geography, I'll just ask you in the future."

"I would appreciate it. It is my job, Mr. Rathkey."

Milo thanked Martha and returned to the gallery. Holding out the two bottles for Lana's inspection, he asked if she preferred German or domestic.

"My goodness, two different late harvest Rieslings. I'm in America. Let me try the domestic," Lana said. "I will need a tour of that wine room."

"Sutherland better show you. Apparently, there is a secret decoder ring involved. Only he and our chef have one," Milo said.

Milo mixed his gimlet in the family room, returned to the gallery, handed Lana her wine, and sat down across from her. "Have we ever met? I grew up here."

"Once, years ago, but you were quite young. I was also here for Laura's funeral."

Milo nodded. "I was already in the Navy and couldn't leave."

"John called me when he was thinking of leaving you a pile of money and half this house."

"Did he?"

"Yes, he wanted my opinion."

"Which was?"

"I knew Laura had willed all her money to Sutherland. I told him Lakesong was his house, and what money he had was his to leave to whom he chose. What do you do with John's money, Mr. Rathkey?"

An aggressive question, Milo thought. He was hit with a dizzying moment of déjà vu. As a boy, he had many discussions with Laura McKnight who also asked pointed questions. Now, sitting here as a man, being questioned by an older Laura McKnight clone, he was taken back to that other time.

He debated on his reply. Part of him wanted to tell her it was none of her business. He wasn't a young boy, and John did what he did for his own reasons. Instead, he turned it back. "I bought a new old car, three suits, a few assorted shirts, pants, and expensive shoes. What do you do with all your money, Ms. Freskin?"

"Good parry. Does all that shopping take up your days?"

"I'm trying to remember my fencing moves here. Would that be a lunge on your part?" Milo questioned.

"More a thrust I'd say. So, the cook's son is a fencing enthusiast?" Lana was amused.

"The cook's son is a man of many talents. As a boy, I was attacked by The Three Musketeers."

Lana smiled again. "Your humor is a good riposte. Most people just tell me to go to hell and stomp off."

"Stomping off is counterproductive. I'm learning who you are."

Lana cocked her head. "Whether you know it or not, Laura influenced you. She wouldn't let a few insulting comments throw her off her game either. I was the stomper—missed opportunities. By the way, I'm learning who you've become. I looked you up. You're a somewhat famous detective. I even read a book about you."

"I prefer to be a not so famous detective."

"Noted. Are you doing any detecting at present?"

"I found you, and I'm helping the police solve a murder."

Lana moved toward the edge of her chair. "Certainly not my every day. Tell me about it."

"Not much to tell. A local radio station is holding a contest that involves puzzle pieces, clues to a hidden treasure. It appears that one treasure seeker was murdered."

"How do you begin to solve something like that?"

"We talk to everybody involved. Eventually, a solution is floating in front of us. This one is a little more complicated because we're dealing with a family that doesn't want to talk to us."

"Can they do that? Refuse?"

"They think they can. I think a judge is going to force them to talk."

"Can't you just break down their door like they do in the movies?"

"Not that simple. They live in a compound with a very sturdy gate."

Lana's eyes grew wide. "Family compound?"

"Yeah, I guess."

"Are you talking about Greer Campbell's family?"

"I don't know a Greer Campbell, but the family name is Campbell. We want to talk to a Mazy Mason. She owns the radio station. Do you know the Campbells?"

Lana settled back in her chair. "Mr. Rathkey, this is your lucky day."

§

Gramm was reaching for his coat when his phone startled to life. "It's Doc Smith," he told White.

"Are you going to answer it?"

"I have to. I hope it's short. Amy is making lasagna." Gramm put the phone on speaker. "Hey Doc, kinda late in the day."

"Right. Your boy drowned. As you know, he was struck twice by a blunt object, maybe a pipe, but he was breathing when he went into the river."

"Water in the lungs?"

"Look at you, a junior coroner."

"How long was the body in the water?" White asked.

"Less than twelve hours." The phone went dead.

"Did you and the doc go to the same school of bad phone etiquette?" White asked.

"Why?"

"You both fail to say goodbye when you finish talking. You just click off."

"He had nothing more to say."

"Should I call Milo?"

"Sure, why not? You can say hello and goodbye and all that phone etiquette stuff you learned in good phone school." Gramm rushed out of his office.

"I won't get the chance," she yelled after him. "He just clicks off, too."

§

Milo's phone lit up with the song *Happy*. "Robin, kinda late, isn't it?"

"I have news from the doc. Are you on speaker?"

"Yup. I'm here with Sutherland's Aunt."

"Could you take it off speaker?"

"So secretive." Milo pushed the speaker button, putting the phone to his ear. "The doc says our floater drowned after being struck on the head twice with a pipe-like object."

"So, accidental death?"

"See you in...damn it! Again!" White put her phone in her pocket and prepared to follow Gramm out the door.

§

"Uncle Chip told me the police were here today looking for me," Mazy told her husband Michael as she walked outside with her predinner wine. The night was warm with a soft easterly breeze. Mazy stopped to inhale the smell of spring growth.

Michael brought the marinated steaks out to the large propane grill on the back patio. "The police? What did they want?"

"I don't know. Chip gave orders not to let them in. Don't overcook my steak."

"Do I ever? Why would Chip do that?"

Mazy shook her head. "Because he's Chip. He's a Campbell. He thinks it puts him above everyone else."

"Did the police just leave?"

"Yes. I think they are going to get a warrant, but Chip's lawyer is going to fight it. I think it's all nuts, but Chip insists we make it as difficult as possible for the police to invade our privacy."

"What's Chip afraid of? What's going on?"

"I have no idea, but I wondered the same thing."

Michael thought this was a good opening to press his usual demand. "You know, this would be a lot easier if I were in the board meetings. I'm a lot smarter than any of those people. I have great ideas!"

"Michael, we've been through this. I don't decide who's in and who's out."

"Can't you get your Aunt Greer on your side?"

"Aunt Greer? Quite frankly, why would Greer take on Chip and Clay for you?"

"Shouldn't she be running the family, not Chip? She's the last of her generation."

Mazy shook her head. "This is a family of misogyny. You're right, she was older than her brother, but my great grandfather installed him, my grandfather, over Greer. If she objected, he could have thrown her off the board, which is what happened to her older sister. I'll tell you one thing: I'm running this family before any of my cousins."

"Good luck with that. You need me on the board—my vote." Michael turned the steaks and poured himself a beer.

Mazy took out her phone and began scrolling through her social media.

"I found a good mechanic." Michael blurted.

"What?"

"For my Ducati."

"What about it?"

"Get your head out of your phone. I found a good mechanic for my Ducati."

Mazy scowled. "How much is that going to cost me? I'm not funding your hobby forever."

"It's not a hobby. And you wouldn't have to fund it if I were on the board. Then I'd get paid like you. I could fund it myself."

Mazy sighed. "Why do you need a mechanic?"

"I need a mechanic to travel with me to the tracks. Some guys have entire teams of people."

"Some guys win races."

§

Milo escorted Aunt Lana into the family room, freshened her wine, and the two sat down on the sectional as Martha arrived with hors d'oeuvres. "Do you do this every night? Have a sit-down dinner?" Lana asked.

"Almost every night. Before I returned here, dinner for me was a cardboard container from the Chinese Dragon Restaurant," Milo said.

"I love Chinese food," Lana said. "You must take me there."

"I will only if you promise to not listen to the proprietor. He lies."

"Lies? About what?"

"Me, primarily."

"Hello again," Agnes said to Lana as she bounded in from the upstairs apartment. "Sutherland will be here in just a minute." She sat down in one of the chairs.

Lana nodded. "Milo has promised to take me to the Chinese, ah..."

"Dragon," Milo added.

"Yes, the Chinese Dragon Restaurant," Lana said.

"I'm impressed. He has yet to take me or Sutherland there."

"Take us where?" Sutherland asked as he entered the room.

"The Chinese Dragon," Agnes said, but Sutherland didn't hear. He was staring at Lana. The hair was whiter and longer, but the face was an older version of the woman who left him when he was ten. His eyes began to water. He quickly shook it off.

"Aunt Lana, it's so good to meet you," Sutherland said, using his best. friendly realtor mode. He took refuge behind the bar. "Can I get you a drink?"

Agnes caught Sutherland's unease.

"Milo has supplied me with wine," Lana said.

"Martha found it. I couldn't get out of the Ripple section in the wine room," Milo quipped.

Sutherland wanted to quip back, but his mind was swimming. He was frozen, looking at his mother, but it wasn't his mother. *Get it together, Sutherland! You're not ten!* He chided himself.

Agnes walked over to Sutherland and put her hand on his. He smiled at her. "Dirty Martini?" he asked.

"Always. Three olives please."

Sutherland busied himself with making their drinks and then sat down in the chair opposite Lana and Milo. Agnes perched herself on the chair's arm, leaning into Sutherland. He needed to know she was there.

"John always wondered why I didn't come to visit," Lana said. "I know my appearance must disturb you, yet there's nothing I can do about it. I came now because you're an adult. I hoped we could overcome the *identical* problem. It would have been confusing and upsetting when you were young."

Sutherland said nothing for a second, thinking about his younger self seeing Aunt Lana after his mother had died. Everyone waited.

"Thank you. I think you were correct, and I'm sorry it kept us apart all these years. Mom told me about you but only referred to you as her sister, never her identical twin."

"You will find I'm quite different from your mother. She held a tight tiller and rode the waves. I run with the wind, most of the time swamping the boat."

Sutherland smiled. He never thought of his mother that way, but thinking about her now, he realized there was truth in what Lana said. He took a sip of his martini. "Tell me about you and her."

Lana took a deep breath. "We're twins, always close, until Laura moved here and married your father."

"Didn't you approve of my father?"

"Me?" Lana laughed. "I thought John was great. Our father disapproved, but I had already plowed the road—ran with the wind. He had already disowned me, you know."

"My mother had mentioned that."

Lana laughed. "I'm sure she did. The point is, father couldn't disown both me and your mother, or he'd have no children."

"Why did he disown you?" Sutherland asked.

"My morality interfered with his money making. He owned a shipping company. It was a major polluter—the worst of the worst. He and I constantly fought about that.

Finally, I turned him into the maritime authorities with documentation. It cost him a lot of money in fines."

"Running with the wind!" Sutherland smiled.

"Exactly."

"My mother's money still exists. Half of it is yours if you want it," Sutherland offered.

Lana shook her head. "I've gotten my share."

Sutherland wrinkled his brow. "How?"

"Sutherland, are you running a large shipping conglomerate?"

"No," Sutherland said, laughing.

"After our father died, Laura sold me the company for one dollar. We make less profit, but do not pollute." Lana put her hand up to her ear. "That faint whirling noise you hear is my father spinning in his grave."

Martha announced dinner, and all moved to the family room table. Broccoli and bacon salads were awaiting the trio. An iceberg wedge with blue cheese dressing had been placed in front of Milo's chair.

"Not a fan of broccoli, Mr. Rathkey?" Lana asked.

"Milo is not a fan of green," Sutherland explained.

The troupe dug into their salads and listened to Aunt Lana fill in the blanks of Sutherland's family. Milo was silent, thinking about his earlier discussion with Aunt Lana about Greer Campbell and the Campbell family.

8

Mazy Campbell was reading through her emails while downing her kefir and fruit breakfast. The last email was from her Uncle Chip telling her about a possible hearing to block the police from coming onto Campbell property. Chip said his aim was to make the process long and annoying.

"Why?" Mazy shouted.

Her outburst made Michael jump. "Why what?"

"It's Chip. He's going to court to stop the police from interviewing me here on the compound."

Michael poured more syrup on his toaster waffles. "So go to them."

Mazy smiled. "Sometimes, Michael, you pay for your keep. That's exactly what I'm going to do."

"I've told you. I am so much smarter than your uncles. You need me on that board!"

Michael's constant nattering about being on the board was becoming background noise to Mazy. She emailed her uncle, informing him of her intent to go to the police. Her phone lit up immediately.

"Gee, it's Uncle Chip. What a surprise."

"Tell me why you would circumvent the family's wishes?"

"They're not the family's wishes, they're your wishes and quite frankly they're stupid." In her mind, she could see his upper lip tighten.

"There's more at play here, Mazy dear, than just a police interview."

"Please stop. In your mind, what's at play?"

"Our privacy. We must safeguard it at all costs."

Because we come from a long line of paranoid men, she thought. "I'm going to the police."

"You are your father's daughter. I insist you take our lawyer, Kimberly McKenna, with you."

"She's not my lawyer, and she wasn't my mother's lawyer," Mazy protested.

"She is your lawyer! Your mother, may she rest in peace, did not have need for her. Ms. McKenna doesn't do wills and such, and my sister never needed to talk to the police. You can blame your reckless father for this."

Mazy wanted to rip into Chip but held back. "I'll text you with a time and place. If you want her there for the family, you tell her." Mazy hung up.

Michael smiled. "You're a bad ass this morning." He popped another two waffles into the toaster, deciding this was not the time to again bring up the cost of a full-time mechanic.

§

"Why do you buy coffee?" Gramm asked White. "We have coffee."

White smiled as she sat down in her usual chair. "You're just wondering that now? I've been bringing in my own coffee since I started on the force."

"But why?"

"It's Thursday. This week Thursday is caramel macchiato day. As extensive as our coffee services are, caramel macchiato is not on the menu."

"What about Friday?" Gramm asked.

"I don't know. It's not Friday yet."

Milo arrived carrying his own cup of coffee.

"What's in your cup?" Gramm asked.

Milo sat down. "Do you have a warrant to grill me about my coffee?"

Gramm groaned. "A lot of that's going around these days."

"Okay, don't beat me. It's Ilene's with cream, no sugar."

"You go to Ilene's for coffee?"

"I go to Ilene's for a cream puff. As long as I'm there, I get a coffee. Are you thinking about writing a book, *The Duluth Police Coffee Choices*?"

White turned to Milo, "Lying to the police is a crime."

"I told the whole truth. Type it up. I'll sign it."

"You said, a cream puff. We know, Mr. Rathkey, that you have never stopped at one cream puff."

"I want my lawyer."

"Can we get to work here?" Gramm insisted.

"You're the one that went off on a coffee tangent," White charged.

"I drink the office coffee if anybody cares," Preston offered.

"We don't," Gramm said. "Tell us what you've learned about the Campbell family."

Preston opened her pad. "They own a variety of businesses, originally in mining and agriculture, but they have been branching out into electronics. They are known for their secrecy. None of their holdings are public. Duncan Campbell IV, known as Chip, runs the family along with his younger brother Clayton."

Milo raised his hand.

Gramm sighed. "Please tell me somebody has something besides Milo."

White and Preston shook their heads.

"Okay, Milo, whatcha got?"

"Sutherland's Aunt Lana."

"Okay, I'll bite. What about Aunt Lana?"

"She went to school with Greer Campbell."

Preston scrolled up on her pad. "Greer Campbell, aunt to Chip and Clayton. She's also on the family board of trustees."

"Aunt Lana told me, as a girl, she visited Greer in the family compound. They weren't allowed to run free around the compound. They had to stay in special areas. Lana says Greer used to complain about all the family rules."

"Such as not allowing the police in?" White said.

"Greer told Lana that the original Duncan Campbell made his money in mining, and he had a partner who died in a mine cave-in the early 1900's. The partner's family apparently claimed foul play and insisted that Duncan stashed the body in Campbell Mine Number Two."

"Where is this Campbell Mine Number Two?" Gramm asked.

"Up the shore, north of Culver," Milo said.

"Did anyone ever find a body?"

"I don't know...something to check out."

"Do we think this Harold Gilbert has anything to do with that old legend?" Gramm asked.

"No clue. It's just information."

Gramm turned to White. "What about the dead man's phone?"

"It's a waterlogged pay as you go," White said. "It's going to take time."

"It's been two days. How much time do they need?" Gramm grumbled.

"I'll check," Preston offered.

"Have we at least found Milo's friend, this Shawn guy?" Gramm asked.

"Shane," Milo corrected. "Shane Bell."

White shook her head. "We have a BOLO out for him. One other note: I talked to Ralph at the Coast Guard last night and told him the body had been in the water for less than twelve hours. Ralph called back this morning with a launch point."

"Launch point?" Milo questioned. "The guy wasn't a boat."

"I'm just the messenger. Ralph said launch point."

"Stop it!" Gramm shouted. "Where did the victim go into the water?"

"At or near Jay Cooke State Park."

"No surprise there. That's where the county found his car," Preston said.

Gramm was about to grumble again when his desk phone rang. He picked it up. "Gramm."

"Lt. Gramm, this is Mazy Campbell. I understand you've been looking for me."

Gramm's eyebrows shot up. "We have. Thank you for calling."

"What is this about?"

"A man has died, possibly murdered, and we have reason to believe that he was one of the people looking for your puzzle pieces."

"They aren't my puzzle pieces, Lieutenant. They were my father's."

"I am led to believe they are yours now. We simply need to know about the contest. Seeing as how we can't visit you unless a judge gives us permission, could you visit us?"

"Certainly. I will be there within the hour. I might have an attorney with me if that's okay with you."

"It's your right."

"Goodbye."

"Goodbye," Gramm echoed, smiling at White.

§

Shane Bell lived in his car most of the time. Every three or four days, he would rent a cheap hotel room to get a good night's sleep and a shower.

That's where he was now, repacking his traveling kit and looking for his last clean shirt and pants. *Time to find a laundromat,* he thought.

Shane checked his wallet. He had enough money for breakfast and laundry, but it was time to find a few more moving jobs. Movers were always looking for cheap labor to carry the big stuff. He scratched his chin beard and smiled. There was a new deal on the horizon. With luck, he could get out of this back-breaking business forever.

The knock on his motel door startled him. "Mr. Bell, police, please open the door and keep your hands where we can see them."

Shane ran to the bathroom, but the only way out, a small window, had bars. Police blocked the front door. He froze, unable to move.

The banging continued. "Shane Bell, we know you're in there. Open the door!"

A younger Shane Bell would try to fight, but he was too old to fight and work on the same day. He opened the door.

He stared at two Duluth cops—one tall female and a shorter male, both in uniform. "Shane Bell, you are wanted for questioning in the death of Harold Gilbert. You have the right to…"

"Harold Gilbert? I don't know any Harold Gilbert!" He tried to run through the two officers. They pushed him back, slapped cuffs on him, and began leading him out of the motel—reading him his rights.

"What about my stuff—my clothes? I need my clothes."

"We'll pack you up," the male cop said.

"Throw everything in the red duffle," Shane said. "The green one is for clean clothes."

"Do you want me to iron anything for you too?" the cop said sarcastically.

Shane wanted to head butt the guy, but he was cuffed and being shoved into the back seat of the cop car. Several of the motel's other customers stepped out of their rooms to gawk.

"I don't know anybody named Harold!" Shane kept shouting, ducking as his head went under the open door of the car.

§

Michael Mason insisted on driving Mazy to the police station for her interview with Lt. Gramm. She agreed to his driving but told him to stay in the car. He wasn't needed and would get in the way. That did not sit well with Michael, but Mazy didn't care.

The day was cloudy, and the promised drizzle had just begun. Mazy exited the Cadillac Escalade, popped her umbrella, and hurried around the parking lot puddles.

"I'm Mazy Campbell here to see Lt. Gramm," she told the desk sergeant while folding up the umbrella.

"How do you spell Mazy?" the sergeant asked.

"One z one y."

After signing her name into his log, the sergeant alerted Gramm, who escorted her back to his office. "Can I get you coffee?" he asked.

She declined.

He introduced her to Sgt. White, who noted her expensive, well-tailored, black suit. Mazy referred to it as her nondescript, family approved, blah attire.

"Thank you for coming in, Ms. Mason. Your visit saves us a lot of trouble," Gramm said.

"The family does love its privacy," she quipped. "Now, what is this about?"

Gramm, settling into his chair, opened a fake interview folder. He started doing that several months ago and liked the effect. "The body of a man named Harold Gilbert was recovered in the St. Louis River two days ago. We have reason to believe he had found one of your puzzle pieces before he died."

"I told you, they are my late father's puzzle pieces." Mazy crossed her arms.

"We understand, but thought he might have shared his ideas about the contest, such as the purpose."

"Ratings. My father owned KDDW. He told me he wanted to pump up the ratings for something called the spring book. The station was basically his toy."

"Getting back to the contest, we understand it has two parts—find the first part, win a hundred dollars and a puzzle piece that can lead to more money. Why that complicated?"

Mazy smiled. "I wondered the same thing. I questioned him about the two parts to the contest. He said he wanted to see what people would do. My father was always a student of human behavior."

"What were their options other than looking for the treasure?" White asked.

"My father said they could look for the treasure themselves, join with other puzzle holders and share the treasure, or sell the puzzle piece."

"Sell it? Who to?" Gramm asked.

Mazy smirked. "He suspected my family, for one. My father was convinced the Campbells would buy as many of the pieces as they could to stop the contest from going forward."

"And are they? Buying puzzle pieces?"

"Don't answer anything!" A female voice shouted from the bullpen area.

Gramm's head shot up. Kimberly McKenna strode toward his office, with the desk sergeant sputtering behind her.

Mazy groaned.

Gramm's bushy eyebrows knitted together.

"Lieutenant, I'm surprised that you are attempting to interrogate my client before I could get here."

Gramm shrugged. "First off, Ms. McKenna, I would have to know you were definitely coming. Your client didn't mention it as an absolute."

Mazy turned to McKenna. "I'm not your client."

McKenna was taken aback.

Turning back to Gramm, Mazy said, "Ms. McKenna represents the Campbell family, not me. I personally do not feel I need a lawyer."

White was amused at the game that was unfolding. Gramm was not.

"Ms. Mason, if you wish Ms. McKenna to leave, she'll leave."

"I advise you to let me stay," McKenna said.

"You can stay, but if you start spouting off *Chipisms*, you're gone," Mazy said.

McKenna smiled and looked around. "I seem to be without a chair, Lieutenant."

"Grab one from out there," Gramm directed.

McKenna continued to stand next to Mazy.

Gramm stretched his back and his neck. "So, we were asking you if your family was buying puzzle pieces."

McKenna began to object. "I…"

"Yes, they are," Mazy broke through.

McKenna pursed her lips.

"How does that work?" White asked, enjoying Mazy's stifling the lawyer. "How do they know the identity of the people who have found the pieces?"

"The radio station has offered to interview anyone who finds a puzzle piece," Mazy explained. "People love the attention. The station gets more buzz. My father also expected that."

"How many pieces does the family have?" White asked.

"Lieutenant, as Ms. Mason does not head the family, how would she know?" McKenna interrupted.

"I'm on the board, Ms. McKenna. On Tuesday, Chip showed us two pieces."

"Out of how many?" White asked.

"Twelve. The family has two. The last we heard, a group calling itself 'The Consortium' had three. I have been told there are three people who will not sell, at least not yet, and have not joined with others. As of Tuesday, that leaves four yet to be found," Mazy said.

"I really must advise you to not answer any more questions," McKenna insisted.

"Why? They just want to know how the contest works. A man was murdered, for goodness' sakes. That was not an outcome my father foresaw."

"Who are the members of this Consortium?" White asked.

"Chip said it was an older woman, a bald guy, and a younger woman. I don't know names."

"Who does?" White asked.

"I think they've been interviewed on the station. Talk with Larry Latto. Chip may know their names, but I doubt he'll talk to you. He did say the younger woman was volatile."

"Volatile?" Gramm questioned.

"Chip said the family's gopher tried to buy her piece, and this woman went off on him. Come to think of it, Chip did have her name. It was Kayla something or other. I think she threatened to stab the guy. Good for her."

"Gopher?"

"Yeah, the family has someone trying to buy the pieces. I don't know for sure who, but probably the Major—you know, the guy who wouldn't let you in."

"How much are they offering?"

"That's not your business," McKenna said.

"Five thousand dollars," Mazy said. "Maybe it's gone up. They just want this contest to go away because it threatens their precious privacy."

"What's the final treasure amount?" White asked.

"I don't know. My father never said. I assume it's something in the thousands."

"Have you ever heard the name Harold Gilbert?"

"No."

"Thank you, Ms. Mason, for coming in. Please give your phone number to Sgt. White before you leave, in case we have further questions," Gramm said.

"Are you going through with that silly idea of getting a warrant?" McKenna asked.

"We may. At some point, we will need to talk with other members of the family. If they cooperate, as Ms. Mason has, a warrant will not be necessary, but if we need to enter their compound, then yes, we'll be asking a judge to grant a warrant."

McKenna handed her card to Sgt. White. "I would appreciate a call first. I may be able to save you some embarrassment and convince my clients to cooperate. If not, we'll see you in court."

"I look forward to it," Gramm said.

McKenna and Mason left, being led through the bullpen area by Officer Preston.

"Five thousand dollars!" Gramm said to White. "I'd sell that puzzle piece in a heartbeat."

"I'd need at least that to keep up with those two," White complained. "Mason's black suit was expensive, as was McKenna's brown suit with that fancy coral blouse. Did you notice that it was similar to what she wore at the Milo killer-reveal last fall? Is that a uniform with her? I can imagine twelve of them hanging in her closet."

Gramm laughed. "Speaking of the same old, same old, a young woman named Kayla who threatens to stab people.

That couldn't be our old friend, Kayla Maki, could it?" Gramm asked, referring to a suspect in an earlier murder case.

White looked at her feet. "Should I change into running shoes?"

9

"I just got a call from Harry on the desk. We've picked up Shane Bell," White said to Gramm, Milo, and Kate Preston. "Fast work. We only put the BOLO out this morning. Harry says we have him in holding. He's loud and annoying, insisting he doesn't know our victim, yet his fingerprints are all over Ham Gilbert's car. This might be another quick case."

"Let's not make it that quick. Let him stew for a while." Gramm said. "I'm hungry. Let's eat."

"I hate to say this," White said, "but I'm thinking Chinese food."

Preston smiled. "Oh, good, I'm not that hungry now, but by the time Milo and Hank finish their banter, I'll be famished."

"I'm right here, you know," Milo insisted. "The problem is Hank, not me."

The group piled into Gramm's Police Interceptor for the trip down the hill. "This was much quicker when the station was across from the restaurant and not up over the hill," Gramm complained.

After parking in a nearby public parking lot, they walked the drizzly two blocks to the Chinese Dragon. White and Preston brought umbrellas. Gramm and Rathkey kept their heads down, setting a fast pace. White was the first to see the folding signboard in front of the building. She walked over to it and began laughing.

The other three followed. "What the hell?" Milo yelled.

The board featured a picture of Milo at the group's favorite booth, a picture taken by the proprietor, Milo's good friend, Henry Hun. The sign read: *The Chinese Dragon is a favorite of famed Duluth Detective Milo Rathkey.*

"Are you kidding me?" Milo sputtered. "It's that damn book." That *damn book* was Ron Bello's national best seller about the Harper Gain case and Milo's sensational solution.

White patted Milo's shoulder. "If your friends can't exploit your fame, who can?"

"Can we go inside?" Gramm groused. "I'm getting waterlogged."

As they walked in, Hank rushed to meet them. "I have a booth for you right up front."

"We want our usual booth in the back," Milo said.

"No can do. Last time you were here, too many people wanted you to sign books. It created a bottleneck. Up front there's plenty of room," Hank said.

"If Milo isn't with us?" Gramm asked.

"Then you get the booth in the back."

"Thank you for your support, Ernie," Milo said.

Gramm shrugged. "I didn't say we would do that. I just wanted to know our options."

Hank led the foursome to an alcove on the left, usually a spot where people waited for a table or for their takeout. The benches had been moved outside, and a lone booth set up apparently for Milo and company.

"This is a hallway!" Milo complained. "You've moved us to a hallway."

Hank feigned hurt. "I provide you with your own special alcove, and you complain. Here you can eat in private, undisturbed."

"I'm hungry. Let's do it," White said, sitting down.

Hank left, but the group heard his voice on the restaurant speaker system. "For those awaiting a Milo Rathkey autograph, he's sitting up front in our special alcove to the left. Enjoy."

"Of all the…" Milo began his tirade but was cut short by people lining up to get his autograph.

Hank returned with tea, complimentary sticky baked Chinese chicken wings, and spring rolls for Gramm, White, and Preston. When Milo complained about being left off the appetizer order, Hank told him he was a sloppy eater and would get grease on people's books.

"If the food wasn't so greasy, it wouldn't be a problem," Milo yelled after him.

"Mr. Rathkey," the next lady in line said while setting her book in front of him, "I love that you support local small business. Could you sign to Florence? It's for my grandmother."

Milo turned to his picture in the book and signed his usual: *Florence. Book clubs can be dangerous. Milo Rathkey.*

"These chicken wings are fabulous!" White said to Preston.

Preston agreed. "Milo, aren't these chicken...oops."

After fifteen minutes, Hank returned to take their orders. "We are having Dim Sum Thursday. You can order dim sum from the special menu or order the usual from the usual menu."

Milo finished with the last autograph seeker and picked up a dim sum menu. Hank grabbed it back. "Not for you. You won't order dim sum. You'll just ask a bunch of jackass questions and then order your usual chicken egg foo yung."

"I saw other people ordering dim sum," Milo said. "The plates seem kinda small. Did the bank repossess your big plates?"

"You're in an alcove, you can't see other patrons," Hank said. "Robin, what is your pleasure?"

White ordered vegetarian shumai, Preston ordered pork and prawn shumai, and Gramm opted for the regular menu—chicken and broccoli, which he thought to be healthy. "Allow me to order for our celebrity," Gramm said. "Chicken egg foo yung, and as much as it pains me to say this, don't skimp on the gravy."

"I may want dim sum. I am, after all, a celebrity and a man of the world." Reading off the special menu, Milo said, "I could want feng zhua, chicken feet in black bean sauce."

"But you don't," Hank said, pulling Milo's menus.

"I could."

Hank smiled and left.

As Milo signed another fan's autograph, White bet Gramm a dollar that Milo would get chicken feet.

Gramm noted the book-hugging line of fans had dissipated. "Good. We're alone…finally. Let's do some business. We have Milo's good buddy Shawn Bell in lockup."

"Shane Bell," Milo corrected.

"Yeah, him. There is mounting evidence against him, but we have to do our due diligence. That means interviewing Kayla Maki and the other members of this so-called Consortium."

"You take the back door," White said to Preston.

"What does that mean?" Preston asked.

"She's a runner."

Hank and a server returned with the food. Dim sum bamboo baskets were set in front of White and Preston. Gramm's dish came under a silver dome. Milo's was just a plate…one chicken foot sticking out of a jellied bean broth.

Gramm handed White a dollar.

"What is this?" Milo shouted.

"What you ordered."

"I can't eat this. I'll be thinking of a poor one-footed chicken on crutches!"

Hank sighed as a second server came to the table with Milo's chicken egg foo yung in heavy gravy. Hank was about to take away the chicken foot, but Preston said she'd love to try it. Hank took it from Milo and placed it in front of Preston.

"You don't know some people until they are presented with a chicken foot to eat," Gramm mumbled. "I miss my booth in the back."

People clutching books interrupted their meal, and police business, several times. Milo signed without complaint. When Hank returned to the table, Milo allowed as to how his meal should be comped for bringing in all this business.

Hank looked at an imaginary spreadsheet. "Let's see, Milo owes me $5,390.28 for all the meals I provided when he was dead broke. Let me remove the cost of this meal from that total."

"That's fair," Milo said. "I'm glad my debt is going down."

"On second thought, I'll just charge you," Hank said, handing Milo his bill.

"What about our checks?" Gramm asked.

"On the house. You have to put up with Milo."

"Wait, they get comped, and I don't?" Milo complained.

"You catch on fast. I guess that's why you're a world-famous detective."

On the way out, Milo noticed Hank had hung an old picture of the two of them riding the bench on their high school baseball team.

"Aw," White said. "He likes you."

§

The off and on drizzle was on again and drove Chip and Clay from the back patio to Chip's study. "I received another one of those notes," Chip complained.

"How?"

"Same way, tacked to my front porch. It says 'Old secrets. New problems.'"

Clay laughed. "What did they do, cut out letters from an old magazine?"

"Computer printer."

"Someone's having you on, Chip. He is sending you these cryptic messages, and you are filling in the blanks. They don't say anything."

"Who besides the family would know about an old secret? A LaPointe? And what makes you think it's a man? It could be a woman."

Clay thought for a moment. "You may be right. What about Mazy? Her father started this mess. Maybe they were in it together. Embarrass the family because of some imagined slight."

Chip's upper lip began to quiver just thinking about it. "Mazy went to talk to the police today after I specifically told her not to. That damn contest. Exposing the family. Breaking traditions. Kim says Mazy ignored her advice—answered all their questions."

"Questions? About what?" Clay asked.

"The damn contest, how it worked, that sort of thing."

"Sounds pretty innocuous."

"Clay, you named her as the betrayer! She ran to the police. She couldn't wait to answer their questions. Campbells don't do that. We're above that. It is time we distance ourselves from her."

"Distance?"

"She's the enemy. She should not be in the inner circle. We have the votes. She's gone!"

"It's been done before," Clay agreed.

§

Gramm, White, Milo, and Preston looked through the one-way glass at Shane Bell in the interview room, still cuffed, still angry. "Recognize him?" Gramm asked Milo.

"He's older, has that chin hair, but that's him. Benny was right. Those are bad tattoos." Milo said.

"Tell me again what you remember about him," Gramm asked.

"I was doing shore patrol in Norfolk. Shane was a grunt. He had lost his ride for fighting…"

"Lost his ride?" Preston asked.

"His boat," Milo explained. "The Navy assigned him to a submarine as a mechanic, but he was a discipline problem. If I remember correctly, he was thrown off the boat and was doing grunt work at the base. I remember arresting him every other week. Then he was gone."

"Boat?" Gramm questioned. "Shouldn't it be called a ship?"

Milo shook his head. "Not a sub. Subs are boats."

"You were a cop in the Navy?" Preston asked.

"Yes, why does that surprise you?" Milo asked.

"Did you have a cute uniform with wide cuffs and a natty hat?" White asked.

"You watched too many Popeye cartoons."

"Popeye?" Preston asked.

"Stop!" Gramm growled. "You're making me feel older than I am. Milo, I think you and I should grill this guy."

White made a "be my guest" gesture.

Bell noticeably startled when he saw Milo walk in with Gramm. "Milo Ratface—just like old times."

"I'm Lt. Gramm. You know, police consultant, Milo Rathkey. We're going to ask you questions about the death of Harold Gilbert."

Shane sneered and pushed his chair away from the table. "I keep telling ya, I don't know any Harold Gilbert."

"Ham Gilbert," Milo added.

Shane sat up. "Ham? Somebody killed Ham?"

"Oh, so you do know him," Gramm said.

"Yeah, I know Ham, not Harold. No one called him Harold."

"How do you know him?" Milo asked.

"He's my partner, my buddy. We work together."

"Doing what?" Gramm asked.

"Mainly furniture moving, but we would do heavier stuff if we could get it. Pays better. I'm still strong, unlike you, Ratface. You look like an old man."

Milo ignored the gibe. "Were you looking for puzzle pieces together?"

Shane stared but didn't answer.

Milo sat back. "You were overheard talking about it in the Rasa Bar, just before you threatened your buddy Ham."

"We were kidding around. That's what guys do. You never understood that, Ratface, you wuss."

"So, Ham found a puzzle piece in the hats and wouldn't share?" Milo accused.

Shane blinked rapidly, wondering how Milo knew about the hats. "Well…well, we both followed the clues. The puzzle piece had to be in one of those hats. I had an important thing to do, so I sent Ham to buy the hats. Figured he could handle that part. Big mistake. He told me at that bar there weren't any pieces in the hats. I didn't believe him. I think he found one and was going to sell it on his own. Ham was stupid that way."

"So, you killed him," Gramm said hopefully.

"Ham was stupid. I ain't stupid," Shane spat. "If I did that, I wouldn't get the puzzle piece, would I?"

"Let's say I believe you," Milo said. "If Ham had the piece, how do you know he wasn't going to try to find the treasure all by himself?"

"Ham? Nah. He couldn't find his ass with a flashlight. Like I said, he was going to sell it, skip town, and cheat me."

"Sell it to who?"

"That's sell it to *whom*, moron. I had the connection with the guy who's paying big bucks for those pieces. Ham and I were going to split it. Then Ham says the hats were empty. I smelled a double cross."

"Who's your connection?" Milo asked.

Shane gave him a nasty smile. "None of your business. I ain't a rat, Ratface."

"Your fingerprints were all over the victim's vehicle," Gramm said.

Bell laughed. "We were partners. I rode in it every day. We took his car to jobs. Better gas mileage. We were supposed to take a job a couple of days ago, but Ham never showed. I've been callin'—no answer. I figured he was gone, and I got screwed again. Damn!" Shane slammed his hands on the table and stood, as did Gramm. An officer raced into the room. "I'll tell you one thing, Ratface," Shane began as the officer's hand pushed down on his shoulder, forcing him back into his seat. "I'm going back to that bar and kick some ass. They stitched me up. They're all ratfaces, just like you!"

Milo smiled and looked at Gramm, who said to Shane, "I would strongly advise you to stay away from the Rasa."

After Shane was taken back to holding, Milo remained at the interview table, deep in thought.

"Tell me you've solved this," Gramm said.

"Just the opposite. None of this makes sense. Once again, if Ham Gilbert was murdered for his puzzle piece, why did the murderer leave it?"

"He panicked or didn't see it. Mazy Mason told us about those radio station interviews. The murderer noted his name and tracked him down."

Milo nodded. "And then killed him?"

"Well, maybe someone got to him before the buyer. Or he changed the deal, and the buyer offed him."

"We need to go to that station again," Milo said, "to see if Ham Gilbert made an appearance."

"Others could be in danger," Gramm said.

"There's one other possibility."

"What?"

"Ham's death has nothing to do with the contest."

Gramm groaned. "Our easy case just got complicated."

§

Kayla Maki sipped her iced tea and bit into another of Charlotte Lane's mint green frosted sugar cookies. Kayla smirked. Charlotte, a retired teacher in her seventies, had matched the cookies with her mint green and orange-striped eye glasses. *And people think I'm odd,* Kayla thought.

Ben Heikkinen, the third member of the KDDW Puzzle Consortium, returned from the bathroom. He was wiping his hands on his overalls. "Charlotte, your hand towels are too pretty to use. I left a message for this Ham Gilbert to join us, but I haven't heard anything. He probably sold his piece."

Kayla shook her head. "You didn't read the blog this afternoon?"

"No, why?"

"The police pulled a Harold Gilbert out of the St. Louis River Tuesday morning. I assume Harold and Ham are the same person."

"Oh, my!" Charlotte closed her eyes as she shook her head. "How awful. Did he fall in?"

Kayla crinkled her face. "I'd go with murder."

"Why would you think that?" Ben objected.

"The blog said that homicide cop Gramm is involved. He doesn't do accidents," Kayla explained.

"You talk as if you know him," Ben said.

"I've met him. I think Gilbert was done in for his puzzle piece."

"If that's true, we all need to be careful," Ben said. "Last night, my guard llamas attacked someone lurking in my barn. He got away. I don't know what the guy was doing. The llamas were putting out their shrill warning call, so I ran to the corral. A pickup with a camper on top was pulling out of the parking area. I couldn't see the make. It's dark at my place."

"You have llamas?" Charlotte asked.

"Alpacas, mainly. The llama's guard the herd. They're fierce when upset, and they were upset."

"No one has messed with me," Kayla said. "They better not," she added, pulling out a three-inch folding knife.

"Stop! Stop!" Charlotte waved her hands in front of her face. "I wanted this afternoon to be pretty. This is not pretty. It's murder, and knives, and…"

Ben stared at her. "Are you all right, Charlotte?"

Charlotte looked down. "I get so few opportunities to entertain. So many of my friends are dying, and now people I don't even know are dying. It's ugly. I like pretty."

Kayla put her knife away. "Sorry, Charlotte." The three talked about getting at least one more member into their Consortium and decided that Charlotte would get another chance at entertaining next week.

"Yellow," Charlotte said. "I shall do yellow. I have yellow polka dot glasses, a recipe for lemon cookies, and a lovely, yellow, frilly blouse. I will even add yellow flowers! It will be so pretty."

Ben said he was looking forward to it. Kayla thought about her usual look of red lipstick, long, stringy, dirty-blond hair, and oversized jean jacket. None of that screamed pretty yellow. *But I like lemon cookies,* she thought.

§

The leggy receptionist at KDDW once again tore herself away from TikTok videos to tell Larry Latto that the police were in the lobby. Before this visit, White had called Latto to inform him of the information the police needed. Latto joined them in the lobby.

"I think we have what you want," he said. "Follow me to the production room."

The three followed Latto past the gold record, down the hall, past his office, into a smaller room on the right. He sat down at a control console. Latto pressed a button, and the interview with Ham began.

"Where did you find your KDDW Puzzle Piece, Ham?" The DJ asked.

Gramm was looking for a tape deck, but there wasn't one. "No tape?" he asked.

"Not for years," Latto said. "It's all digital."

The interview continued. *It was hidden in a hat at a hardware store. The clues led me there.*

When you say hidden, what exactly does that mean?

It was sewed into the hat.

So, Ham, what are you going to do with your piece? Find the treasure yourself, join a group of people with pieces, or sell it?

I wanna sell it.

Well, I think you have a good chance of doing just that. What would you do with the money?

I just wanna to go home. I'm tired of the big city.

The DJ stifled a laugh at Duluth being called a big city. *Where's home?*

Fortuna, North Dakota.

Well, all of us here at KDDW in the big city wish you the best of luck.

"That didn't happen," White said.

"What do you know about these people offering to buy the puzzle pieces?" Gramm asked.

Latto shrugged. "Not much other than we hear they are offering up to five grand. So, they have to have deep pockets."

"Did Gilbert tell you anything else?" Gramm asked.

"No. That was the one and only time we talked to him."

§

Kayla Maki lived over her father's garage, several hundred yards from the main house. A single bare bulb at the top of the garage threw a dim light over the outside wooden stairway. She parked her old electric-blue Hyundai Elantra in the driveway and was walking toward the stairs to her apartment when a rotund, hooded man crashed through a stand of tall bushes and shoved her down on the hard concrete.

"What the...ow!" she screamed as her body bounced on the hard, wet driveway.

Her attacker was on top of her, holding her down. Kayla smelled his rancid breath as he hoarsely screamed, "I want your piece!"

"What?" Kayla stuttered, turning her head away.

"Your puzzle piece, give it to me! Now!"

"Sure...sure. Just don't hurt me," Kayla whimpered.

"Hurry up!"

"I can't get my hand in my pocket. You're on top of me!"

The attacker was in the process of standing up, pushing off her, when the sharp pain of her blade pierced his skin. "No!" he yelled, falling to his right, trying to avoid her knife. But Kayla had caught him, and his movement continued the slice—not deep, but messy and painful. The man screamed, grabbed his midsection, and stumbled to his feet.

Kayla sprang up, knife still in hand. The rotund man was stumbling down the driveway. A year ago, Kayla would have followed and cut him several more times, but she had been taking court ordered anger-management classes. She could hear her teacher saying, 'Kayla if you stab him again, you're in for trouble. Let him go.'

"Loser!" she yelled into the night.

Kayla two-stepped it up the stairs, placed the knife on the counter, and called the police, congratulating herself for remaining so calm.

10

White loved her job but mourned the fact that TGIF is never a thing when working an active homicide. So, this Friday she treated herself to a double-espresso-pistachio latte. Strolling into the bullpen, coffee in hand, she sat down at her desk and turned on her computer. She put her long, black hair into her work mode ponytail, and glanced at the overnight log which was part of the department's homepage. White did a double take. "Wow!"

Gramm lumbered in a few minutes later, poured himself a cup of department brew and turned toward his office only to be flagged down by White.

"Have you read the overnight log yet?" she asked.

"All members of this department are required to read the overnight log," he responded officiously.

"And?"

"I'm a little behind."

"How behind?"

"1995, but I'm catching up."

White rolled her eyes. "Maybe I should wait to have this conversation in 2042, but it's time sensitive. Someone tried to mug Kayla Maki last night."

"Oh man! Dead?"

"Kayla's fine, apparently."

"I was talking about the mugger."

"Well…we're not so sure about that. Kayla cut him and watched him bleed all the way down her driveway."

"She only cut him once? Was she carrying groceries?"

"She told the responding officers about taking anger-management classes. This gets better."

Gramm arched his back, rolled his neck, and took a sip of his coffee. "I can't imagine how."

"The mugger wanted her piece of the puzzle."

"Our Friday starts early. Call Kayla. Tell her we're stopping by to chat. Did they let her keep the knife?"

"Yes. The blade was legal, barely."

§

Agnes thought she would be the first one down for breakfast. She was wrong. Lana had arrived first and was sitting at the morning-room table checking her email on her phone.

"Good morning," Agnes said, sitting down, catching the glassy stillness of the big lake.

"Am I sitting in your place?" Lana asked.

"Oh, no, I'm just enjoying the lake. That's an unused chair."

Martha arrived with toast and one egg over easy for Lana. "Mrs. McKnight, what is your pleasure this morning?"

She's loving this, Agnes thought, smiling inside. "That egg looks good."

"Just one?"

"Okay, two eggs over easy and toast."

Martha smiled and returned to the kitchen.

"So, being Mrs. McKnight feeling a little more comfortable than it did yesterday?"

"Martha and I are friends. She's doing that just to drive me crazy, but it's fine."

"You are the lady of the manor," Lana said.

"Oh, please! We're not in the Middle Ages. This may be a mansion, but I'm still trotting down the hall to take a bath."

"Why?"

"Sutherland's bachelor suite has a small shower. When we renovate the north end of the second and possibly third floor, I want a bathtub—in the apartment—not down the hall. He kids me that I am being unreasonable and extravagant."

Lana smiled and then took a sip of her coffee. "Let me ask you an indelicate question."

Agnes inhaled and pleasantly responded, "Of course." *Here we go again.*

"I know it's none of my business, but like I said, I run with the wind. I'm curious. Did Sutherland have you sign a prenup?"

Agnes exhaled and took time to think, sipping her coffee. "Up until a couple months ago, I would have asked you why he would need such a thing. It wasn't until *after* we were married that I learned about your sister's money."

Lana laughed. "Oh, my God! You didn't know?"

"Well, in my defense, he had a delightful house he inherited and a good job. He seemed stable except for a few quirks. And I really loved him. I never thought to ask for his complete bank account."

"Did he have you checked out?"

Agnes laughed. "I was pretty upfront about the $375.46 in my checking account. In retrospect, I should have had him sign a prenup. That kind of money attracts the wrong sort."

"Am I the wrong sort of whom you are speaking?" Sutherland asked as he arrived at breakfast.

"You are," Agnes said. "I was about to tell your aunt about my first meeting with Creedence."

Sutherland winced. "Not my finest hour."

"Who is Creedence?" Lana asked.

"Our financial advisor," Sutherland said.

"I was wondering why we were going to a financial advisor. I was quite capable of managing $375.46 without any help," Agnes said.

Milo appeared in time to suggest that, if Agnes had that kind of money, he was paying her too much.

"This is the oddest household I have ever been in," Lana said. "It makes me want to stay longer."

"What prevents you from staying?" Milo asked.

"I miss my home in Scotland. This may be a good time for me to confess—I'm here on a mission."

Sutherland raised his eyebrows. "Which is?"

"I am in good health, but at my age, it is natural to look for a successor to run the business. My father would absolutely hate both you and Agnes, so I would love for either of you to take it on. However, I don't think that's something either of you would want to do."

Agnes looked at Sutherland, who shook his head. Agnes agreed.

"So, here's my thought. You're both newly married, and like I said, I'm in good shape. We'll revisit this after your kids are out of college. Maybe one of them would like to run a shipping line."

"Kids?" Agnes asked.

"College?" Sutherland responded.

"Oops, I can see you're not there yet," Lana joked. "Mr. Rathkey? Do you want to run a shipping company?"

"My nautical knowledge ends with captaining the *Laura*."

Lana sat up straight. "Is the *Laura* still in the family?"

"Oh, yes," Sutherland said. "She's just out of dry dock. We keep her in the boathouse. It's Milo's favorite. I prefer the sailboat, the *Lakesong*. The *Laura* and the *Lakesong*," Sutherland smiled. "My father named his boats after two things he loved."

"No, he didn't!" Lana objected. "The *Laura* was your mother's boat! My mother, your grandmother, bought two identical boats, the *Laura*, and the *Lana,* one for each of us. A gift when we turned sixteen."

"I like that!" Agnes said. "She named them after her daughters."

"Where did she get the money?" Milo asked. "Those are two expensive boats."

Lana laughed. "For all my father's swagger, he wouldn't have made millions without my mother's inheritance. She lent him funds to use as seed money."

Sutherland nodded. "A family tradition, or so it seems."

"Except your mother, Sutherland, had a lot more than *seed* money," Agnes kidded.

"Where's the *Lana* now?" Milo asked.

"At my home in Scotland."

"Pity. We could race them," Milo suggested.

Lana smiled. "We did as teenagers. I usually won."

Milo's phone did it's *da dunk*. He excused himself, went into the gallery, and answered.

"Am I interrupting your breakfast?" Ernie Gramm asked.

"I haven't started yet."

"Well wolf it down and meet White and I at Kayla Maki's house. I'll text you the address."

White walked into Gramm's office just as he was offering to text. *He's texting. They grow up so fast.*

"Can I ask why the urgency to visit Kayla?" Milo asked.

"She was mugged last night. Some guy assaulted her for her piece of the puzzle."

"Is the guy still alive?"

Gramm laughed. "I asked the same thing. They stitched him up. We arrested him last night at the ER. He's not going anywhere, so I want to talk to Kayla first." Gramm hung up and turned to White. "Amy worked last night. Let me see if she tended to our mugger. Maybe she heard something."

"Isn't she sleeping?"

Gramm looked at his watch. "Not quite yet." Gramm called Amy.

"I was waiting for your call. Yes, I saw the guy come in. We knew right away something wasn't right."

"How did he say he was cut?"

"He was making a sandwich."

"Really?"

"Slipped on some mayo that fell on the floor."

Gramm could not stop laughing.

"Easy for you to laugh. We have to keep a straight face for these jokers, so they don't get suspicious. Besides, his sloppy sandwich making skills didn't account for the other injuries."

"Such as?"

"He had a dog bite on his leg, and a severe bruise on his chest. We could see the imprint of what looked like a hoof where an animal struck him."

"So, we're looking for an angry sheep with karate skills?"

"Yes, you are. Have a good day. I'm going to bed now."

"Did we haul him to jail, or is he still there?"

"He's resting comfortably, handcuffed to his bed."

"Did he say anything that I should know?" Gramm asked.

"I got the idea that if you know a woman named Kayla, be careful. Apparently, she was making the sandwich."

"Sweet dreams, Amy. Thank you."

"Kayla's ready for us," White said, looking at an incoming text. "She's waiting at her house."

§

No breakfast buffet or coffee urn was visible. Bottled water had been hastily dumped into a large ice bucket placed in the center of the large conference table. Chip Campbell's hands were folded in front of him on the table, and his face was grim.

When all were assembled, Chip called the emergency board meeting to order. "This is not easy for me, but in light of disturbing recent events, I feel we have no choice but to remove Mazy from our board."

Mazy smirked. "What disturbing events, Uncle Chip? Did you get skunked in your fishing hole again, and decide to take it out on me?"

Chip's upper lip was quivering. "You disclosed family business to the police after I warned you not to," Chip challenged.

Mazy's temper flared. "And who the hell are you to tell me what to do?"

"Now, Mazy, there's no need for histrionics," Clay admonished.

"Oh, my! Chip's lap dog speaks," Mazy sneered.

Greer absently played with the jewel on her necklace but did not join Clay in admonishing Mazy. That should have been the first sign that this meeting was going south, but neither Chip nor Clay noticed.

"If anything needs to be discussed today, it should be Clay's continuous bad deals on the nineteenth hole which have been losing money for two quarters."

Clay's shoulders snapped back as if he had been pulled up short.

"Did you think I wouldn't notice? I can read a spreadsheet," Mazy continued. "Along with Clay's bad deals, we also have several divisions that are underperforming—all under your leadership, Chip."

"Enough! We're not talking about money!" Chip yelled. "I move that Mazy Mason be removed from the board, and that she and her husband vacate their house on the Campbell compound within the week."

"I second the motion," Clay shouted.

Mazy mocked Clay's lapdog status. "Good boy Clay. Treats for you later."

"Greer, take notes. I want a record of everything she said," Clay snapped.

Greer's note pad flew across the table into Clay's lap. "Be my guest," she spat.

Clay's eyes widened with apprehension. Chip's complexion went from pasty white to burning red. "All those in favor of the motion signify by raising your right hand."

Clay and Chip responded. Mazy and Greer did not.

"Greer, this is where you raise your hand," Chip barked.

"Chip, this is where I don't."

"Aunt Greer? What is going on?"

"Revenge, Chip dear."

"Revenge? For what?"

"My sister." Greer's look hardened.

"Oh, not that again! This vote is important. Vote yes!" Chip demanded.

Greer stared him down. "No! I won't! My sister McKenzie should have taken over as the oldest. Instead, she was banished. Not again, nephew. History will not repeat itself."

"As you very well know, Greer, Clay and I were not on the board when that happened."

"Sins of the father and all that." Greer sat up. "As to the removal of Mazy, I vote no. Mazy dear, how do you vote?"

"I also vote no. It appears we're at an impasse."

Greer laughed.

Chip glared at her. "Fine. We will break this *impasse* soon enough. My Amanda turns twenty-one in a week. She will take her rightful place on the board, and she knows how to behave."

"Are we going to discuss Clay's bad deals and the under-performing divisions?" Mazy asked.

"No!" Chip shouted.

"So, privacy before profit, uncle dear? Not a business model I've ever heard of."

Chip rose from the table. "We're done here." He and Clay left.

Greer looked at Mazy. "I'm afraid my company Christmas gift will be coal this year."

"My mom told me I had an Aunt Mackenzie who was banished from the family. Tell me more."

"She was the oldest of my siblings and bristled at being passed over when my brother, your grandfather, was named chairman of the board. Mackenzie was much brighter than our brother. She lodged her complaint at each board meeting while pointing out every mistake Duncan made. He and my father engineered her removal and banishment from the family. That was before I was on the board. I've sat in silence until now."

"It was a wonderful moment, Greer," Mazy said, "but I'm afraid Chip's right. In a week, he will have enough votes."

Greer smiled. "Don't be so sure. Tell me, what did the police want?"

"Nothing really. They wanted to know why my father started the contest, how it works, and whether or not the family is buying up puzzle pieces."

"Why would they care?"

"A man was murdered several days ago. He apparently had a puzzle piece."

"Oh, my."

"Why would Chip care about the contest enough to buy up the pieces?" Mazy asked.

"The short answer is the contest is an embarrassment. The actual answer is Chip is afraid the clues will lead people to Campbell Mine Number Two. Do you know the family history of that mine?"

"I know that the partner of the first Duncan Campbell, some guy named LaPointe..."

"Hayden LaPointe."

"Hayden LaPointe died in the mine—a cave-in," Mazy said.

"The LaPointe family claimed the original Duncan murdered him and left his body in the mine," Greer added.

"Is it true?"

"I wouldn't doubt it. Chip believes it. He doesn't want people entering that mine."

"Why not just post guards? Or board it up?" Mazy asked.

"The original Duncan allowed local people to hunt and fish on the land as long as they stayed away from the mine. He told everyone that it was unstable. We've continued that policy. If we post guards now, the locals will become suspicious about what are we guarding?"

"Well, I don't think that's a worry anymore. The police are convinced the puzzle leads to Jay Cooke State Park," Mazy said. "That's where that poor man was murdered."

"Too bad. Chip's paranoia is amusing."

§

Back at Chip's house, Clay and Chip mixed themselves stiff drinks to calm down and digest the recent mutiny. Normally Chip wouldn't imbibe this early in the day, but he was frazzled.

"What has gotten into Greer?" Chip demanded as Clay handed him a whiskey and water—more whiskey than water. "That goddamn Rutledge! I've got people attacking me from inside and out! Now Greer, my own aunt, is challenging me. She's never opened her mouth in the forty years I've known her." Chip downed his drink and made a second.

"Dear brother, we didn't realize how deep Greer's anger went?" Clay said with smug satisfaction.

Chip was angry and flustered. "What are you talking about? Just spit it out Clay! I'm not in the mood for more puzzles."

"She said 'sins of the fathers' to your face. She told you who has been sending those notes."

"Greer?"

Clay nodded. "Could be a coincidence, but I doubt it. I think she said it on purpose. She's the one who has been messing with you."

11

Kayla Maki was not an early riser. She set an alarm to get her head ready to be interviewed by the police. At least this time she was the victim, sort of. He had attacked her first. It wasn't her fault he was bad at it. The police had bagged up the clothes she had been wearing last night, including her favorite jean jacket. She didn't want them back. Her attacker had bled on them.

Eero Maki, Kayla's dad, had come over with breakfast to check in on his little girl. In the past, stress, such as being attacked or arrested, would bring on killer migraines, but the daith ear piercing had been doing its job. Plus, it looked cool—only one migraine since January and that was when she had to fill out an unemployment report. The mini mall where she had been selling candles banned her for her aggression toward customers. She was in the process of finding a new job.

Gramm stood outside the garage, looking up at the steps. He sighed. "Let's do this."

White scampered up the single flight. Gramm trudged and was halfway up as Milo turned his Honda into the driveway. Eventually, they were all seated in Kayla's small but comfortable garage apartment.

"I have one of those pod coffee makers in the kitchen if you want some," Kayla said, not offering to prepare it or bring it. All three passed.

"So, Ms. Maki, we meet again," Gramm said.

White was taken by the change in Kayla's appearance— yoga pants with matching fitted crop shirt. Her dirty-blond hair was pulled back and caught in a soft knot, but the red lipstick remained the centerpiece of her makeup.

"I was told you arrested the jerk," Kayla said. "What do you want from me? I was the victim. See, look at my face," she said, pointing to her scraped chin and nose.

"*Oh, there she is,*" thought White, "*as defensive and argumentative as ever.*"

"Yes, you were the victim, but we're here this morning hoping you could help us with another case that could be connected to last night's attack."

Kayla eyed Gramm with suspicion. She had not prepared for this.

"Where were you before you came home?" Gramm asked.

"I was meeting with my puzzle group."

"The Consortium?" White asked.

Kayla sneered. "No! That idiot blogger gave us that name. We don't like it—we don't use it."

"Who else is in the puzzle group with you?"

"They're nice people. They didn't do anything wrong."

"I'm sure they didn't," Gramm said.

Kayla was not convinced. She stared at Gramm. Her eyes shifted to White and then Milo. They must have passed the Kayla test because she began to relax a bit. "Charlotte Lane, older than my dad. She was a teacher, I think. Her clothes match her cookies—good cookies. Ben Heikkinen shaves his head because he's going bald, and he loves alpacas. He owns a farm outside of Hermantown."

Gramm glanced at White, making sure she was getting all this. "Where were you meeting?"

"At Charlotte's. She lives in a fourplex off Woodland. You might want to know this," Kayla offered. "Ben told us that someone had been messing with his animals—he calls them his babies—a couple of nights ago, but the llamas kicked the guy's ass."

"I thought you said alpacas," White said.

"The llamas guard the alpacas. It's a thing, I guess. Ben says they spit, strike with their front legs, and charge at humans in their pasture and body slam them."

Gramm looked at White. "Karate sheep?"

"More like killer sheep from hell," Kayla grinned. "Ben has lots of stories about them taking on coyotes and wild dogs. He says you don't want to mess with them. They're really strong."

We could say the same for you, Kayla, White thought.

"Do you think your attacker followed you home from your meeting?" Gramm asked.

Kayla's eyes narrowed as if she were thinking about Gramm's question. "Don't know. Ask him."

"Tell us about the attack."

"I already told the cops that came last night. Remember, I called them." Kayla boasted.

"They were here to deal with your attacker. We're here to deal with a homicide that occurred several days ago." Gramm said.

Kayla jumped up. Anger flashed. She stopped and took several deep breaths before pacing into the kitchen and returning—five times. On the last run, Kayla returned to her seat.

"Kayla? Are you okay?" White asked.

"*I* did not kill anyone."

Gramm smiled. "We weren't accusing you. We're wondering if your attacker might be involved in this murder we are investigating."

"Yeah? Well, you arrested the guy. Ask him."

"The murdered man was named Harold or Ham Gilbert. Ring any bells?"

"Yeah. I heard him on the radio. He found a puzzle piece. I contacted him—left a message."

"Tell us about the attack."

Kayla sighed, rolled her eyes, and began, "Not much to tell. I came in, parked in the driveway. I was walking toward my steps when that creep came up behind me and knocked me flat."

"Did he say anything?" White asked.

"I remember his bad breath."

"Yes, but did he say anything?"

"He demanded my puzzle piece. I gave him a nice slice to his midsection instead. After I cut him, he ran away. I've got his blood all the way down my driveway. Who's cleaning that?"

Milo noticed the compound bow hanging on the wall of the living room and remembered the pictures of Kayla at her dad's archery range—pictures of her holding marksmanship trophies. "Keeping up with the archery?"

"Dad and I do."

"We are told your attacker was a man named Jimmy Pleski. Do you know him?"

"There's lots of Pleskis around, but I don't know a Jimmy."

"How did you get your puzzle piece?" Milo asked.

"I followed one of the clues. *Lions and tigers and bears, oh my! My friend rides the sky. Who could it be? You'll have to pay to see.*"

"That was the clue?" Milo asked.

Kayla nodded. "Most people went up to Hawk Ridge, which I thought was stupid. You don't have to pay to see anything up there, and no one was going to ask a hawk to hang on to a puzzle piece."

"Hawks are so unaccommodating," Milo agreed.

"I went to the Lake Superior Zoo and found a backpack-wearing stuffed owl tucked behind other stuffed animals in the gift shop. The hundred dollars and my puzzle piece were in the backpack." Kayla sat back.

Milo applauded. "Well done."

Kayla beamed.

"Can I ask what you were doing a little while ago," White said, "with the walking and the deep breathing?"

"I was agitated. I thought you were accusing me of murder—again. I went through my steps: Think before I talk.

Breathe deeply. Exercise, and most important, use *I* statements. *I* did not kill anyone. Anger management—court ordered."

"Anger management. That's good," White said. "When did that start?"

"After I dumped Ike. He was a loser," Kayla revealed, referring to her biker boyfriend. "He made my headaches worse, always yelling at me. I got help for the headaches, too." She showed the ring in her ear.

"That's pierced in your ear." White was amazed.

"Cuts down on migraines. Doesn't work for everybody—works for me."

"I've been told," Gramm began, "that you can do one of three things with a puzzle piece: try to find the big treasure on your own, combine with others as you have, or sell it. Apparently, people are offering thousands of dollars. Why did you join with others?"

"Kinda out of character, isn't it?" Kayla smiled. "Charlotte reached out to me on that blog. My gut reaction was 'screw you,' but then I did my breathing and stuff. When I called her, the first thing she did was offer me cookies and was real nice to me. After talking for a while, I realized that two of us would have a better chance of finding the big prize. Ben joined us shortly after."

"Where do you three think the treasure is buried?" Gramm asked.

"Nice try." Kayla smirked.

§

"I'm told the horde is digging up Jay Cooke State Park."
Chip laughed as he joined Clay in the Island Lake Restaurant.
Chip bought the failing restaurant for the family so they
could have a private room when they wanted it.

"Is Jay Cooke where that guy was killed?" Clay asked.

"Yes. Lucky for us."

Clay flicked a crumb from his golf pants.

§

Preston called just as Gramm was parking the Interceptor
in the hospital parking lot. "The attacker of Kayla Maki,
James William Pleski, is 47 years old," Preston told Gramm
and White by phone. "He played semi-pro hockey years ago.
Until recently, he was a switchman for the railroad but is now
on disability. Not married, no kids."

"What's wrong with him?" Gramm asked.

"Pardon?"

"You said he's on disability. What's wrong with him?"

"I talked to a couple of people at Duff's bar in West
Duluth where the railroad guys hang out. A switchman has
to jump on and off trains. Pleski couldn't do it anymore, so
he faked an injury, according to a couple of the guys."

"You went to Duff's?" Gramm asked. "How would you
even know about Duff's?"

"My dad and two uncles worked the railroad. I've got
Duff's rights."

"Comes in handy. What else did you learn?"

"No one seems particularly fond of Pleski. They're glad
he's gone."

"Any particular reason why?" White asked.

"He's a whiner, thinks the world owes him. Also, one guy said he was accused a couple of times of having sticky fingers, stealing watches and stuff like that out of lockers."

Gramm hung up.

"See that? That's rude," White said.

"What?"

"You hung up. Preston is going to think she got cut off."

Gramm huffed, called Preston back. "Did you have more?"

"No. I…" Preston looked at her phone.

Gramm smiled at White. "She gets it."

Milo was already out of his car, having found street parking, and was walking toward the hospital entrance.

Duluth is a regional medical center for northern Minnesota, Wisconsin, and Upper Michigan. The hospitals tend to be on the large size for such a small city, and they're getting larger all the time.

"Big place," White said, looking up at the massive building.

"Sick people are big business, as Amy always says," Gramm added.

Milo met them in the lobby. He and White followed Gramm because he knew where to go to get the help they needed. The nurse on duty at the Special Services desk greeted him. "Inspector Gramm," Nurse Thompson said with a pronounced British accent.

"Helen, it's *Lieutenant* Gramm."

"Of course, Leftenant." She said, giving it a decidedly British air.

"We need the room number of a Jimmy Pleski, P-l-e-s-k-i."

Thompson entered the name into her computer. "Room 321 left tower. The elevators are on your right."

As they approached room 321, Milo questioned the lack of a police guard. "On TV they always have a police guard."

"On TV the police have unlimited manpower and overtime budgets," Gramm said. "What we have is a spare set of cuffs. If Pleski escapes, we'll put a BOLO out for a man dragging a hospital bed down the street."

"Do we shoot Pleski or the bed?" Milo questioned, but Gramm had already entered the room.

"Jimmy Pleski, we meet again," Gramm said to the man handcuffed to the hospital bed. "Last time you were trying to run past us in Jay Cooke."

"Screw you," Pleski spat. One bandaged leg was outside the sheet.

Gramm pulled up a chair and sat down. "You know, Jimmy, you could have mugged any number of people and come out the winner, but you picked the one woman who could do you damage."

"And she did," White said.

"I understand you wanted your victim's puzzle piece. How did you know she had one?" Gramm asked.

Pleski looked at Gramm as if he were stupid. "That blog. Some woman was advertising for puzzle piece holders to join her. I just staked out her house. When that young woman left, I followed her. She slit me open like a watermelon." He lightly moved his hand over his belly for effect. "I was the victim."

"You were mugging her at the time, Jimmy," White said.

"That's her story."

"What's yours?"

"I was trying to buy her piece when she attacked me for no reason, out of the blue."

"Were you also trying to buy a piece from that llama whose hoof is imprinted on your chest?" White asked.

Jimmy absently touched the place on his chest where the animal had kicked him. "I ran into a parking meter."

White rolled her eyes.

"Let's get to the real reason we're here. You probably read on that blog that a man was killed and his body dumped in the river near Jay Cooke Monday night. We're thinking that was your work, Jimmy," Gramm charged.

"No way! I ain't talkin' no more."

"In case no one has informed you, you're being held on robbery and assault charges," Gramm said.

"She stuck me!"

"You were attacking her at the time. She was defending herself," White laughed.

Pleski stalled, sipping water from his cup. "If I help you, do I get a break?"

"Possibly. Whatcha got?"

"Have you found the blogger yet? The guy doing the Duluth Puzzle Blog?"

"Do you have a name?" White asked.

"What do I get?"

"We tell the DA and the judge that you cooperated with our investigation. That should cut some time off your sentence," Gramm said.

Jimmy huffed. "Time off? No fair!"

"Right, Jimmy. It never is. Give us the name."

"Brandon Park. He lives on 16th Avenue East in an old barn-like house. What do I get for telling you that?"

"Up to the judge," Gramm said over his shoulder as they left.

§

"Jimmy wasn't lying," White said, looking at the brown, cedar shake house with the gambrel roof. "It does look like a barn."

Gramm and Milo were already on the porch. "It's a duplex," Gramm said, looking at the two intercom buttons. He pressed the one that had the word "Park" below it.

"Yes?" a voice inquired.

"Brandon Park?"

"Yes."

"Police. We want to talk to you."

"Come on up." The invitation was followed by the buzz of an electronic lock being opened.

Gramm shook his head. "Why do all these people live on the second floor?"

White laughed. "I do too. It's a better view."

As Gramm mounted the steep steps, he allowed as to how he was only going to interview suspects who lived on the ground floor from now on.

Brandon Park met them on the second-floor landing. His jet black, heavily pomaded hair was shaved on the sides, and swooped up on the top. "Hey, come on in."

"Nice hair," White said as she, Gramm, and Milo followed him into the apartment.

"Thanks," he said, turning around. "My mother and grandmother are hair stylists. I get this done for free. There isn't a curl to be found in my family, and I wanted a wave. They turned me on to dry pomade. I am Duluth's most edgy Korean American."

The apartment was 1920s old with original wood floors and woodwork. In stark contrast, Brandon had furnished the place with light, contemporary furniture. Gramm sat down in a modern recliner with a footstool. White chose the sofa with high metal legs. Brandon sat in an egg chair that hung from the ceiling by small chains. Milo stood and stared out the window.

"We understand you are the man behind the Duluth Puzzle Blog," Gramm said.

"Guilty."

"Not a very catchy name," White noted. *Especially for someone with that hairstyle.*

"It's a specific sub blog from my main blog."

"What?" Gramm was confused.

"I'm an orienteer. That's what I usually blog about."

"Orienteer?" Gramm asked.

"It's a sport," Milo said, turning to the group. "People hide things and provide a map and clues. You try to navigate the best way you can."

Brandon nodded.

Gramm and White looked at Milo.

"I did it for a while when I lived in Brainard. Fun."

"I do it as much as I can. I blog about my experiences and get paid to advertise other contests," Brandon continued. "When this radio station puzzle started, I loved it. I mentioned it a couple of times in my orienteering blog, and it got a huge response, so I decided to create a separate blog for it. Naming it the Duluth Puzzle Blog got to the point and did well in the search engines. My advertisers like that."

"Let *me* get to the point, Mr. Park," Gramm said. "You published details about a murder in Jay Cooke State Park before we released them. How did you know about them?"

"First let me read you your Miranda Rights," White said.

Brandon Park was shocked and barely heard what White was saying. When she finished, he asked, "Do you think I did it?"

"Mr. Park, you knew details about the murder even before we did. How is that possible unless you're the killer?" Gramm asked.

"I got an email."

"From whom?" White asked.

"I don't know. It was signed *The Riddler*. It told me that a guy with a puzzle piece was murdered in Jay Cooke State Park because he was getting too close to the treasure."

"That was it?"

"Well, the email said the guy was hit in the head and fell into the river."

"Based on an email, you published that information?" Gramm asked.

"I'm a blogger, not a newspaper reporter. It didn't mention any names. If the email was wrong, so what? I didn't believe it. I just thought it was part of the fun. Maybe a false clue or a dangerous one."

"Do you still have the email?"

"Of course."

"We will need to see it."

Brandon shrugged, stood up, and walked toward the door. When no one followed, he turned and said, "My computer is in my office on the third floor."

"Of course it is," Gramm mumbled, slowly rising from the recliner.

Another flight of stairs later, Gramm, White, and Milo were standing in a large, mostly vacant room with framed maps on the walls. A long computer table held Park's laptop, three screens, and several computer hard drives.

"How do you afford all this?" White asked. "The apartment, the computer, and these drives?"

"I trained as a physical therapist, but I do a lot of different things—most of them make money. And this is where I spend my money. You should make an appointment, Lieutenant. I see you wince a lot. Back problems?"

Gramm nodded and took his card.

Park sat down at his computer and called up the email.

"Do you mind if I forward it to myself?" White asked.

Park stood up, moved to the side, and gestured for White to sit down. She read it out loud first, so Gramm and Milo didn't have to crowd around. *"Duluth Puzzle Blog Master: A puzzle piece holder was murdered this evening at Jay Cooke State Park. He was hit over the head and fell into the river.* It's signed The Riddler."

White sent it to herself. "What did you write about it on your blog?"

Park leaned over her right shoulder, moved the mouse, and called up his blog.

Exciting vibes in the air this morning. Your faithful servant got word late last night that one of our puzzle brethren was laid low in the St. Louis River. What did he know? Rumor has it that he held a piece to the treasure. What, oh what has happened to that piece? As of this writing, it is in the wind. Do you have the cajones to stay in the hunt?

Blog Master

"St. Louis River?" Milo asked. "The email didn't mention which river."

Park shrugged. "What other river is there near Jay Cooke?"

"Do us a favor. If you get another note from The Riddler, let us know immediately," Gramm said.

"Sure, but I'll still publish it."

"We ask you not to, but you have that right."

"How many puzzle pieces do you have?" Milo asked.

"Two."

"Two?" White asked.

Park smiled. "I'm very good at sorting out clues."

"Or maybe killing people who are very good at sorting out clues," Milo said.

"I heal people. I don't kill them."

"Do either of your puzzle pieces say State or Park on them?"

Brandon called up scans of his pieces on the computer. One piece showed parts of four lakes. In Minnesota, the land of ten thousand lakes, it provided little useful information.

The other piece was even more limited, showing a small creek. Both appeared to be corner pieces.

"Not much there," Milo said.

"More than you think," Park said. "One piece, the one with the lakes, has a small white road. I'm trying to match that road. That same piece has a river running through the little node, which fits into the adjacent piece. It runs northwest to southeast."

"Not the St. Louis River," Milo said.

Brandon smiled. "Nope."

"So, not Jay Cooke State Park?"

"Nope."

"When did you get this piece?" White asked, pointing to the piece with the lakes.

"Weeks ago."

"So, you knew the treasure wasn't in Jay Cooke State Park," she charged.

"No, I didn't. Someone could have gotten to my pieces before me and left dummies to throw me off the hunt."

"Does that happen?"

"It does in orienteering all the time."

12

May in Duluth could be a delight, or it could be a throwback to winter. This day in May was heaven—deep blue skies, warm temps, and a slight breeze. Stepping off Brandon Park's porch, White took a deep breath. "I feel sailing in my future."

"Makes me want to stay outside," Gramm agreed.

White turned. "Food truck! There are food trucks at Canal Park."

"And it's early in the season, so it won't be packed with tourists," Gramm added.

"Milo?" White asked.

"What?"

"Food trucks? Are you in?"

"How do they work?" Milo asked.

"You go up to the truck, order your food, and then you pay. Complicated, but we'll guide you through it."

"Okay, you get your food. Where do you take it?"

"You run around the parking lot, taking a bite when you can," Gramm interjected. "Keep dodging cars."

"I'm in!" Milo said with enthusiasm.

Gramm and White, in the marked police car, found a parking spot, causing Milo in his Honda to grumble. "They could have left that for me. They can park in no-parking zones." After driving around the full parking lot for five minutes, he finally found a person leaving. He waited for the car to back up. A young guy in a jacked-up Jeep drove up on the other side of the parking space and gunned his engine. Milo calmly put his blue light on the roof of his car and sounded the siren once. Mr. Jacked Up got the message and moved on.

Gramm shook his head. "How am I going to explain to the Deputy Chief about Milo using lights and sirens to get a parking space for lunch?"

"Sanders loves Milo," White said. "Milo does interviews and mentions the department."

"Good point."

"You guys could have parked in that no-parking zone and left me the parking space," Milo complained as he walked up to Gramm and White.

"We could have, but we didn't," Gramm said. He looked at the three food trucks, all with growing lines. "Which one?"

White read the signs, "Diamond Max's Barbeque, Pizza Wheels, and Tank's Taco Truck. I think they're all safe. Milo can't possibly know any of these people. He's an inside kinda guy."

Gramm said he remembered trying Diamond Max's brisket last fall. "Melts in your mouth. No need for sauce, it's all in the rub."

"I don't even want to know what 'rub' means," Milo said.

The three stood in line for ten minutes, during which time Milo suggested he return to his car and get the blue light and remote siren. "You know, just to move past this line."

"I'm really regretting getting you that equipment," Gramm said.

Milo reached the counter first—a clear mistake. "So, Diamond Max, I assume you are Diamond Max," Milo said to the bald, large African American man with a salt and pepper beard.

"I am Diamond Max. Thanks for asking, sir." The man smiled.

"My friend here says your brisket will melt in my mouth. How do I know it won't melt on my plate? I don't want a plate full of melted meat."

White turned to Gramm. "How did we let him go first? Can't he just order his food?"

"If the meat melts on your plate, drink it," Diamond Max said. The smile didn't disappear.

"Do I need a beverage, then?"

"I would recommend it, just in case the brisket doesn't melt in time."

"Milo, if you don't order something, I will turn you over to the angry crowd behind you," Gramm threatened. "It's growing."

"I'll take the brisket, mac and cheese, and coleslaw with a Diet Coke. If it doesn't melt, I'll leave a less than favorable review."

"I'm quaking," Diamond Max said as he piled Milo's plate.

White stepped up next, ordering the same thing Milo did. "I am so sorry for him. He does this at all restaurants."

"Except to Maude at Everybody's."

White took a step back. "You know him? You've eaten with him!"

"Milo? Of course. He's my less than silent partner."

White looked around in confusion.

"It's all right. Milo is just being Milo," Max said, taking Gramm's order.

Milo took his food to a nearby picnic table. He smiled when he saw Gramm and White approach. "Fabulous food. Melts in your mouth."

White sat down and stared at Milo.

"What now?" Milo questioned.

"You're his partner?"

Milo nodded his head. "You picked it. You could have picked a different food truck. I don't know Pizza Wheels or Tank's Taco Truck, but both look tasty."

White turned her stare to Gramm. "Did you know?"

"I think we should talk about the case," Gramm said, clearing his throat.

"You did!" White accused Gramm. "It wasn't me. You're the one who chose Diamond Max!"

"Try the brisket," Milo suggested. "It's worth the aggravation."

White took a bite and closed her eyes to savor the taste. "Okay, you're right, but you could have let me in on it, partner."

§

The waitress took the Campbell brother's orders as they finished their second drink, a perfunctory exercise as they always ordered the same thing. Clay had the club sandwich, Chip the French dip.

Chip handed the menus back to the waitress and waited for her to leave. "We have our third piece."

"Did you reel that in from the lake this morning?" Clay mocked.

Chip moved his silverware around. "As a matter of fact, I did."

"So, dear brother, show me the new piece," Clay requested.

Chip retrieved the piece from his shirt pocket and set it on the table. It was green except for a round blue blob at the top and a thin blue line extending down through the piece.

"Not much there," Clay said.

"You're wrong! That blue is Round Lake, and the thin blue line coming down from it is the Arrow River, right by the mine."

"Oh, come on Chip. That could be any lake and river."

Chip shook his head. "Do you think Lewis picked some remote spot to bury his treasure? I doubt it. He's leading people to the mine and the body of LaPointe."

"So what? Let's say he is. What's the worst that could happen?"

"The LaPointe's are starting another lawsuit, and let me point out, little brother, that could be expensive."

Clay laughed. "All we have is a letter from a lawyer threatening a lawsuit. Who are these mysterious LaPointes? We haven't met one in years. Much ado about nothing, dear brother. They're your boogiemen. Our grandfather bought them off generations ago."

"We have no proof of that, but let's move on to the other problem…" Chip stopped talking long enough for the waitress to deliver their food.

"The other problem?" Clay asked as he bit into his club sandwich, wiping the remnant of a juicy tomato from his mouth.

"Mazy's accusations and Greer's betrayal."

"I've got to admit, I didn't see that coming," Clay said. "But your Amanda joins the board in a couple of weeks, then we can vote them both off the board."

§

"Something about this puzzle bothers me," White said, sampling the mac and cheese. "So good!" She rolled her eyes.

"What bothers you?" Gramm asked, letting more brisket dissolve in his mouth.

"Park said the treasure is not at Jay Cooke, but the piece that we have says *Cooke*. Shouldn't there be another piece that says *Jay* or *State Park*? Where are those pieces?"

"Duh!" Milo laughed. "I asked him that. Remember?"

"We need to see all the pieces found so far," Gramm said. "I assume we will need a judge to order that."

"Especially because Cooke doesn't necessarily mean the Park." Milo said.

Gramm laughed. "Do you think it refers to John Cook, the pirate?"

"No 'e' on the end," White countered.

"Rutledge misspelled it," Gramm joked.

"If you two are done, I will explain," Milo said.

Gramm did a sweeping hand gesture. "Explain away, oh wise one."

Milo took his time, sampling the brisket, the mac and cheese, and the coleslaw, before taking a long drink of his Diet Coke. "Well, Duluth is filthy with Cooke's. We have a Cooke Street, and the Jay Cooke statue in Jay Cooke Plaza at 9th Avenue East and Superior Street. That's not too far from Lakesong. I go there sometime to eat my lunch. Just me, Jay, and the pigeons, and let's not forget the Jay Cooke Plaza Tunnel."

"Crap!" Gramm said. "This puzzle piece could refer to any of that."

"But Ham Gilbert was murdered in Jay Cooke State Park," White argued.

"Maybe he got it wrong. Maybe he was looking in the wrong place," Milo suggested.

"Then why kill him?" White asked.

"We need to know more about Ham. Maybe he was killed for some other reason."

"Maybe your buddy Shane killed him because the dead guy stiffed him," Gramm said.

White erupted. "Maybe, maybe, maybe. I'm tired of maybes. We don't have enough information. We need to see more puzzle pieces."

"We also need to talk with Charlotte Lane and Ben Heikkinen," Gramm said, "the other two members of Kayla Maki's little group. Meanwhile, I'll get the DA going on subpoenas to see those pieces. It's the only line of inquiry we have right now. If our victim was killed for another reason, we're in the dark as to what that could be."

White called Preston. "Kate, find out as much as you can about Ham Gilbert. Where he grew up, any enemies, prior run-ins with the law—you know, the usual."

"I've already run a check, Sarge. Harold 'Ham' Gilbert grew up an only child of Harold senior and Helen Gilbert, nee' Smith in Fortuna, North Dakota. His parents are dead. He inherited a small house and supports himself by doing manual labor. He and Shane Bell linked up two years ago, hiring out to moving companies around the country. They didn't travel together, just met at the job. I got the idea that Shane was the contact person and when he needed help, he called Ham. That's it. No arrests, no girlfriends, boyfriends, nothing that pops up."

"Girlfriend or boyfriends? You checked?" White asked.

"I called the county sheriff. The woman who answered the phone went to school with Ham. She was mildly upset at his passing. She wanted to talk. We talked. She knew of no one in Fortuna that would wish him ill. I got the impression that Ham was 'just there,' that guy who doesn't take up space. She knew he wasn't in town anymore but did not know when he left."

"Well, that's a dead end and this puzzle thing is just a pain," White said.

"I asked if the deputy knew of anyone who would claim the body," Preston added. "She didn't."

"Sad."

"What happens now?" Preston asked. "Does someone ship the body home? What about his truck and possessions?"

White sighed. "St. Louis County buries him and probably auctions off his stuff."

"That is sad." Preston echoed.

§

"Charlotte Lane agreed to talk with us. She seemed almost eager," White said. "It was like she had something to tell us."

"Let's hope she knows the identity of the murderer," Gramm mused as he ran a red light.

"That light back there was red!" White admonished.

"It was yellow. I don't stop for yellow lights. I almost got rear-ended once."

White looked back at the intersection. "Milo stopped."

"He was behind us. For him, the light was red. Tell me about this Charlotte Lane."

"Preston said she's a retired schoolteacher. Her husband died five years ago. She found her puzzle piece in the downtown library. That's all I know."

"And Kayla Maki says she matches her cookies with her clothes. We could arrest her for that," Gramm joked.

"I think it's sweet."

The color of the day was pink—pink glasses, pink blouse, pink flowered capris, and pink sandals. Charlotte led Gramm, White, and eventually Milo into her living room where she invited them to sit down around a large, wooden coffee table complete with a plate of four pink sugar cookies and a pitcher of pink lemonade.

"I don't think I've ever entertained the police," Charlotte said. "Please have some refreshments."

White declined. "We've just eaten."

Gramm took one cookie and poured himself a glass of lemonade.

"Apparently, Sergeant White has just eaten," Milo said, taking two cookies and the lemonade. "I'll have hers."

Charlotte tittered. "How can I help you?"

"We understand you have a puzzle piece," Gramm said.

"I do. Would you like to know how I found it?"

Gramm nodded while biting into the cookie.

"Well, Thursday is my library day. I visit all of them. That week, it was the main library. That's where I found the one hundred dollars and the puzzle piece."

"Did you solve a clue?" White asked.

Charlotte laughed. "I do enjoy mysteries, but no, I just happened upon the puzzle piece while checking out *The Doorbell Rang*. I am reading Rex Stout's Nero Wolfe Mysteries. I do love all those wonderful characters that Nero Wolfe has about him: Fritz the chef—oh, I do wish I could cook some of his meals. I love flowers, so Theodore—the orchid man—is a particular favorite. And I enjoy Archie Goodwin so much. He's such a clever boy...."

"Ms. Lane, we are wondering about the puzzle piece that you found," said White, trying to get back to the reason for their visit.

"Oh, I'm sorry. I do get carried away sometimes. Where was I? Oh, yes. I was checking out *The Doorbell Rang* and there was an envelope in the book. I thought it was a leftover bookmark, and I was going to throw it away but saw the words: *Congratulations—Open Me* on the front. I opened it and found a one-hundred-dollar bill and a piece of a cardboard jigsaw puzzle. The woman at the checkout desk filled me in on the radio station contest. After I checked out and dropped the books in my car, I headed down to that same radio station. It was only two blocks down the hill."

"Why go there?" White asked.

Gramm finished his cookie and wondered if there were any more. He didn't care how Charlotte Lane found her puzzle piece, but thought it best to keep her talking.

"I couldn't imagine someone meant to leave a hundred dollars in a book. I understood the puzzle piece, a bit of fun, but not the money, at least for me. I just happened upon it by accident. I didn't earn it. When I arrived, they insisted the money was mine, and requested to interview me on the air. Seeing as how they just gave me a hundred dollars, to refuse would be rude."

"What made you decide to form the Consortium with Ms. Maki and Mr. Heikkinen?" White asked.

"On the radio, they asked me a rather intriguing question. Was I going to sell the piece? Apparently, people are offering a ridiculous amount for them. The other choices were to go on the treasure hunt by myself or join with other puzzle piece holders. Well, I certainly wasn't going treasure hunting by myself. My days are full. I don't have time to be traipsing around looking for buried treasure. My mother would have called that unseemly." Charlotte laughed. "But then my mother would have thought my chair yoga and Pilates to be unseemly."

"Did anyone offer to buy the piece?" Gramm asked.

"I did get several calls. The first was a man named Park. He offered a ridiculous amount of money. I didn't think I earned the hundred dollars, much less thousands. Another caller, also a man, was rude and bullying. I hung up."

"How did you meet Kayla Maki and Ben Heikkinen?"

"Would you like another cookie, Lieutenant?"

"Yes, I would. They're excellent!" Gramm answered.

Charlotte rose, picked up the plate, and disappeared into her kitchen. She returned with four more cookies. This time, Gramm grabbed two.

"How did I meet Kayla? Well, when given those choices on the radio station, I thought why not meet new people, so I said I would be open to joining a group and included my number. Kayla called almost immediately. Such a delightful young woman, fresh, full of sass. We agreed to meet the next day. My Friday was open."

"Where does Mr. Heikkinen come in?" White asked.

"Kayla put out whatever you call it on Tweeter, and Ben answered. As we say, the rest is history."

"So, you three hope to solve the puzzle."

"Kayla and Ben hope to find the treasure. I provide cookies and encouragement. Such fun. I'll be sad when it ends."

"Can we see your puzzle piece?" Milo asked.

Charlotte wagged her finger. "Ah, ah, ah. Kayla said you would ask. She has advised us to wait for a court order." Charlotte took a sip of her lemonade. "This is exciting. It's like being in the middle of a police drama."

"Do you know a Ham Gilbert?"

"Is that the unfortunate young man who is no longer with us?"

"It is."

"Kayla tried to talk to me about that, but I waved her off. It is part of the ugly I do not allow in my life if I can help it."

"Do the three of you have a theory of where your puzzle piece leads?" Milo asked.

"To tell you the truth, it could be anywhere. Although Kayla is looking at satellite photos to see if she can match the features on our pieces. She is so smart—knows all today's technology—reminds me of myself when I was her age."

I wonder if Charlotte wielded a three-inch blade when she was that age, White thought.

"Do any of your group's puzzle pieces spell the words *State* or *Park*?" Gramm asked.

"I assume you are referring to Jay Cooke State Park. I haven't been there in ages. That would be good for an outing one day."

Gramm thought that was the politest non-answer he had received in a while. Charlotte filled up his lemonade glass.

"I was quite distressed about dear Kayla being attacked. Should I be concerned for myself or Ben?"

"We have that man in custody," Gramm said, "but there may be others. I would advise you to be careful."

White handed Charlotte her card. "If anyone contacts you, or you think of anything else, please call me."

"I hate that you didn't sample my cookies. Would you like those two for later this afternoon—that four o'clock slump?"

"I would," White said, smiling, scooping up the two remaining cookies and folding a pink paper napkin around them.

§

Ben Heikkinen's alpaca and sheep farm was off of Maple Grove Road between Duluth and Twig. "Why would anyone name their town Twig?" White asked, as she, Gramm, and Milo drove up Highway 2.

"It's named after the town's founding father," Milo said from the back seat. "Cosmo J. Twig. He laid out the subway grid in Twig."

White checked her phone. "Subway grid? There are only sixty people in Twig!"

"Not many stops along the route."

Gramm turned in at the *Blue Ribbon Alpaca Farm* sign. It was the first in a series of multicolored signs. The first, orange dominant, said, *The Alpacas and Sheep are Friendly.* The second, neon green, advised, *The Llamas Can Be Crabby.* And the third, blue on yellow, read, *The Sheep Don't Care Either Way.*

The last sign featured a red arrow pointing the way to parking, office, corral, and barn. The farm offered a petting tour for twelve dollars per adult and half that for children under fourteen.

"Six bucks just to pet mutton?" Milo questioned as the three emerged from the police car.

"Twelve, unless you are planning to pass for thirteen," White sneered.

"I've been told I have a young face."

"You were told lumpy, not young."

"So cruel."

"Can we get this done?" Gramm grumbled. "Farms make me nervous."

White stared at him. "Farms make you nervous?"

"As a kid, a cow stepped on my foot," Gramm offered.

"Hallo there!" A middle-aged man with a friendly face emerged from the barn, wiping his hands on a handkerchief.

"You must be from the Duluth Police Department. You don't look dressed for the tour. I'm Ben Heikkinen."

Gramm shook his hand and introduced the others. "We understand you had a trespasser here a few nights ago."

"Sure did. The damn fool." Heikkinen rubbed his bald head with the same kerchief as he thought. "I've got big, gaudy signs all over. Solar lights on them at night warning people. I imagine he was hurting pretty badly."

"Did you get a good look at him?"

"Nah. He was driving away by the time I got out here. Do you want to see the llamas? I told them you were coming and to be nice." Ben smiled.

A thin, fortyish, blond woman left the barn and joined them. "I'm Lois, Ben's wife."

Again, Gramm did the introductions. "Did you happen to see the prowler from several nights ago?" he asked Lois.

"Nah, I was sleeping. It was the middle of the night, but he riled up the herd—caused quite a commotion. Woke me up. We didn't see him. Why would anyone just walk into a corral guarded by llamas unless they were up to no good?"

"I guess he didn't know llamas were dangerous?" White said. "I didn't realize that anyone raised llamas and alpacas in Minnesota."

"It's a tricky business," Lois said. "We moved up here from Albert Lee about five years ago when Ben inherited his dad's farm."

"Dad raised cattle. Lois crunched the numbers and said llamas, alpacas, and sheep would make more money and be easier."

"Along with the wool, we make a pretty patch with the tours—we're exotic. No one wants a tour of a cattle farm."

"We're here because we're investigating the death of a man who had one of those puzzle pieces," Gramm said, changing the subject.

Lois rolled her eyes. "Oh, save me from that contest. A man called, offering Ben five thousand dollars for his piece. Five thousand! I screamed at Ben to sell the damn thing!"

"She did." Ben nodded and put his hands in his pockets.

"Why didn't you?"

"I still might."

Lois gave Ben a playful nudge. "He wanted to meet that cute, young girl with the puzzle piece that called him. What's her name?"

"Aw Lois, I didn't want to meet Kayla. She said our group would have three puzzle pieces if I joined. I just thought three pieces were better than one. Maybe we'll find the big prize—go to Hawaii."

"How much is the big prize, Ben?" Lois asked.

"Don't know."

Lois rolled her eyes again. "I bet it's not anywhere close to five thousand dollars. That will take us to Hawaii."

"It's got to be worth something. Some guy attacked Kayla last night, maybe the guy who ran into Nukua our llama. Kayla called Charlotte and me to tell us," Ben said.

"You didn't tell me that. Is she okay?" Lois asked.

White nodded. "Her attacker is in the hospital. Kayla finished what your llama may have started."

"At first, I just figured he was drunk and got lost," Lois said. "Do you think he was after Ben's puzzle piece? Why would he go into the corral?"

"Good question. We didn't ask him, but we will," Gramm said.

"Where do you think the treasure is located?" White asked.

Ben looked at his boots. "Don't know. We have three pieces, can't tell if they go together, but we photographed them. Kayla is checking to see if they match any satellite maps. The problem is we don't really know how far one piece is from another. We need more people to join our group, but the people offering thousands of dollars for pieces will probably get to them first."

"Did the man who offered money for your piece leave a name or a number?"

"No name, but the number is on my phone." Ben removed his phone from his overalls and scrolled through it. He showed the number to Gramm, who motioned for White to write it down.

"Do you know a Harold or Ham Gilbert?" Milo asked.

"That guy who died? Nah, Kayla was trying to reach him to join our group."

Several curious alpacas wandered over to the fence and proved irresistible to White, who went over to pet them.

"See," Lois said. "People can't resist our babies. They're nice too. No one wants to pet a heifer."

§

"Forensics says they are finished in Jay Cooke. Nothing found, at least nothing pertaining to Ham Gilbert," White said as she slid into the police car.

"So, we can pull everyone?" Gramm asked.

"Not quite. The park people ask that we keep some uniforms on to help them protect the park. They don't want it dug up by all those crazy treasure hunters."

Gramm sighed. "There goes the overtime budget. I'll talk to the deputy chief."

"This weekend seems pretty clear," Milo said.

"If we're free, I get the grandchildren," Gramm added. "Sunday is Mother's Day. Our daughters are taking Amy out for brunch."

"I plan to visit mom in Leech Lake," White said. "What do you do, Milo?"

"Although I'm motherless, I still do what my mother told me to do."

"Such as?"

"Go to Zeke's soup kitchen on Lake Avenue and help serve people. Mom took me there a couple of times a year. She always said it helped to right my selfish little ship. I was a teenager at the time."

13

"I hope this misty soup burns off before we start to play tennis later today. Should we be concerned we are abandoning your aunt?" Agnes asked Sutherland as they sat down to breakfast. "Maybe we should invite her to come and watch this afternoon."

Sutherland shook his head. "I think she would be bored. Let's check with her. She probably has something she wants to do without you or me tagging along."

"Are you talking about me?" Lana asked, walking into the morning room.

"We were," Agnes admitted. "Sutherland and I have a commitment to play tennis this afternoon, and I was concerned that we were abandoning you."

Lana smiled. "I'm abandoning you. Martha and I are taking her brothers to the Steam Festival at the Duluth Depot,"

Lana said, proceeding to the coffee urn to get her coffee like a regular.

"Hey! Watch where you're going!" Milo yelled as Jet ran under his legs to get to the morning room windows. A quick look outside, and Jet was off again, running over Milo's feet to get to the family room windows.

"You never apologize!" Milo yelled after him.

"What's got into him?" Sutherland asked.

"Young love," Milo said. "There's a cat named Cinnamon out there. She stands by the windows and lets Jet make a fool of himself."

"How does she get onto the estate?" Sutherland asked.

Milo sat down at the table. "I don't know. She walks through the fence? Maybe Jet has that app that opens the gates."

"How do you know her name?" Lana asked.

"It's on her collar. She comes up to me when I'm sitting on the terrace. I won't say this in front of Jet, but she may be out of his league."

Agnes was about to suggest that maybe Milo was projecting about his own relationship with Mary Alice Bonner, but thought better of it and said instead, "He is a bit immature."

Having returned, Lana sipped her coffee and stared out the window at the lake obscuring fog. A high pitched, single note horn sounded in the distance. It was answered by a shrouded ore boat that was probably passing in front of Lakesong.

"Peanut Whistle," Sutherland said.

"Peanut Whistle?" Lana asked. "I've never heard of that."

Martha arrived with blueberry pancakes for Agnes and Sutherland and took Lana's order of eggs over easy and toast. Milo changed his usual breakfast to a peanut butter, jelly, and banana sandwich with bacon on the side. Martha knew the sandwich was Milo's tennis playing fuel, and the bacon was for the cats.

"Peanut Whistle is the derogatory term for the reduced-volume foghorn that replaced the old foghorn whose blast could be heard for twenty miles." Sutherland explained while pouring the blueberry compote on his pancakes. "Hillside residents complained that the horn blast rattled windows, disrupted conversation, and woke the sleeping, if not the dead. But there are still plenty of people who miss the old two-toned 'Bee-oh' sound."

Annie, the cat who ignored Jet's running escapades, waited patiently for Milo's breakfast to arrive—something a proper cat should do. After a few minutes, Jet returned, spurned by Cinnamon once again. Annie batted at him, a sign that he should go into the kitchen, turn his charm on Martha, to speed up the bacon delivery. Doing as he was instructed, Jet walked up to Martha, rubbed against her legs, and squeaked.

She looked down and said, "Keep your fur on, it's coming."

Once delivered, Milo's breakfast bacon was shared between the cats. Annie ate her share. Jet played hockey with his.

"So, both Jamal and Darian are going to the Steam Festival?" Sutherland asked Martha.

"They are. We are going to see Darian's experiment in the Future Engineers of Duluth activity tent. After that we're going treasure hunting on a train. Darian is sure he's figured out one of those radio station clues."

"That sounds like a fun day. And Jamal?" Sutherland asked.

"He's also interested in engineering," Martha said, "Engineering and Kelly, the cheerleader who has volunteered to help in the activity tent."

Agnes laughed. "Should he be giving Jet pointers?"

"Maybe Jet should give Jamal pointers," Milo suggested, nodding to one of the floor-to-ceiling windows that featured a tan and white cat. "Cinnamon has returned to ignore Jet."

As if on cue, Jet came running up to the window, leaving a saliva mark. Cinnamon turned her head toward the window, showing off her little pink bowtie collar while wrapping her tail around her body, just because she could.

"You're a fixed indoor cat," Milo said to Jet. "It's never going to happen for you, buddy."

§

Shane Bell slammed the door of his hotel room and flopped down on the bed. What he really wanted to do was trash the place, but he knew that would only cause more problems. "Don't mess up the sweet deal," he kept repeating to himself like a mantra.

The cops had released Shane from police custody this morning, but they did not provide a ride to the motel. Not having extra money for a cab or a rideshare, Shane walked the five miles to his West Duluth motel. Once there, he discovered the motel was charging him for two nights, the one he wanted and the one he spent in jail.

After settling up with the motel, he stayed to do his laundry and figure out his finances. He had enough for dinner tonight, and he could sleep in his truck, but he would need some help for Sunday. Waiting for his clothes to dry, he picked up a discarded newspaper and read a feature article on the pending closing of The Lake Avenue Soup Kitchen. The article mentioned a free breakfast for Mother's Day.

"I had a mother," Shane said to the dryer. He had a moving job on Monday. They were expecting two people. Maybe he could pick up a helper at the soup kitchen.

First, he had to check in with his future boss to make sure everything was on track for Thursday. "Hello, Mr. Mason?"

§

Milo called Mary Alice. "Hi Blue. I'm bored."

"We're playing tennis this afternoon. You should loosen up."

"I am."

"In your library chair?"

"I'm rotating my wrist. It's all in the wrist."

"I would love to amuse you this morning, but I am entertaining Richard and his latest tall, blond girlfriend, whose first name ends with Y."

"Cindy?"

"So before Christmas, Milo. This one is Aubrey. She came after Bailey."

"You should make them wear numbered jerseys. Then you could just refer to the latest as number seventy-two. What time should I pick you up?" Milo asked.

"I think play begins at one. There will be food afterward and, of course, a sign-up for the season."

"Let me repeat my question for those that found it too complicated the first time. When should I pick you up?"

"Noon. Don't be late. Even though it's just for fun, I still like to warm up, unlike yourself."

Milo's phone did the *da dunk* sound. "Gotta go. The police are after me."

"Such a criminal!" Mary Alice joked. She hung up.

Milo hit the green button on his phone. "Ernie, it's Saturday, my day of rest."

"We've been through this, Milo. You are not Jewish or Muslim. It's not your day of rest."

"I wasn't being biblical, just lazy. Didn't we have the weekend off? I have a tennis tournament this afternoon."

"Well, who doesn't? This won't take long. I have Robin and Kate on here. We had to let Shane Bell walk, even though I'm sure he had something to do with Ham Gilbert's death."

"And I need to know this, why?" Milo said.

"In case you run into him at your country club, I didn't want you to be surprised."

"So considerate."

"Speaking of considerate, the reason I called, the DA got a judge to subpoena the puzzle piece holders."

"Yay!" White cheered.

"Not so fast. We have to get on the Campbell property to serve the subpoenas, which requires a hearing before Judge

Murphy on Monday. So, buckle up, we're taking a ride on the legal express on Monday."

Gramm hung up without a 'goodbye,' as was his custom, taking White and Preston with him.

§

While Milo was deciding on which outlandish t-shirt to wear at the country club round-robin tennis tournament, his mind was mulling over what Brandon Park had said about people leaving fake puzzle pieces. Is somebody selling fake pieces? Was Ham Gilbert selling fake pieces?

Minutes before noon, he edged the top-down Mercedes onto London Road. The air was a little chilly for the convertible, but the car had a great heater. He turned onto Mary Alice's drive at exactly noon. The gate was open. He was expected.

Mary Alice bounced out in a modern-art-explosion of a tennis skirt, flashing periwinkle blue, yellow, hot pink, black and orange.

Milo only noticed her long legs.

§

Jimmy Pleski's plans did not include spending Saturday in a hospital bed. He was in pain. Out the window, he watched the fog burn off as the early morning clouds moved out over the lake. He was antsy. Not fully grasping his predicament, Jimmy vacillated between groaning about the pain and grousing about not being able to get back to Jay Cooke park in search of treasure.

A nurse had gotten the cops to remove his handcuffs after assuring them that Pleski was in no shape to get up and run. After she left the room, he tried to prove her wrong, but the instantaneous pain was sharp and debilitating. He laid back on the bed.

Shortly before lunch, a young man in a dark, cheap suit stopped by his room. Reading off a sheet of paper, he asked, "James William Pleski?"

"It's Jimmy! Who the hell are you?"

"I'm Cody Cookson, your public defender."

"Public defender? Why the hell do I need a public defender?"

Cookson looked at his assignment sheet. "Let's see, hmm, it says here you, James William Pleski, are charged with assault, robbery, and trespass."

"It's Jimmy! And you got the wrong guy."

Looking again at his sheet, Cookson read, "Pleski attacked a woman named Kayla Maki from behind, attempting to rob her." Cookson looked up at Pleski. "I would say the police are cutting you some slack. They could have added sexual assault or attempted murder."

"What?"

"You grabbed her, and your motive is somewhat unclear."

"Did you say you're *my* public defender?"

"I did."

"Does it say there she stabbed me? No? Let me make it clearer," Pleski yelled, lifting his hospital gown to show his injury. "She sliced me!"

Cookson winced. "Please don't flash me, Mr. Pleski." Cookson walked over to the chair to sit down out of eyesight of Pleski's halting attempt to cover himself. "As ugly as that cut is, I don't think we are going to get anywhere claiming you are the victim."

Jimmy was stunned. "So, I get sliced, and I'm the bad guy?"

"According to this report, you initiated the attack, so the short answer is yes. Now, tell me what you were doing in Kayla Maki's driveway last Thursday night."

Jimmy took some time, sipping his water, thinking about how to make this work for him. "I was celebrating. I solved one of those clues on the radio—you know, a hundred bucks and a puzzle piece. The piece was in my hand when, out of nowhere, this woman grabs it and runs. She was a lot faster than I was. I was just trying to get my property back."

Cookson rolled his eyes. "You chose to celebrate in Kayla Maki's driveway?"

"Yes, I did." Jimmy smiled, showing his bad dental work.

Cookson shook his head as if to dislodge a bit of illogical information. "Why?"

"I was hitching, and that's where my buddy dropped me."

"Buddy's name?"

"I don't know. I called him Tank."

Cookson put his hands over his eyes. "Let me get this straight. Your buddy, who has no other name but Tank, picked you up while hitchhiking and dropped you off at Kayla Maki's driveway—a stranger to you. Yet she knew you had a puzzle piece and tried to steal it."

"Small world, isn't it?"

"What was the clue, and how did you solve it?"

"I...I...don't remember right now."

"Where did you find the puzzle piece?"

"Jay Cooke State Park."

"Mr. Pleski, are you aware that the police are investigating a murder in that park, and you just put yourself at the murder scene?"

Jimmy began to sputter. "No, no, I get confused. I found it at a farm with deformed sheep."

"Deformed sheep?"

"Tall, long necks that slammed into me like a linebacker. It also hit me with its front hoofs."

"Llamas?"

"Sure. That's where I found it. On that llama farm."

"Mr. Pleski, you have now put yourself in line for a second trespass charge. When you flashed me, I saw the purple bruise on your chest. Let's stop with the lies. You went to that woman's house and tried to take her puzzle piece by force. Why?"

Pleski looked at the man like he was insane. "To get a puzzle piece." He paused after each word as if he were speaking to a child.

"It wasn't yours."

"So what? I tried to solve those riddles—too hard. I deserve to get a puzzle piece anyway, and the treasure."

"A judge will not see it that way."

"I hope I'm not paying for this. You don't seem to be on my side."

Cookson sighed. "Here's my advice. You admit to the attack…"

"What? Are you crazy?"

The attorney held out his hand to stop Pleski from interrupting. "We paint this contest as if it was an attractive nuisance. In other words, the radio station made this contest so lucrative that anyone might have been compelled to break the law to gain the prize. We make the radio station the bad guy."

"Can I sue them?"

"Possibly, but that's not my territory. I'm just trying to get your jail time reduced."

"Jail? I'm the victim!" Pleski began to pull up his hospital gown again, but Cookson insisted he'd seen enough.

"I'm afraid that's the best we can do."

"I shoulda gone after that old lady. Course, with my luck, she's a former Navy Seal."

§

To Darian's delight, steam floated in and around the crowd of people standing by the tracks where the huge, black, iron and steel locomotives were displayed. The whoosh of escaping steam could be heard above the din of voices. Darian, waving his hands to struggle through the steam, insisted on bypassing the various tents and displays in order to buy tickets for the next run of the North Shore Scenic Railroad. He explained that he thought the train hid the clue to the prize he was after.

"What is the clue?" Lana asked.

Darian took a piece of paper from his pocket and read,

Buy a ticket for the train
Don't work hard or strain your brain
Ride that ride of long ago
Be polite and just ask Joe

"Just ask Joe?" Lana questioned. "You know, Joe is slang for a cup of coffee. Do you think that puzzle piece could have a connection to coffee?"

"There's also GI Joe," Martha said. "Although I don't know how that applies here."

"There's Kelly! I'll see you later," Jamal said.

"We're talking about Joe!" Martha countered.

Jamal smiled. "But I like Kelly." He sprinted to the young lady in the STARBASE tent.

"Kelly is Jamal's true interest in engineering," Martha told Lana. "She is helping out, guiding the younger set with engineering experiments."

"Let's buy those tickets!" Darian urged.

Martha let herself be pulled to the ticket window. The man behind the window tugged at his shirt sleeve garter as he told Martha the prices for the three levels of service, first class, diner car class, and coach class.

"My treat!" Lana insisted, handing the ticket man her credit card. "Four first-class tickets, please, on the Zephyr."

"Make it three," Martha said. "We will pick Jamal up after the ride."

"Three first-class tickets, please," Lana said, smiling.

"The train boards in fifteen minutes," the man said, handing Lana the tickets. She dispensed one each to Darian and Martha.

"We have time to check out Darian's experiment," Martha said, leading Lana and Darian back to the main area. Jamal was standing back, arms folded in front of him, admiring Kelly, who was helping several fourth graders create a volcano.

"My group did an invisible ink project," Darian said, pointing to a nearby table.

Martha rolled her eyes. "He kept handing me notes in invisible ink. I had to drop grape juice on them in order to read them. He thought it was so much fun. It was amusing for a while, then annoying. I locked up my baking soda."

Several kids were writing, using the baking soda and water mixture. "It doesn't work. There's nothing there!" a girl said with attitude.

Darian walked up to her and pointed to an eyedropper. "Load that up with grapefruit juice and drop it on the paper."

"That's cool!" the girl exclaimed, as her writing suddenly became visible.

"Future spy," Lana said to Martha.

Martha informed Jamal of the train trip, which he did not have to take. He nodded and smiled. "Kelly gets a break in five minutes, and we're going to grab some food. Don't worry. I have money for both of us."

An announcement on the overhead speakers informed the throng of the imminent departure of the North Shore Scenic Railroad Zephyr. It was now boarding. Ticket holders were asked to please make their way to the back of the museum.

Darian ran to the train, knowing well the location of the boarding area. Lana and Martha caught up, and the conductor directed the three to the dome car. "This car is neat!" Darian proclaimed, looking through the wide curved windows on the right and left of the aisle as they found their seats. After a brief wait, the train pulled out of the station.

Lana and Martha were taken with the high view they had of the lake as the train proceeded along the shore. Darian looked at the lake, but kept an eye out for the conductor. A man dressed in an old-time conductor's outfit was making his way down the aisle when disaster struck. A gravelly voiced man in front of them asked the conductor if his name was Joe. The conductor nodded.

"You've got my puzzle piece!"

"I'm sorry. What sir?" the conductor smiled. His conductor's hat slipped slightly down his forehead, and he pushed it back up.

"If you're Joe, I found you, so give me the piece!" the man demanded.

"Sorry," the conductor said and moved on.

He arrived at Darian. "Ticket please."

Darian handed him the ticket. "Joe?"

"Yes?" the conductor said, as he punched a hole in the ticket and handed it back to Darian.

"May I please have a puzzle piece?"

The conductor smiled, reached into his black coat for an envelope, handing it to Darian. Darian turned it over and read, *Congratulations! You won!*

"Enjoy," the conductor smiled.

Darian held the envelope up. "Really? Really?"

"Yes really. You're a very polite young man."

"Hey!" the gravelly man shouted. "I asked you for the puzzle piece before that kid did!"

The conductor turned. "But sir, you were not polite."

Darian tore open the envelope to find a hundred-dollar bill and a piece of the puzzle.

Martha was stunned. "That was it?"

"Ask Joe and be polite. So simple," Lana said, shaking her head. "We adults look for hidden meanings."

"Yes ma'am. It's gotten quite messy at times. Several people spilled coffee grounds on the floor of the train thinking the puzzle piece was in the coffee urn," the conductor said. "They ignored me or, worse, rudely pushed me out of the way. I had the envelope the whole time."

Lana watched Darian inspect the puzzle piece. "What happens now?"

"I don't know, but I'll take this bill for safe keeping. Do you want to keep the puzzle piece, Darian?"

"No, you can keep both for me. I want to enjoy the ride."

Lana leaned over and whispered to Martha, "Maybe call that radio station when we get back."

§

Mary Alice and Milo checked their upcoming tennis matches on the big board in the dining room of the country club before sitting down for a pre-tennis drink. As they discussed the new tennis season, Milo noticed he was still getting stares from a number of club members. He wasn't the new kid on the playground this year. He thought the staring might stop.

"Are they staring at me because I'm a world-famous detective or because they feel you could do so much better?"

"So insecure. They're staring at me because of my new colorful tennis wardrobe. Get used to it. Tennis whites are so establishment," Mary Alice said.

"Maybe they're staring at my tennis attire," Milo suggested.

Mary Alice looked at Milo's black shorts and Grateful Dead t-shirt. "Did you ever attend a Grateful Dead concert?"

"Of course not."

"Or even listen to their music."

"Can't say I have, but I'm sure they are a great group and good to their mothers."

"What happened to your Metallica shirt? The one you wore when you humiliated poor Sutherland. I haven't seen it since."

"I feel if I wear the same ratty shirt twice, I'll become predictable."

Mary Alice laughed. "Milo, no one can accuse you of being predictable."

"It's my charm."

"You kid, but it is."

The stares and murmurs moved from Milo and Mary Alice to the couple who just walked into the dining room, Agnes and Sutherland, both dressed in predictably pristine tennis whites. As they looked over the match board, someone at the table behind Milo and Mary Alice whispered, "That's her, the wife."

"Well, she certainly cashed in," another said.

"How long will it be before she cashes out? He's cute, but kind of dull. I suggested my Brooke chat him up, and she said no way."

"Does the wife come from money?"

There was a laugh. "Not a penny."

"Well, she's got a penny or two now. I know that tennis dress. It doesn't come cheap."

Mary Alice, overhearing the chatter, excused herself. "I have some petty business to take care of." Milo watched her stroll over to Agnes and put her arm around her. "Come with me. We have ribbons on ponytails that need straightening."

Agnes followed as Mary Alice floated from table to table, making small talk and introducing her as Mrs. Agnes McKnight. Agnes knew what she was doing and remembered the words of Sunny Upton: "No one wants to disappoint Mary Alice."

Sunny's was the last table Mary Alice came to. She said in a loud tone, "Sunny, I would like to introduce Mrs. Agnes McKnight, but then, of course, you two already know each other."

Sunny smiled. "Of course, we do. So nice to see you again, Agnes. I'm pleased we get to play each other today."

Sutherland walked over to Milo and sat down. "Remind me to thank Mary Alice."

"For abandoning me?"

"No, this little dance is not about you," Sutherland smiled. "She's making life easier for Agnes."

"Who is that woman they're talking to?" Milo asked, gesturing toward Sunny Upton's table.

"Sunny Upton. There are two powers at this country club, Milo, Mary Alice Bonner, and Sunny Upton, and it appears as if both are making the room know that Agnes is an accepted friend."

"It's easier to be a guy," Milo mused.

"Do you think the men aren't gossiping about you?" Sutherland charged.

"Me? Why me?"

Sutherland laughed. "How should I put this? Mary Alice is, well, gorgeous while you, Milo, are just a charming schlump."

"I'm a better dressed schlump than I used to be," Milo defended himself.

"Ha! Not today."

The bell sounded, signaling the beginning of the first match. Milo was playing with Sunny Upton on court three. Their opponents were Brad Nelson, Mary Alice's former partner, and a woman named Naomi Olsen.

"I'm Milo, Milo Rathkey." Milo shook Sunny's hand.

"Oh, you're Agnes' boss."

"And the annoying guy who lives downstairs."

Sunny nodded. "Glad to meet you."

Brad and Naomi walked over to the net for the sportsman-like handshake. Brad looked down at Milo with disdain. "Milo Rathkey. Mary Alice is keeping you on for another season?"

"I've heard I made the cut."

Brad sneered.

Naomi extended her hand to Sunny and Milo. There was no need for introductions, as Naomi knew them both.

Milo and Sunny moved to center court to talk about strategy. "Do you like him?" Milo asked, nodding his head toward Brad Nelson.

Adjusting her visor, Sunny said, "He's an ass. He'll be gunning for you. It's personal. Not only did you grab Mary

Alice as your partner, but he couldn't find one last season, so he didn't play."

"Pity," Milo said. "Ad or deuce?"

"Deuce court," Sunny said.

Milo nodded and stood waiting for Brad to serve to Sunny.

It was a hard serve, but she handled it. Brad cut in front of Naomi to slice the ball toward Milo, who fought it off, placing it in the empty space where Brad should have been standing.

Naomi shouted, "If you can't put it away, stay where you belong."

Brad, the petulant child, protested. "That was a winner. He got lucky!"

Retreating to take Brad's anger-driven serve, Milo was not disappointed. It was fast and spinning. Milo smashed it with his backhand for a cross court winner. Brad threw his racket into the net, garnering a warning from the club's sportsmanship official.

Sunny walked over to Milo to touch rackets—a *well done* gesture between tennis partners.

Milo and Sunny won the first three games before Milo got a chance to serve. Brad was standing midcourt to receive. Naomi urged him to back up. "I've played against him. This guy has a wicked serve."

Brad sneered. "Nothing I can't handle."

Milo bounced the ball three times, tossed it up, and sliced through it with his maximum force. The ball hit the service line and chirped away, hitting the side fence before

Brad could move. Brad threw his racket onto the court and stormed off. "This is bullshit!"

The official moved to eject Brad.

"Don't bother!" Brad shouted. "I'm leaving."

Milo looked at Sunny. "Was it something I said?"

Sunny laughed. "You are fun."

14

Two pills tumbled out of Milo's green bottle. After downing them with his orange juice, he sat up straight, pulled his shoulder blades together, and turned his head right and left. He was stiff, but nothing abnormal.

"Excedrin morning?" Mary Alice mocked.

"Beginning-of-the-season soreness. I have to work the kinks out," Milo explained, scooping two large spoonfuls of scrambled eggs and one of hash browns onto his plate. He found room for three pieces of bacon and topped it all off with an orange marmalade laden English muffin.

Mary Alice watched in awe at Milo's breakfast mountain building. Milo enjoyed her interest. "I'm a growing boy."

Mary Alice's cook always fashioned Sunday morning breakfast as a brunch buffet, even though most Sundays featured only one or two people. "Were does all this food go?" Milo asked.

"Cook takes it home. She has a large family. Today, it's my contribution to her Mother's Day Celebration." Mary Alice took a small dollop of eggs and one piece of toast.

"Not eating much—saving room for Mother's Day celebration with Richard?"

"Yes, he's coming over again this evening—just he and I—no girlfriend. This afternoon I plan to pamper myself at the spa with my masseuse who is going to work out *my* kinks."

"Should I be jealous?"

"Yes, of course. I'd be upset if you weren't. You could always join me."

"Have you met me? I'm not a get-naked-in-fron t-of-strangers-for-a-rub kind of guy."

"Nor am I. I usually introduce myself first."

Milo smiled and shook his head.

"Are you going to retire to your library?" Mary Alice asked.

"I have a guy named Zeke who will work out my kinks and I don't have to get naked.

The blue eyes danced. "Zeke's loss."

§

Milo looked up at the black-on-white, hand-painted sign over the Lake Avenue Soup Kitchen. At least it used to be the Lake Avenue Soup Kitchen, but the word *soup* had been crossed out with black paint. Milo couldn't wait to get the skinny about what led to that action.

Zeke, the tall, former First Gulf War Marine who ran the kitchen, had the plywood that covered the windows decorated by local street artists. If gang members tagged the artwork, Zeke would whitewash the boards and invite more artists to go at it again. Milo always wondered if the artists were the ones doing the tagging in an effort to replace a rival artist's work.

Three hard knocks brought Zeke to the front door. "Good to see you, Milo," Zeke said. "Gloria is in the back."

As he entered, Milo asked about the sign. "You run out of soup?"

Zeke looked puzzled.

"The word soup is crossed out—your sign. What gives?"

Zeke smiled, "Oh that. The landlord thinks the word *soup* with *kitchen* is derogatory, so I changed it to Lake Avenue Kitchen. He keeps coming up with crap like that, hoping we'll move."

Milo remained silent.

"I coulda done that sign better, but I was in a mood," Zeke explained as he resumed wiping down the long tables. "He wants to sell. If we're outta here, he can get a better price, so he's making life difficult. First the sign, now the rent's going up. The truth is, it's working. We're going to have to move."

"Sucks," Milo said as he walked to the back hallway to hang up his jacket.

Gloria yelled, "Oh it's a Milo Mother's Day! Good day to play my lotto numbers." The strong, stocky cook with short, gray-white hair gave Milo one of her infrequent smiles.

"Whaddaya need Gloria?" Milo asked.

"I need to win my numbers!"

"What else do you need?"

"Get me two boxes of tomato sauce and one box of kidney beans—the spicy ones. We got chili today along with lasagna—big day."

Milo went to the storage area piled high with boxes of food, loaded two boxes of sauce and one of kidney beans onto a dolly, and rolled them into the kitchen. Although each box weighed forty pounds, Gloria tossed them onto the prep table as if they were an individual sized can of tomato soup.

"You should try to work out, Gloria. You know, get a little stronger," Milo teased.

Milo got no smile and no comment. He took no offense. Time had always been in short supply in the soup kitchen. Milo's mother was the fill in cook here and brought young Milo along to snap beans and hand out rolls. He progressed to carrying large cans from the storage area to the kitchen, washing dishes, and clearing tables—tasks he still performed.

"Next, get me twenty onions," Gloria said.

"Going a little spicy today?" Milo asked.

She stared at him. "Onions, not Jalapenos. Chop chop. Doors open at one. We've got people to feed."

§

Chip waited for the golf cart to arrive at his front porch. He handed the latest note to Peters. The man, dressed in camouflage, read it out loud, "Time's up!" He handed it back to Chip.

"Like the others, tacked to my porch."

"It wasn't here when I delivered the papers this morning. Any idea yet what it could mean?" Peters asked.

"I don't know if it's a threat to me, my family, or it's just nothing. I want to know how these notes are getting by you! We have a long history of looking out for each other. I pay you to make sure things like this don't happen."

Peters stood almost at attention. "Sir, I suggested placing a camera or a 24-hour guard at your house after the first note, but you declined."

"I don't want Grace to know about this. She thinks she and the kids are safe. We're living in a closed compound. That should keep these notes from happening."

"Not if they're coming from inside the compound, sir."

"Who do you suspect?"

"If I may say sir, I understand your attempt to unseat Mrs. Mason did not take hold. She would be my first suspect."

Chip exhaled. "Mine too. Put her under surveillance. Maybe we should confront her."

"Leave it to me."

§

Shane Bell tried to sleep in his truck in the motel parking lot, but he was told to move along, forcing him to drive around in the middle of the night looking for a new place to park. The lot across the street from the Lake Avenue Kitchen filled the bill. When the soup kitchen opened, he would have a meal on Sunday.

Milo was behind the serving counter, spooning bowls of chili and handing out corn bread. Even though this was a special

Mother's Day lunch, homeless men were also arriving. Zeke did not turn away anyone unless they were causing a problem.

"Women and children sit on the left, men on the right, unless they are with their family," Zeke explained to each person as they entered. Most were regulars and already knew the routine.

Gloria's grandchild was standing by Zeke, handing each woman a flower, wishing them a happy Mother's Day.

"Could I get another cornbread, please?" A little boy in a blue striped shirt asked Milo. "I love cornbread. It's like cake."

Milo looked around as if he were doing something illegal and dropped a second cornbread on the child's tray. "Don't tell anyone. Gloria back in the kitchen will yell at me."

"No, I won't!" Gloria shouted from the kitchen.

The boy laughed and moved on to the lasagna. His mother offered to skip her cornbread, but Milo refused. "We have plenty."

A bell on the door jingled each time the door was opened. Through habit, Milo would glance up to check out the next customer. Although Zeke could handle any out-of-control customers, Milo would assist from time to time. Today's crowd was well mannered.

The jingle sounded. Milo looked up in time to see Shane Bell come through the door. He wondered if Bell was this hard up, or did he just want to horn in on a free meal?

Zeke directed Shane to the serving line, where he picked up a tray and moved past the volunteers who handed out silverware and napkins. He arrived at Milo's station and stopped. "What the hell are you doing here?"

"Language!" Zeke yelled. "You get one warning. That was it."

"Sorry!" Shane yelled back.

"I volunteer here," Milo said. "What are you doing here?"

"Eating. That da...that motel charged me for the day I was in jail. I'm a little low on cash until tomorrow."

Milo put the chili and cornbread on his tray. "What happens tomorrow?"

"I start a three-day moving job. I get paid daily. I'll be flush and I won't have to come here and see your ugly face. I'm getting back to being a mechanic on the motorcycle circuit."

"I just saw a flier for motorcycle races at Brainerd," Milo said.

"Yeah, MotoAmerica races. I hope to be there working on a Ducati."

"Why are you moving furniture if you're a mechanic?"

Shane drew a long breath. "Why did I get drummed out of the Navy, Ratface? I got suspended from the track for slugging a guy who needed slugging. I've been reinstated."

"If I remember, most people you slugged really didn't need slugging. You just like to slug them."

Shane white knuckled his tray but moved on. Milo served the next person.

An hour later, the crowd had thinned out. The food service was over. Volunteers were bussing the last of the dishes. Shane was still seated at his table, finishing his second dessert.

Milo walked over and sat down across the table from him.

"You're upsetting my digestion," Shane snarled.

"Tell me about Ham Gilbert."

"Why?"

"I want to figure out who killed him."

"Why?"

"It amuses me."

Shane sneered. "He was a boring little man with a strong back."

"Did you kill him?"

"Why would I do that?"

"I don't know. Maybe you got mad, hit him, and he fell in the water."

"And what would Ham do that would make me that mad, dumbass?"

"Sell your puzzle piece, dumbass."

Shane stared at Milo. "You're telling me he had that piece all along? Friggin' liar!"

"We found one on the dashboard of his car." Milo waited to see Shane's reaction.

Shane shook his head as if clearing his ears of water. "Why would someone kill him and leave the piece?"

"Good question." Did Shane really not know about the puzzle piece? Milo remembered how good Shane had been at playing dumb.

"If he was selling, who was buying?" Shane asked. "That's your murderer."

Milo realized Shane had zeroed in on a key question. *The family has two pieces which they bought. Who else has more than one? Brandon Park!*

§

The sun was warm as the *Laura* cut through the waves of Lake Superior. The spray carried by the breeze made the day perfect for boating up the shore. Lana Freskin took her turn at the helm. Watching her from behind, Sutherland had a flashback to his mother at the wheel, her blond hair pulled back through a baseball cap. Being at the helm was something Laura insisted on most of the time. Sutherland's father, John, piloted the sailboat, but the *Laura* was, well, Laura's.

Agnes watched him watch his aunt. "Are you okay?"

Sutherland smiled. "Yeah. Mom's cap was blue too."

At Sutherland's suggestion, Lana had motored up the shore to Two Harbors where his company and Mary Alice's were doing a joint project to restore an old dry dock facility and marina.

"Slip 12," he told Lana, who expertly turned the craft into the open space.

"She handles just like mine," Lana said. "You've kept her in beautiful condition."

A catering van met them at the pier. The server came aboard and began to deliver lunch. "You're catering this?" Agnes laughed.

Sutherland nodded. "Well, until we finish the marina project, the nearest restaurant is a mile away. I didn't think we wanted to walk."

"We could have packed a picnic," Agnes said.

"It's Martha's day off."

Agnes rolled her eyes. "I could have packed a picnic. For that matter, you could have packed a picnic."

"I would have you know, dear wife, that I have no picnic packing expertise nor experience."

"PB&J sandwiches take neither expertise nor experience," Agnes quipped, watching the caterers bring aboard several bottles of wine, plus grazing boards, filled with sliced apples, pistachios, figs, olives, grapes, cornichons, orange slices, kiwi, and assorted meats and cheeses. Her eyes darted from the food to Sutherland. "On second thought, dear husband, it's best you continue to order from the caterer."

A waiter uncorked the first wine bottle and filled three glasses. Lana held hers out for a toast. "To clear skies and prevailing winds to you both for all of your lives."

"Hear, hear," Sutherland said, clinking his glass, locking eyes with Agnes.

Lana took a sip and then inspected the bottle. "Not my Riesling, but nice."

Sutherland leaned back, letting the warm sun bake his face.

"Where's Milo?" Lana asked, picking from the grazing boards.

"He has a Mother's Day Tradition, helping at a soup kitchen," Agnes said.

"How would you know that?" Sutherland mumbled from his reclined position.

Agnes shook her head. "I was hoping we could have this conversation when you're ready, but I guess it will have to be today." She sighed. "I work for Milo. It's my job to know his schedule. I'm good at my job."

"Why does he work there on Mother's Day?" Lana asked.

"He told me his mom cooked at the kitchen from time to time and made Milo come along to help serve," Agnes said. "She was Martha at Lakesong before Martha."

"Oh, that's right. That's the connection," Lana said. "Which reminds me, I have a little tidbit about the Campbells I forgot to tell Milo. I thought he would be with us."

"Murder tomorrow," Sutherland said. "Today we enjoy the sun, the lake, and these tiny pickles."

"No poker game tonight?" Agnes asked.

Sutherland shook his head. "It's Mother's Day. Besides, we have company."

"You didn't need to cancel because of me. You could have just dealt me in," Lana said. "What are the stakes?"

"Nickle, dime, quarter," Sutherland said.

"Tedious, but safe."

"I've been called worse."

Both Lana and Agnes laughed.

"Feinberg also has company," Sutherland added. "Kimberly McKenna is in town."

"What brings her to town?" Agnes asked.

Sutherland shrugged, spearing another pickle. "I don't know. Saul's pastrami?"

§

In the early evening, after all the soup kitchen cleanup was finished, Milo returned to Lakesong. On a mission, he rushed into his office, said hello to John's spirit, whose presence he could still feel, and turned on his computer.

He typed in "Brandon Park" and waited. There were thousands of Brandon Parks. Milo refined the search to Brandon Park, Duluth, Minnesota. There was only one.

Milo began to read:

Park, Brandon.
Coder, blogger, physical therapist
Estimated Net worth, $5 Million

"Grandma must have sold a lot of pomade for him to be worth that much," Milo said to the empty room.

Milo went on to read that Park created several successful apps which he sold, creating the bulk of his fortune. He ran numerous blogs which were listed as being quite successful, making money with advertising.

Checking on his address, Milo answered his next question: why was Brandon living in a duplex? The answer was simple—he owned it, along with many other properties.

Milo looked at the chairs by the fireplace. It was where he imagined John McKnight to be sitting. "If Brandon wanted to compete with the Campbells, he could."

Lana Freskin startled Milo as she entered the office. She sat down in John's fireplace chair and announced, "We missed you today. I remembered a bit about the Campbells you may want to hear."

Milo joined her and flipped on the gas fireplace.

"Gas? You have a gas fireplace in Lakesong? Isn't that some sort of sacrilege?" Lana joked.

"It is but seeing as how John installed it and not me, I feel I can use it without too much guilt," Milo said.

Lana chatted on about how she had been contacting various old friends to tell them she was in town. "The conversation of interest to you was the enjoyable and interesting afternoon with Greer Campbell. We reminisced about a lot of things, but you will want to hear about the summer I visited her at the family retreat."

"On the compound?"

"Of course. That's where she lives."

"So, what did this stroll down memory lane with Greer Campbell produce?"

Lana rubbed her hands together and gave Milo a Cheshire grin. "Remember, I told you about the Campbell mine, and that guy named LaPointe?"

"I do."

"During my visit with Greer, I got to thinking that maybe I shouldn't have shared all that information with you about the mine and the dead body. I confessed my possible faux pas to Greer and..."

"She wasn't happy."

"That's the interesting thing. She seemed quite pleased, even happy, about it."

Milo cocked his head, much like a dog trying to hear a new sound. "Happy? Really?"

"I told Greer that I didn't divulge our teenage trip to the mine, but she urged me to tell you everything."

"Tell me everything? Aunt Lana, what did you do?" Milo teased.

Lana's eyes twinkled. "Well, you know how you do dumb things when you're young?"

Milo nodded.

"Well, Greer, her sister, and I hitchhiked to the mine one summer day to find the dead body."

Milo was surprised. "Hitchhiked? To find a dead body?"

"Yes, Milo. Young and dumb. We found the mine and snuck in between the boards that were blocking the entrance, but some rocks fell down in front of us. We got spooked and ran out—our hearts racing. Greer slipped and fell, skinning her leg. Luckily, we got picked up by a couple of cute guys who tended to Greer's knee, bought us slushies, and dropped us off at Island Lake walking distance to the compound. Concentrating on the cute guys all afternoon took our minds off of being scared."

"This mine, do you remember where it was?" Milo asked. Lana shook her head.

"Do you really think there's a body in the mine?"

"I don't know, but back then, in our imaginations, there was a body and at least one ghost who threw the rocks at us—so young."

"Do you remember how long it took to get to the mine?"

"Traveling up, we hitched a ride from a couple that was going camping. It seemed to take forever. Coming back—did I mention the cute guys? It passed in an instant."

§

Saul Feinberg handed Kimberly McKenna an after-dinner ice wine and poured a glass for himself. She was sitting on his expansive deck, looking out at Duluth and its harbor. The clear night gave them a full view of the Aerial Lift Bridge, glowing in its array of spotlights. A salty, approaching the bridge, sounded one long and two shorts, the signal for the bridge to raise. The air was right for the sound to travel up to Feinberg's deck.

"Lovely," McKenna said.

The bridge responded, and its deck began to creep upward. Even up on the hill, they could hear the clanging of the chains lowering the counterweights as the bridge deck lifted to let a salty pass under.

McKenna sipped her wine. "I have a court date in the morning."

"As do I," Saul said, sitting beside her.

"I bet mine is more intriguing than yours," McKenna teased.

"Yours may be intriguing, but I can describe mine as puzzling."

McKenna sat up. "Judge Murphy, ten o'clock, courtroom three."

Saul, who was rarely surprised, was surprised. "Do we have the same clients?"

"I doubt it. I cost a lot, so my clients have money." McKenna laughed. "All your clients have is righteous indignation."

"They can't complain they're not getting their money's worth," Saul said.

"Black or blue suit?"

"Black. Let me guess, for you, your traditional brown tweed with coral silk blouse?"

"You men have it so easy. You can wear that black suit with the same shirt all week and no one would notice. If I wear the same blouse two days in a row, someone will make a comment. So, tomorrow's blouse is more of a light sage."

"I won't be able to recognize you," Saul joked.

15

"Can I spend my hundred dollars?" Darian asked Martha as he sat down for breakfast. "There's a mega cyborg hand I want to buy. You build it yourself! It runs on hydraulics, pneumatics, water, air, stuff like that."

Martha was torn. Her gut reaction was to save the hundred dollars, but she knew that was silly. John McKnight had left her siblings more than enough money in trust to pay for higher education. Martha looked at Darian's phone, which displayed the hand and read over the specs.

"Have you run this past Jamal?"

"Yeah, he says it's legit and he would help me if I get stuck."

"Okay. Tonight, we'll order the hand. Right now, I have to call that radio station to see what we do with that puzzle piece," she said to Darian. He didn't seem to care. The hand was more important.

"KDDW, home of the hits," a female voice answered.

"Yes, my name is Martha Gibbson. My young brother found a piece of your puzzle on the Zephyr, that train that runs up the shore. I'm calling to find out what he should do with it."

"Just a moment, ma'am." Music replaced the voice.

Jamal lumbered into the cottage kitchen. "What's for breakfast?"

"I'm getting the hand!" Darian shouted proudly, displaying his phone to Jamal.

"Cool bro," Jamal said. Martha was pleased that Jamal took the role of big brother seriously. Even though he probably wouldn't want to spend his money on a robotic hand, he didn't put down Darian's joy. Looking at the stove, Jamal asked if the bacon and eggs were for him. Martha nodded and pointed to the phone at her ear.

"Hello there," a male voice said. "I'm Candler Jones, morning man here at KDDW. I understand you found our last puzzle piece."

"Not me, my young brother, Darian."

"How old is he?"

"Ten."

"Would he like to be interviewed? We could do it now over the phone."

"What do you mean, interviewed? What are you going to ask him? I'm his guardian. I need to know."

"It's pretty simple. We'd like to know how he found it and what he plans to do with it."

"Well, that's why I'm calling. We don't know what to do with it." Martha put her phone on speaker so Darian could hear.

"I'll tell you what I've told everyone. He could look for the treasure himself—with your help, of course. He could sell the piece. When we last checked, two separate parties were offering to buy them. Or he could join with others who have pieces."

Darian thought for a moment as Jamal sat down to devour his breakfast. "Take the money," Jamal advised.

"No, I think I want to join other people," Darian said. "It sounds like fun."

"Would he like to talk to me on the air?" Candler asked.

"Darian, do you want to be on the radio?" Martha asked.

He looked at Jamal, who shrugged in an inaudible teenage language.

"Cool!" Darian shouted, echoing his brother's favorite word.

§

Gramm, with his phone to his ear, trudged into the police bullpen area. With one hand, he secured a Styrofoam coffee cup and poured out the last of a fresh brew. His sour expression did not change as he walked into his office and back kicked the door.

Officer Preston watched her boss take the last of the coffee and slam his office door. The empty pot gurgled and spit on the warm burner. She scowled, thinking this Monday was starting out on the wrong foot. Reluctantly, she stood up and moved to the coffee area to make another pot. Another officer named Marcy, walked past her. "Don't complain. Today I'm on my way to direct traffic at Lake and Fourth in the rain—public works is fixing the traffic lights."

On Preston's first day on the force over a year ago, she pushed to help Sgt. White, not knowing that was unheard of by a rookie. Through sheer dumb luck, it landed her a spot on Gramm's homicide team—no traffic patrol or other usual rookie duties, except coffee making.

Sergeant White arrived with her coffee cup in hand.

"What's today's brew?" Preston asked.

"Vanilla sweet cream nitro cold brew," White crooned. "The super boost!"

Gramm reemerged from his office barking, "White, Preston!"

White looked at Preston. "Happy Monday."

Gramm was adjusting his chair, a recognized sign of agitation. White and Preston sat down and waited for Gramm to finish fiddling with his chair.

Several minutes later, he looked at the two. "Our trip to court just got easier except for the hiccup. The Campbell's attorney has agreed to accept the subpoena for the puzzle pieces on behalf of her clients."

"Meaning?" White asked.

"We don't have to get a subpoena in order to serve a subpoena."

"Oh good, when do we see the pieces?"

"Not so fast—the hiccup. The Campbells want a hearing on our request to see the pieces."

White shook her head. "I thought the judge already agreed to let us see the pieces."

"She did, but now she has rescinded that order and set a hearing for this morning to hear the Campbells' objections. The Consortium has joined with the Campbells. They gave us cookies and now they're taking us to court!"

"I get the Campbells," White said, "but the Consortium? Does that sweet little old lady have a dragon lawyer on retainer?"

"Let me call the listed dragon and find out how he ended up on this case." Gramm pushed his speed dial button for Saul Feinberg and put it on speaker. Before Gramm could even ask, Feinberg charged ahead.

"Charlotte Lane was my high school honors English teacher," Feinberg said, in place of the usual greeting. "I anticipated your question."

"I'm glad you went to high school, but that doesn't tell me how you ended up representing her," Gramm insisted.

"You bullies served that poor lady with a subpoena. Retired high school English teachers do not expect to be served when they open their doors in friendship. She called me. She always liked me. I believe in the Oxford comma. See you at ten." The phone went dead.

"I applaud his ability to sneak in the fact that he was in *honors* English," White commented. "I wonder why our blogger buddy Brandon didn't also file."

Gramm's phone rang. He answered, laughed, nodded several times, and hung up. "To answer your question, the District Attorney has just heard from Pat Wautkin. Remember, he was Mary Alice Bonner's attorney a while ago. He is joining the suit on behalf of Brandon Park."

"That's odd," White said. "Park let us see his pieces when we questioned him."

"That is odd."

Milo chatted with several of the cops in the bullpen and then strolled over to Gramm's office. He leaned in the door. "What did I miss?"

"Some of us have to be in court at ten to justify our request to see the puzzle pieces," Gramm explained.

"Some of us?" Milo asked.

"Not you apparently."

"I'm hurt, left out, feeling…"

"Yada, yada, yada," Gramm cut him off.

"Who filed? The Campbells?"

"The Campbells, the Consortium—yes, that nice lady with the cookies—and Brandon Park."

"Ah, Brandon Park," Milo said. "Last night, I did a bit of digging and discovered that Mr. Park is rich. I wonder if he found his pieces with a checkbook."

"Something to ask him today, when we finish with court," Gramm said.

§

With Gramm and company leaving for court, Milo retreated to the vending machine area and selected an egg salad sandwich. He checked the date on the plastic tray. It expired today. "Close enough," he said, ripping open the package and taking a bite.

Remembering his conversation with Zeke yesterday, Milo called Creedence. "I wanna buy a building, but I don't want anyone to know I own it."

"Okay," Creedence began with hesitation, not sure if this was a continuation of Milo's *batteries* complaint. "What building and why?"

"The Lake Avenue Soup Kitchen, only there's no Soup. It's a big building on Lake Avenue."

"Why is there no Soup?"

"Zeke painted over Soup."

"You know Milo, after talking to you, my head hurts."

"Extra Strength Excedrin, works for me."

"You didn't let me finish. My head hurts because I bang it into the wall."

"Don't do that. What about my building?"

"The one with no soup."

"Yup."

"How can a soup kitchen have no soup?"

"The current building owner doesn't want soup. He's trying to sell the place."

"Let's not talk soup anymore."

"Fine with me. I wasn't calling about soup. I want to buy the building."

"Okay. To what end?"

"I want to make sure the soup kitchen stays there free of charge. And I want everything upgraded."

Milo wants to buy a soup kitchen, Creedence thought. "That's different. Okay, give me the particulars and I'll check it out."

§

Martha was putting in her orders for the week with the butcher, her produce vendor, and Mr. Polmish, her fishmonger, when her phone vibrated. She didn't recognize the number. "Hello?"

"Is Darian there?" a male voice asked.

"Who's calling?"

"I need to speak with Darian."

"Well, that's not going to happen until you tell me who you are and what you want," Martha said indignantly.

"I want to buy his puzzle piece."

"I'm sorry, but Darian has decided not to sell."

"Five thousand dollars can buy a lot of ice cream."

"Who are you?"

"You have my number on your phone. If he changes his mind, call me."

Martha stared at her phone for a minute before deleting the number.

§

Judge Olivia Murphy was relatively young, especially when compared to the ages of the other judges in St. Louis County. At forty-five, she had already handled several controversial cases and, from most accounts, received high marks for being tough but fair. She sat behind the bench, finished cleaning her blue flecked, tortoise-shell glasses, and looked at the assembled attorneys and police officers.

"Well, this is a new one on me. Apparently, we all are gathered here today to discuss a treasure hunt based on puzzle pieces. As I understand it, the Duluth Police Department would like to take temporary possession of these pieces. How many are we talking about, Mr. District Attorney?"

Duluth District Attorney, Dutch Wilson, stood and lifted his chin—a move that he thought made his five-foot-four frame look taller. "Your honor, we count eight. Two with the Campbell family, two with blogger Brandon Park, three with the group calling itself The Consortium, and one with the police department."

"Your honor," Saul Feinberg stood, "my clients would like it on the record that they do not call themselves The Consortium."

Murphy smiled. "I don't care what they call themselves, Mr. Feinberg. For this hearing, they will remain The Consortium. Now, is this an accurate count? Ms. McKenna?"

McKenna stood. "In the interest of full disclosure, the Campbell family now has three pieces, your honor."

Wautkin stood next. "Your honor, my client, Brandon Park, has four pieces."

White looked at Gramm and whispered, "Milo was right. He must be buying them."

"Lieutenant Gramm, are you going to tell me *you* have more than one?"

Gramm stood. "Just the one, your honor."

"So, by my count, there are eleven pieces, out of how many?"

District Attorney Wilson responded, "We are told by the radio station that there are twelve. One is missing." Wilson described the contest.

"And why do you want to take possession of these puzzle pieces, Mr. Wilson?" Judge Murphy asked.

"A man named Harold Gilbert was found murdered last Tuesday by two fishermen in the St. Louis River. The police have forensic evidence showing he was bludgeoned in or near Jay Cooke State Park and his body dumped in the river. The police found one puzzle piece in the victim's car, a piece with the word *Cooke* on it. The police need to know if the puzzle piece found in the car was the motive for this man's murder, or was it some other factor, especially in light of the fact that

Gilbert's puzzle piece was left behind. The police believe the completed puzzle is a necessary clue for solving this murder."

McKenna jumped up. "You honor, handing over my clients' puzzle pieces to the police would cause them irreparable harm. They have spent a considerable sum securing these pieces…"

"Why?" Judge Murphy interrupted.

"They want to stop this contest."

"Why?"

"Louis Rutledge, a family member, owned KDDW until his death earlier this month. He created this contest to help the radio station gain listeners. From the beginning, the Campbell family has felt this contest to be dangerous and wanted it stopped. The death of Mr. Gilbert proves their point. By buying pieces, they hope people will stop looking for the treasure, interest in the contest will fade, and no one else will become a victim."

"Let's get to the irreparable harm. How would letting the police see the pieces cause harm? I assume, Lieutenant Gramm, that neither you nor your staff are in the treasure hunting business."

"We are not, your honor."

"Your honor, shortly after Mr. Gilbert's death, a blogger was given information that only the police could know. That clearly shows the police have a leak, and, if they were to possess all the pieces, a copy of those pieces could be leaked, and the contest would continue. It would put other people in danger," McKenna said.

Wilson countered, "Ms. McKenna overstates her case, your honor. The police did not leak the information about Harold Gilbert's murder."

"Then who did?" the judge asked.

"The only person who really knows what happened," Gramm interjected, "the murderer. Brandon Park received an anonymous email and placed the information on his blog. We feel the killer of Mr. Gilbert sent that email."

"Mr. Wautkin, you represent Mr. Park. What do you say?"

"Your honor, as Lieutenant Gramm said, Mr. Park received an anonymous email which he provided to police. Mr. Park has already let the police see two of his four puzzle pieces. He feels he has cooperated enough and further cooperation puts him at an unfair disadvantage. He also worries about the ability of the police to keep these puzzle pieces private."

"Mr. Feinberg, you have been uncharacteristically silent," the judge said.

Feinberg stood. "My clients do not have the money to buy pieces. They each found a piece using their wits…"

"Sing the song, raise the flag, counselor. Get to the point."

Feinberg smiled. "They face competitors that are willing to throw money at the matter. One to win the contest. The other to end the contest. Once these puzzle pieces leave my client's possession, they could easily end up in the hands of people who have the means to buy information."

McKenna bristled. "Are you accusing my clients of bribing the police?"

Feinberg shook his head. "Not at all, counselor, and if I implied that, I apologize. I am simply saying that experience has taught me that stuff happens."

"Lt. Gramm," the judge said.

Gramm stood up.

"What assurance can you give the court that these puzzle pieces will remain in good keeping and not be shared with anyone?"

"I will take possession of them and lock them in the department safe."

"How many people have that combination?" McKenna demanded.

"Okay. I think I have the gist of these arguments," Judge Murphy said. "I will rule on this matter tomorrow."

"Your honor?" McKenna stepped forward.

"Yes, Ms. McKenna?"

"I have a court date tomorrow in Minneapolis. I am asking the court to delay the ruling until Wednesday."

"Your honor," Wilson jumped to his feet—chin jutted. "The police are investigating a murder. A delay may let the murderer go undetected."

"I think one day is reasonable. I will rule at one o'clock in this chamber on Wednesday."

Gramm, White, and Preston stood. Wilson joined them. "That went reasonably well. I think you will get to see the pieces."

"But not take possession of them?" Gramm asked.

"McKenna makes a good case."

On the way out of the courtroom, McKenna said to Feinberg, "You made me do all the heavy lifting."

"You jumped right in there," Feinberg laughed.

"Did you know the police had a puzzle piece?"

"I did not."

"Why kill the guy and leave the piece?" McKenna asked.

"I am sure Gramm is asking the same question. If he isn't I assure you, Milo is."

§

"Gustafson's?" Gramm asked, referring to the group's semi favorite downtown restaurant.

"Sure," White said. "I'll text Milo."

"You complain about him, but then invite him," Preston said.

Gramm led the way down the hill to Superior Street. As it was well past noon, Gustafson's was not as crowded as usual. McKenna and Feinberg were just being seated as the police walked in. Gramm nodded and moved on to his favorite booth in the back.

Pat, the waitress, took the Feinberg-McKenna order first and then moved on to Gramm, White, and Preston as Milo arrived. He waved to the restaurant owners, Nick and Nicola Christos, stopped by Feinberg and McKenna, and finally meandered his way to the back booth.

Pat waited for him. "It would help me out if you all came together," she complained, giving Milo the evil eye. "First off, I am forced to tell you that if you want water, you will have to request it."

"Why? There's more fresh water in Duluth than any other place on Earth," Milo complained.

"You know that, and I know that," Pat continued with her evil eye. "But busboy Carl dropped two tubs of glasses yesterday. Until we get replacements, glasses are in short supply. I could simply pour the water on the table and let you lap it up."

"Specials?" White requested, trying to turn the tide of the exchange.

Pat nodded. "Chicken salad on a croissant."

"A croissant?" Milo questioned. "Not very Greek of you."

"Nick did one of those DNA things, discovered he's twelve percent French."

"What comes with the special?" White asked.

"French fries."

Preston laughed. "Of course."

White and Preston ordered the special. Gramm opted for the new pan-fried trout.

"Pan-fried trout?" White questioned.

"Nick is also six percent fish," Pat deadpanned as she turned to Milo.

"I'm glad to see that these new menu items have not come at the expense of my meatloaf sandwich and mashed potatoes."

"Heaven forbid," Pat said. "I suppose you want the green beans."

"Of course. Oh, and a Diet Coke—in a glass."

"At least you drink the Coke," Pat muttered as she moved off to another table.

Gramm looked at Milo. "Brandon Park."

"First, what happened in court?"

"We talked. They talked. The judge talked. Holding pattern until Wednesday."

"Did I ask for the long version?" Milo snarked. "Next time, try to condense it a little."

Pat returned with their drinks, spilling a little of Milo's Coke.

"I swear she does that on purpose," Milo charged.

"I would," White said. "Now tell us about Brandon Park."

"I was wondering if he bought those two pieces rather than figuring out the clues. So, I checked him out on my super-secret PI software. He has done quite well for himself."

"Make that four pieces now, and we think you're right. He bought them," White said.

"Why does it matter, other than he lied?" Preston asked.

"If Ham was selling his piece to the highest bidder, maybe Brandon was the one who was buying," Milo said.

"Why would Brandon leave the piece?" Preston asked.

"Why would anyone leave the piece?" White added.

"Two reasons I can think of. They didn't mean to kill Ham, panicked, and ran. Or Ham's murder had nothing to do with that damn contest," Gramm said.

"A romantic rendezvous gone bad?" Milo asked.

"Did you see Ham Gilbert?" White asked.

"So unkind," Milo said. "I prefer to think there is someone for everyone."

"Don't count on it!" Pat said, returning with their food. She slopped a little gravy on the table in front of Milo.

"I'm starting to admire her ability to do that," Milo said as he wiped the table with a napkin.

"Let's invite Mr. Park to the station."

"Because he lied?" Preston asked.

"Because I don't want to climb those steps," Gramm said, moving his trout through the butter sauce.

Milo pushed his green beans to the side of the plate and slid the mashed potatoes and gravy together.

§

Martha, unhappy that Mr. Polmish didn't have fresh walleye, set her phone down, only to have it vibrate—another number she didn't recognize.

"Hello?" a female voice said. "Is Darian there?"

"No, may I ask who's calling," Martha said, regretting letting Darian do the radio station interview.

"Oh yeah, he's a kid—probably in school, right?"

"May I help you?"

"Maybe. I'm Kayla Maki. I'm a member of the group that is putting our puzzle pieces together. On the radio, he said he wanted to join us, so I'm calling."

"Thank you, Ms. Maki. I'm Darian's guardian. Tell me about your group."

"A guardian? Like not a mom?"

"Yes, Kayla, like not a mom."

"I didn't have a mom either. Bummer."

"Your group?"

"Oh yeah. There are three of us. There's me. I used to sell candles and stuff in Hermantown. Charlotte Lane is old—retired schoolteacher. Nice lady. She makes cookies. The cookies match her clothes. She's sick, totally awesome. Then there's Ben Heikkinen who loves alpacas."

"Alpacas?"

"Yeah, alpacas, llamas, and sheep. He's gotta farm. Gotta be careful of the llamas. They're nasty."

Martha enjoyed the train ride and Darian's discovery. This ride with random strangers, she was not so sure about. "How does this work? Do you meet in person?"

"Oh, yes. We originally planned to share the meetings, but Charlotte loves to bake, so we meet at her house. You can come too."

"When's the next meeting?"

"Tomorrow afternoon, about three. I'll text you the address. Bring the puzzle piece. I'm sure we'll all be eager to see it. One more thing you should know, seeing that he's a kid."

"Yes?"

"I sorta got attacked by a guy who was trying to steal my piece. I kinda sliced him, but he's in jail now."

Martha did not know what to do with that information, but she saw a conversation with Milo in her future.

§

Brandon Park arrived at the police station with his attorney, Pat Wautkin, in tow. They were escorted to interview room A.

Wautkin looked around the sparse, gray space. "You know, Ernie, you really have to brighten up these rooms."

"Maybe some drapes and throw pillows?" Gramm asked sarcastically.

"For starters."

Gramm once again opened his fake folder. "So, Mr. Park, when we interviewed you on Friday, you said you had two pieces. Suddenly, today in court, you have four pieces."

"It was a productive weekend," Brandon smiled.

"Counselor, would you inform your client of the seriousness of this inquiry? Someone is going to be charged with murder. To that end, Mr. Park, I must remind you that you have already been informed of your rights."

Brandon continued to smile.

"If we check your bank records, would we find two withdrawals this weekend?" White asked.

"We won't give you access to my client's bank records," Wautkin said. "and what difference does it make? He admits to buying puzzle pieces. He now has four instead of two. When he bought them is a moot point."

"It speaks to lying, counselor," Gramm said.

Wautkin gave his *so what* shrug. "Move on, Lieutenant. My client is a busy man."

"Can we see the new pieces?" Gramm asked.

"No," Park said simply.

"Come on, Lieutenant, were you not in court today? My client should not have shown you the first two, but you talked to him without advice of counsel."

"We read him his rights. You know how it goes. You have the right to an attorney."

"Why are we here, Lieutenant?"

"Your client misled us. He said he found the puzzle pieces. Buying the pieces puts him in contact with the victim…"

"Do you have any evidence that my client attempted to buy a puzzle piece from Mr. Gilbert? I understand the piece was still in Gilbert's possession when you searched his car."

"The victim's phone was damaged by Mr. Gilbert's trip downriver, but we are repairing that damage. If your client and our victim were in contact, it would be best if he admitted to it now."

Park just shook his head.

"You know, Lieutenant, my client isn't the only one who is buying pieces. The Campbell family is also buying. Have you checked with them?"

"We will. Could you explain something to me, Mr. Park?"

"Maybe. My attorney is doing a pretty good job so far."

"You appeared cooperative three days ago. Today, you arrive with your lawyer, and are seriously uncooperative."

Park smiled. "It's part of the game, Lieutenant. As I told you, I like games. That radio station started this game. I'm just a player. So are you."

"So was Harold Gilbert until someone killed him," White shot back.

"I agree. That murder ups the game. We're all in it to win. I also know you have a puzzle piece."

Wautkin put his hand up to Park's ear, whispering that the police puzzle piece was mentioned in court this morning. Park smiled again. "I knew on Saturday when I got the second email from The Riddler. Stupid name, but the guy has inside information."

Gramm glared at Park. "Now you're withholding evidence."

Park flipped his hand at Gramm as a dismissal. "You need to read my blog. I announced it to the world."

"What did you announce?" White demanded.

"Look it up." Park sat back, arms folded.

White checked her phone and showed it to Gramm.

The Riddler has contacted me again, puzzle hunters:

Ask the police why they haven't told anyone about the puzzle piece they found in Ham Gilbert's car. It's a key piece and has the name Cooke on it. Why are they keeping this information secret? Are the cops puzzle hunters?
    The Riddler

"We need to see the original email." White stated.

"Sure, but you won't get anything from it. This guy is a pro. He's hidden his tracks." Brandon laughed.

"I'm thinking you're the Riddler," Gramm said.

"Then arrest him," Wautkin countered.

Gramm sat back and folded his arms. "Mr. Park, if you are not the Riddler, then you are playing a dangerous game with a dangerous person. This guy has killed once. It's our experience that killing gets easier each time."

Park leaned forward, rubbing his hands together. "Like I said, it ups the game. Now it's interesting."

"This is not the Brandon Park we interviewed last week," Milo said to Preston as the two watched the interview through the one-way glass.

"He's a major gamer. Once that switch is on, they're all in," Preston said.

"Gramm isn't. Notice the eyebrows. When they're that close together, it means he's annoyed. It makes a difference."

"A difference? How?"

"When this is all over, and let's say Mr. Park is not the killer, I bet Gramm charges him with obstruction—those emails needed to be turned over to us as soon as he got them."

"Really?"

"I've never seen the eyebrows that close together. Gramm doesn't do games when it comes to murder."

16

Sequestered in Chip's home office on the Campbell Compound, Chip and Clay were waiting on an early morning call from their attorney, Kimberly McKenna. Clay's wife, Cindy, barged through the patio doors with his requested breakfast basket. She dropped it on the nearest table and left without a word. Her look toward Clay punctuated their earlier argument as to why he couldn't wait to eat until after this meeting with Chip.

Chip also glared at his brother as Clay pulled his chair over to the table and began eating.

"This meeting is important. You could have eaten after the phone call."

"Are you my wife? Tight schedule today. First tee in an hour."

"We could have been discussing family business. Cindy could have overheard something she wasn't supposed to. We can't have outsiders barging in everywhere!"

Clay antagonized his brother further by slowly bringing a forkful of eggs to his mouth and chewing it in slow motion. Chip rose and started pacing, mumbling again about how outsiders were threatening their legacy.

Dabbing his mouth with his napkin, Clay said, "Just stop with the outsider crap! We were all schooled to look for the same things in a spouse, someone who is content to spend our money and not ask too many questions. You did it. I did it. Blair did it. Hell, even Mazy did it."

The desk phone rang. Chip put it on speaker and said, "We're both here."

"Hello, gentlemen," Kimberly McKenna said.

"Why am I here so early?" Clay demanded.

"I have court today in Minneapolis on another matter. I'm on the firm's plane now. It's a short trip, so let me fill you in. I think we made some inroads with the judge yesterday. I suspect the police will be allowed to see the pieces but not possess them. That's a win."

"Can we see the pieces? Other people's I mean," Chip asked.

"I'll ask, but I doubt it."

"Any surprises?"

"Yes, that blogger, Brandon Park, has four pieces, not two."

"Damn! Is he outbidding us?" Chip asked.

Clay smiled. "He's getting to the people before you are. Tell your gopher to step up his game."

"From the count in court, there is only one piece outstanding." McKenna said.

"By the way, Chip," Clay continued to smile, "who is our gopher who has failed to outbid Mr. Park?"

Before Chip could answer, McKenna interrupted. "Oh, there was one other surprise."

"What?" Chip took a sip of his coffee.

"The police have a piece. Apparently, the murdered man, Harold Gilbert, left it behind."

Chip, who was taking a sip of his coffee, erupted into a loud coughing fit that alarmed Clay, who pounded him on the back several times.

"What's happening?" McKenna asked.

"Chip swallowed the wrong way," Clay said.

"Sorry," Chip managed to squeak.

"That piece begs the question of why the murderer would leave it behind. My sources tell me it was on the dashboard of Gilbert's car. I'll be back in town for Judge Murphy's ruling on the warrants tomorrow."

"Thanks Kimberly." Chip hung up.

"What's going on?" Clay demanded.

Chip feigned surprise. "What do you mean?"

"You told me *we* have Gilbert's puzzle piece, and we bought it *before* he died. Tell me your obsession did not get us mixed up in murder."

§

"Getting to know all of you has been wonderful, but all I seem to do is sit and eat," Lana said as she sat down at breakfast. "It's a sunny day, and I need to get active."

"I have all sorts of exercise equipment you could use. Bikes, steppers, treadmills…"

Lana laughed. "I'm sixty something, Sutherland. When I say active, I mean walking."

"You could walk the grounds, and we have a tunnel to the park across the road. It's one of Lakesong's secrets," Agnes offered.

"The park sounds perfect," Lana said.

Martha arrived with breakfast smoothies for Sutherland and Agnes, a poached egg and toast for Lana, and Milo's scrambled eggs, hash browns, and bacon.

Lana watched Milo break off pieces of bacon for the cats. "I've seen you do that every morning. Is that healthy for them?" she asked.

"Jet just plays with his piece," Milo said. "As for Annie, we got her to stop smoking last fall, so the bacon is sort of a reward."

"Any other house, I would think you were kidding," Lana laughed.

"Two packs a day," Milo added. "She finally stopped coughing."

"Sutherland and I have decided on an architect," Agnes announced. "Fair warning. We hope to start remodeling soon. Happy summer everyone!"

"You aren't going to do anything to the gallery, are you?" Lana asked.

"It's due for a cleaning. I suspect the cats will enjoy the scaffolding, but we would never change the glass dome," Agnes said. "We have decided to remodel the second and third floors right above us here on the north end of the house. We are going to extend over the garage as well."

"I remember Laura having a tough time getting someone to sign on to her idea of that gorgeous glass dome—blowing out the third floor to create what she liked to call her indoor park. I'm surprised there is still any of the third floor left."

"Quite a bit, actually, on the north end. I do not know what's on the south end. I think Mr. Teenage Remodeler here must have cut off the stairway from the second floor on that side of the house. I can't find it."

"I can't remember anything ever being said about a stairway," Sutherland sniffed. "I am being maligned."

"You probably are," Lana said. "Look at these old houses. You have the grand staircase for us swells. I assume when this house was built, the servants lived on the third floor."

"She was built in the late eighteen hundreds, so I think they did," Agnes agreed. "I found a staircase from the second floor to the third on the north end of the house. I assume there is an identical staircase on the south end."

"Not necessarily," Lana said. "There were two types of servants in old houses such as these: household staff using your newly found staircase on the north end, and house and grounds people who didn't need to traipse through the house. I bet their staircase goes from the third floor directly to the basement. In fact, Laura mentioned finding a staircase that did just that."

Sutherland stopped slurping his smoothie and looked at Agnes. "Oh no. She has that look in her eye."

Agnes smiled innocently. "Me? A look?"

"Yes, a look," Sutherland echoed. "It's that *grab my crowbar and hunt for those stairs,* look."

"Well, if Lakesong wants us to know, she will show us."

"No crowbars in my wine cellar!"

"Why, dear," Agnes batted her eyes, "I thought it was *our* wine cellar."

Milo jumped in. "It's half my wine cellar. You are welcome to hunt in my half."

"Where is your half?" Sutherland asked.

"Whichever half Agnes is hunting in. I thought that was clear," Milo said.

"Okay, no crowbars. Lakesong doesn't hide things if you know how to find them," Agnes said. "She likes me. I'm sure she will show me the way."

Martha returned to remove breakfast dishes. Lana asked her if Darian had made his lucrative puzzle piece decision yet.

That caught Milo's attention. "Lucrative puzzle piece?"

Martha stopped. "Darian found a hundred-dollar bill and a puzzle piece for a radio station contest yesterday on the train."

"He was polite to Joe, the conductor on that sky car that goes up the North Shore," Lana said.

"The KDDW puzzle?" Milo asked.

Martha nodded. "Darian has decided to join a group of people who are pooling their pieces to find some treasure. His first meeting is this afternoon."

"Kayla Maki's group?" Milo asked.

Martha set the dishes on her cart and turned to Milo. "How do you know Kayla Maki? Is she dangerous? She did say she stabbed someone."

"If Darian isn't planning to mug her, he's safe."

§

Bill Bingham, the head of commercial real estate, poked his head in Sutherland's office. "Got a minute?"

Sutherland closed the Kiner file on his computer and waved him in. "What's up?"

Bingham, tall and wiry, had been with the McKnight Realty firm for years. Bill boasted that he had sold almost every piece of commercial real estate in Duluth twice, if not three times. At least, that was his goal. "We may have to eat some crow."

"I hate cooked crow. Why?" Sutherland asked.

"When Beth got that listing for the old soup kitchen building, we all bet on how long it would take to sell it."

"Yeah, I picked three years."

"You lost, boss, but my pick was worse. I said five years."

Sutherland looked surprised. "Don't tell me we have a buyer?"

"All cash, as is. Beth has been dancing in and out of cubicles all morning."

"You're kidding. Beth disclosed the code violations, right?"

"Absolutely. She said the buyer doesn't care. Creedence is representing the buyer."

"Creedence Durant?"

"You know any other guy named Creedence?"

Sutherland had to laugh. "Who's his client?"

"Wants to remain anonymous. Probably doesn't want to run up the price."

Sutherland thought about Durant's clients. "Well, I know it's not me. It's got to be a tax write off. Thousands will have to go into bringing that building up to code. There's no immediate profit to be made."

§

Mazy Campbell was sitting on her patio, finishing a phone conversation with her cousin. "I'll send you the files by courier, Mandy. Look them over, then decide. See you soon."

"Thanks, Mazy. They loaded my college life into a moving truck yesterday. It should arrive and be unpacked sometime tomorrow. I'd appreciate it if you'd make sure they find the right cottage."

"Will do. See you tomorrow."

A large shadow passed between Mazy and the sun. She looked up to see Major Peters hovering above her.

"We need to talk to you, Mrs. Mason," Peters said.

Mazy looked around. "I don't see a *we*."

Peters tried to stand taller. "I am talking for the family."

"You are talking *to* the family." Mazy stood and glared at Peters. "The family of which you are not a part. You are an employee, sir, and not a good one." Mazy attempted to enter her house by the patio doors.

Peters took a step forward to block her. "We need to talk to you about the notes you've been putting on Chip's house."

Mazy stepped back. "I have no idea what you're talking about. Get out of my way!"

"Are you denying…"

Mazy attempted to move around Peters, who grabbed her arm. "Get your hands off me!" she shouted loud enough for the entire compound to hear.

Her husband, Michael, stormed out of the house, slamming back the patio doors, tackling Peters, sending both of them to the ground. Peters pushed Mason away while scrambling to his feet. Mason sprang up as Peters attempted a swing. He blocked the oncoming fist, spun, and kicked Peters square in the belly. Peters fell to the ground, gasping for breath.

"What the hell is your problem?" Michael demanded.

"Why did you attack him?" Mazy screamed at Michael.

"You needed help."

"No, I didn't! I can handle myself."

Peters stood up, still holding his stomach. "You both just made a big mistake," he said, before stumbling off.

§

Milo walked into the cop shop where Gramm was already holding court in his office with White and Preston.

"Nice of you to join us, Milo," Gramm said, as Milo pushed a chair through the door.

"Darian Gibbson found a puzzle piece," Milo informed them as he spun his chair around and sat down. "He's joining the Consortium with Kayla Maki."

Gramm stared at Milo, trying to comprehend. "Nine-year-old Darian and Kayla?"

"Ten," Milo corrected.

"Well, that makes all the difference."

"Where did he find it?" White asked.

"On that steam train that goes up the shore."

"So, now the Consortium has four pieces?" Gramm asked.

"They do."

"Thank you for that tidbit, Milo. We were just talking about our next step."

"We need to interview the rest of the Campbell family," White said.

"Exactly," agreed Gramm. "I was about to call Dutch Wilson to see how we make that happen."

"Kidnapping?" Milo asked.

"They won't share pieces or even talk to us. Kidnapping may be the only way." Gramm's phone rang. "It's the hotline to the deputy chief," Gramm said, stretching his neck. "I think this day is about to get more frustrating."

"Gramm?" Sanders bellowed.

"Deputy chief."

"Chip Campbell has called the mayor to complain about police harassment. The mayor called the chief. Guess who the chief called?"

"I would bet he called you, sir."

"Good guess."

"We're not harassing anyone," Gramm said. He spent the next ten minutes explaining the case and the need to see the puzzle pieces. "I have to warn you, sir, that we are about to crank up the heat on the family. We need to talk with them."

"Is our consultant in on this one?" Sanders asked.

"Milo is here, yes, sir."

"Good. Keep going but do me one favor. Try to talk to them again before you do anything nasty. We want to say we gave them every chance to cooperate before we hit them over the head."

"Certainly. Does that mean if they refuse, we can hit them over the head?"

"I hate people who try to use influence. Dot your i's and cross your t's and make sure Rathkey is along." The phone went dead.

"He loves me," Milo said.

Gramm's eyebrows slammed together.

"Should I notify the county we're coming this time?" White asked.

"Yup, but not today. Given the Deputy chief's concern, let's contact the family lawyer. McKenna might intercede. Meanwhile, Preston, catch me up on all the family members."

"Duncan Campbell the Fourth is chairman of the board of Campbell Industries. People call him Chip. The other board members are Chip's brother Clayton, Great Aunt Greer, and Mazy Mason, whom we already interviewed. Oh, there's Mazy's husband Michael Mason. Not on the board. He races motorcycles—not well."

White noticed that Preston was not consulting her pad. "Did you memorize the Campbell family?"

"Sort of," Preston laughed. "I…"

"Where does Mazy fit in?" Milo asked. "Is she a child of one of the other three?"

"She's the daughter of Blair Campbell and Lewis Rutledge, both deceased. Blair was a sister to Chip and Clayton," Preston said.

"We can't just sit here all day!" Gramm blurted. "Who can we investigate? How about that idiot playing soldier that talked to us at the family compound? Who is he? Do we know anything about him?"

"Major Peters," White said.

"Is Major his first name or rank?" Milo asked. "His uniform didn't have a rank."

They all looked at Preston. "I'll check. First I've heard of him. Do we know anything else about him?"

White picked up her phone. "Let me call the one Campbell family member who is talking to us."

The phone rang three times before Mazy picked up.

"Mrs. Mason?" White asked.

"Yes."

"This is Sergeant White of the Duluth Police Department."

"Yes, Sergeant, what can I do for you?"

"We are trying to get some information about a Major Peters. I think he does security for you."

"He does things for my Uncle Chip. Funny you should call. I'm seriously thinking of filing assault charges against him."

"If he assaulted you, you should definitely come in and file charges."

"What do you want to know about him?"

"Anything you can tell us."

"Let me go to my office," Mazy said. After a brief pause, she returned to the call. White heard her type, then laughter.

"Mrs. Mason?"

"According to our personnel records, the Major's real name is Elbert Peters. No wonder he calls himself Major.

Chip hired him ten years ago. He lists security expert on his resume."

"Was he a major?"

"Not listed."

"Tell me about the assault."

"He grabbed me and accused me of putting threatening notes on Chip's house."

"What did the notes say?" White asked.

"I have no idea."

"I urge you to file charges."

"I'm considering it. I have something that's pressing right now."

"If you decide to go ahead, come to our station and ask for me, Sergeant Robin White."

"Thank you, Sergeant." Mazy hung up.

"What was that about?" Gramm asked.

"Elbert Peters, the Major's real name. Apparently, he attacked Mazy Mason this morning," White said. "She's thinking of pressing charges."

"She's a family member. Isn't that like attacking your boss?" Preston asked.

"Exactly," White said. "I get the sense he works more for Chip Campbell than the rest of the family."

Gramm smiled. "Disharmony. Nice! I overheard something about notes."

"Yes, Elbert accused Mazy of putting threatening notes on Chip Campbell's house," White said.

"Elbert?" Milo questioned. "Who names their kid Elbert?"

"Who names their kid Milo?" White asked.

"It's a family name."

"Who else in your family had it?"

"I didn't say it was my family."

Gramm shook his head. "Can someone just look up Elbert Peters without triggering a Milo response?"

"Got it," Preston said, opening her pad.

§

Martha picked up Darian after school to take him to the Consortium meeting at Charlotte Lane's fourplex. When they arrived, the others were already gathered. "I'm Darian," he said when Charlotte opened the door.

"Hello, Darian," Charlotte said. "I'm Charlotte Lane. Come in. We've been waiting for you."

Charlotte introduced Darian and Martha to Ben and Kayla. Darian sat down. Martha sat on a chair outside of the conversation circle, trying to be present but out of the way.

"So, Darian, how did you find your piece?" Kayla asked.

"Did you really stab someone?" Darian asked.

Martha wanted to hide. *How does he know that?*

Kayla smiled. "I did! He was trying to rob me."

"Cool."

Ben laughed. "I feel like I don't measure up. All I did was hear my llama scream at someone."

"You have llamas?" Darian asked.

"And alpacas. You can come out to our farm and enjoy the herd if you want. They love to be petted."

Charlotte picked up her plate of yellow cookies and offered it to Darian. "I'm afraid I didn't stab anyone, and my parakeet over by the window hasn't attacked anyone, but I do have cookies."

"This is going to be fun," Darian said, turning back to Martha.

§

Agnes had set Lana and her up on the back patio lounge chairs that overlooked the lake. They were enjoying iced coffee and an assortment of tea sandwiches—smoke salmon and cucumber, egg salad, and tomato and basil. As they indulged, a stiff breeze drove lake waves onto the basalt breakers, sending spray over the agate and sand beach.

"I always wondered why they call these Great Lakes, or lakes at all," Lana mused. "They really are inland seas. I could be on the Moray Shore in Scotland overlooking the North Sea."

"I've never seen the North Sea, but I agree, Superior is huge and yet calming at the same time. Whenever I'm troubled or confused, a session with Lake Superior strengthens me," Agnes said.

"I've always lived near water. I need to see and hear it," Lana admitted.

They lapsed into silence, listening to the waves, feeling the sun, and watching an ore boat edge its way beyond the horizon.

"Thank you for the park," Lana said. "And that secret tunnel under the street is magical."

Agnes smiled. "Lakesong has many wonderful secrets."

"One more of Martha's sandwiches and I'll be up for a stairway hunt," Lana said.

Agnes finished her sandwich, glanced over at Lana, and smiled. Lana's eyes were closed. The fresh air and exercise had lulled her into a catnap. Agnes quietly cleared their late lunch dishes, then returned to join Lana until she roused.

With a start, Lana's eyes opened. She looked around and started to laugh. "Now this is living! I am energized and rested. Let's begin our hunt."

The two descended into the basement with Agnes pointing out the elevator, the hidden kitchen, and the vault before they arrived at the wine cellar.

"Last summer, Sutherland and Milo discovered a tunnel that leads from that vault to the lake," Agnes said. "They think it was for smuggling liquor during prohibition. Do you like whisky? They found some. Also, we discovered a speakeasy room under the stairs. Sutherland bumped into it with his bike when he was a toddler."

"Another prohibition artifact?" Lana asked.

"Actually, no. Milo's ex-wife thought it was built a lot earlier. She visited—that's a whole other story." Agnes opened the doors to the climate-controlled wine room. "Reds to the left. Whites to the right, and what country?"

Lana looked over the vast room filled with rack upon rack of wine bottles. "Amazing. I think if the stairway is in here, it would be in that corner." She pointed to the far south end of the room.

"Portugal reds," Agnes said, opening the door to the red wines. She led the way past various countries, arriving at the red wines of Portugal. Pressing against the wall, Agnes could feel nothing moving.

"There is a secret stair in the upstairs library that leads to the downstairs library. I accessed it by kicking the baseboard," Agnes explained.

Lana kicked the nearest baseboard. Nothing moved. Agnes did the same. Similar result. Lana spied a bottle of Italian wine in with the Portuguese wine. "Why is that there?"

Agnes' eyes lit up. "That's it. That out-of-place wine is a trigger. How clever." She picked up the bottle. Nothing happened.

"Maybe we have to put it somewhere else," Lana suggested.

They spent the better part of the next hour placing the bottle in various slots. If there was a hidden staircase, it remained hidden. The two finally admitted defeat and retreated upstairs to enjoy that Italian glass of wine. Lana defended her choice to call it a day, saying all those bottles made her thirsty.

§

By the time Milo and Sutherland arrived home, Agnes and Lana had enjoyed several glasses of wine and had moved from the gallery back out to the terrace. Duluth was experiencing an unusually warm day in May, warm enough for an outside dinner. Martha put down place settings on the glass-covered, wrought-iron patio table.

"Good idea," Milo said, sipping his recently made gimlet. "Pre-mosquito time."

"Mosquitoes in Minnesota can carry away small children and pets," Sutherland laughed—an old Minnesota joke.

Sutherland offered to make Agnes her Martini, but she declined, saying she would stick to wine. "Aunt Lana and I walked all over Patterson Park and talked about how to find that south side stairway. When we returned, we poked around the wine cellar, but all we found was wine," Agnes giggled.

"Did you kick the baseboards?" Sutherland asked.

"We did. Nothing happened."

"Why would you look in the wine cellar?" Milo asked.

"It's on the south side of the basement and has been remodeled," Agnes said.

"I don't think the wine cellar is the right place to look," Milo said.

"Well, oh great detective, where would you look?" Agnes made a sweeping hand gesture.

"Well, oh mighty-Lakesong-secret-room-hunter, I would ask myself who told Lana about the staircase."

"Laura told me," Lana said.

"Laura. And how would Laura have known about the staircase unless she found it? And how would she have found it? Hmmm? Perhaps, while she was overseeing some remodeling of her own."

"Makes sense," Sutherland said.

"What did Laura remodel in the basement?" Milo continued.

"The pool! She put in the new indoor pool," Sutherland shouted.

"Correct, Sir! Did the Lady of the Manor wish to walk the length of Lakesong to the basement stairs, outside the kitchen, in the dead of winter, and then tread past the furnaces that scare small children to get to the new indoor pool? No, she did not."

Sutherland groaned. "I forgot. She put in private stairs leading from her closet down to the new pool."

Agnes stared at Sutherland.

"It's now in Milo's—I think—unused closet."

"The cats use it," Milo said.

"Don't you use the stairway when you go to the pool?" Agnes asked.

"Yes, me and the cats. It's kinda cute. They're dressed in their little white robes, carrying their pool toys. For the record, I did offer to give up the master bedroom with the His and Hers dressing rooms and bathrooms." Milo nodded to Lana. "The bathroom comes with its own jungle."

Lana laughed. "Of course. There are hidden kitchens, cats that have pool toys, and secret tunnels. Why wouldn't there be bathroom jungles?"

"Someday, I'm going back down to that basement and find that staircase!" Agnes announced. "When she's ready, Lakesong will speak."

"Why not tonight?" Sutherland asked.

Agnes gave Sutherland a side eye. "No more hunting tonight. I will regale you with the complete story of our hunt at a later time. I'm a bit into my cups," Agnes said. "Thank God for Martha and her hors d'oeuvres."

"You're welcome," Martha said as she rolled out a salad cart—strawberry spinach salad for everyone but Milo who received his usual iceberg wedge with blue cheese dressing.

§

The late-in-the-day invitation came at a good time. Brandon Park was getting antsy and needed to get out of his apartment. A nice, breezy drive in his red Audi R8 would blow the cobwebs from his brain. He pulled up to the intercom at the Campbell family front gate, pressed the *talk* button, and waited. After five seconds, he pressed it again.

"Can I help you?" a male voice asked.

"Brandon Park to see Chip Campbell. I'm expected."

"Proceed down the main drive, execute a right turn in the fourth driveway by the elk antlers. Park in front of the lodge. I'll meet you there."

"Who are you?" Park asked, but there was no answer.

The gate swung back, and Park spun his wheels on the oiled dirt road, skidding into the fourth turn, almost taking out the elk antlers. A scowling Major Peters was standing on the extensive front deck of the lodge building. Park jumped from his car and asked if Peters was Chip Campbell.

"I'm Major Peters. Mr. Campbell will meet you inside. Follow me."

Park, annoyed at the pseudo-secret-agent attitude, followed Peters into the large front lobby of the lodge. Peters stopped and looked around at the empty lobby, then keyed his radio. "Mr. Campbell, it's Peters. Your guest is in the lodge."

There was no answer.

"Wait here. Do not leave the lodge," Peters ordered. "I will find him."

Park waited two minutes, then left the lodge.

§

Chip Campbell anxiously paced on the path behind his house. Looking up, he grimaced at the hooded figure approaching. Not bothering with a greeting, he launched into a diatribe. "What have you gotten the family mixed up in? This isn't a goddamn game! I can't believe it! You told me we have that Gilbert guy's puzzle piece, and now McKenna tells me the police have it."

The object of his ire stood silent and motionless until Chip turned to walk away. "It's not how we do things."

The attack was swift, knocking Chip off his feet, face down in the dirt.

"Wha…"

A truncheon came down on his head with a loud thud. Chip lay motionless, blood pooling in his hair, oozing down to the dirt.

17

Michael cracked a third egg into a butter-filled sauté pan and threw two pieces of bread into the four-piece toaster. While searching the refrigerator for the strawberry preserves, he mumbled something about a moving van over by the lake.

Mazy, sipping her green tea, stared at the toaster. "You could offer me toast."

"You don't like anything I make, including toast. So, what's with the moving van?"

"Mandy graduated. She's staying in Raintree," Mazy said.

Michael slid his three eggs onto a plate, buttered his toast, and joined Mazy. "What the hell is Raintree?"

"Geezus, Michael. You live here. They're the cottages on the lake—Loon Call, Pinewood, Raintree, and Birdsong."

"Did Disney name them? Are there cartoon animals skipping all over the place?"

"I didn't name them," Mazy said, standing up. "I'm going to see how Mandy's move is going."

"Why do you care?" Michael sneered.

Mazy smiled. "She's family."

"The same family that's trying to bounce us out of here. Stupid move!"

"Michael, stay in your lane."

"I plan to. FYI, my mechanic is coming here today to go over the bike."

"Am I paying him?"

"Yeah, but he costs less than Clay's golf, and once my bike gets straightened out, Shane's salary comes out of my winnings."

"But I'm not paying for Clay's golf," Mazy said as she slammed the door behind her.

§

Gramm and White met at the coffee machine. "Where's your double Frappuccino soymilk latte?" Gramm asked.

"It's Wednesday," White said, pouring a cup for herself and one for Gramm.

Watching her walk toward her desk, Gramm yelled after her, "What difference does that make?"

"I never buy coffee on Wednesday," White shot back over her shoulder before sitting down and turning on her computer.

Preston walked in and greeted Gramm, who was still standing by the coffeepot.

"Sgt. White didn't buy coffee today," he said to Preston.

"It's Wednesday. She never buys coffee on Wednesdays."

They're putting me on, Gramm thought. He made his way to his office just as Milo walked in. "Hey, Milo!" Gramm shouted, "come in here for a second."

Milo leaned in.

"Notice anything different about White today?" Gramm quizzed.

Milo leaned out and looked at White. "She's a day older than yesterday, but she wears it well."

"Very funny," Gramm offered. "She didn't buy coffee today. I notice these things."

"It's Wednesday. She never buys coffee on Wednesday," Milo said. "I notice these things."

Gramm didn't respond. His attention was taken by the caller ID on his ringing cell phone. "St. Louis County Sheriff's Office. What now?" He slid the green button. "Gramm here."

"Lieutenant, it's Deputy Dennis Blackburn from the Sheriff's office."

"What can I do for you, Dennis?"

"I thought you'd like to know. We're out at the Campbell Compound. Someone attacked Chip Campbell. He's unconscious. The ambulance left for the hospital about five minutes ago."

"Who attacked him?"

"Don't know. The Sheriff is wondering if you guys wanted to pursue this, seeing as how you're..."

"We're on the way, thanks," Gramm said, walking into the bullpen and shouting, "Get in here! All of you!"

"What's up?" White asked.

"We have a way in to the Campbell Compound. No judge required! Chip Campbell has been knocked unconscious. The

Sheriff wants us to take this over. Preston, find out which hospital the ambulance is going to and head over there in case Chip regains consciousness. Milo, you're riding with us."

"I don't do basic head injuries. I'm a world-renowned detective."

"You do now." Gramm was out of his office with White and Milo following.

§

Lights and sirens blaring, Gramm sped up to the now wide open gate in front of the Campbell Compound. A sheriff's deputy was standing guard. Silencing the siren, Gramm stopped and opened his window. "Where do we go?" he asked.

"Chip Campbell's house. It's the third house on the right, the one before the hunting lodge."

Gramm thanked the deputy and proceeded down the road with flashing lights only. As he made a right turn, the lake came into view.

"Big houses on the right. Little houses on the left next to the lake. Interesting," White said.

Gramm was being directed into a driveway by another deputy. He parked behind one of the sheriff's cars. The three got out and walked to Chip Campbell's backyard.

Deputy Dennis Blackburn spotted the group, crossed to them, and shook hands. "Good to see you. The family is at the lodge, waiting for you to interview them."

"What do you know?" Gramm asked.

"Mazy Campbell found her uncle lying here in the backyard suffering from a head wound. She said she came to his house to talk to him about an employee—security guard, Major Peters. He's a strange one—thought he was in charge. I convinced him he wasn't. He's sitting at the lodge with everybody else."

"Have you done any forensics?" Gramm asked.

"Don't have the budget for a non-murder—figured you could do all the heavy lifting. There are a lot of different footprints and ATV tracks, but all of those can be explained away. It's a family compound. The family comes and goes, along with their hired help."

"How far is the lodge?" Gramm asked.

"Next house over on the left. Follow this path."

"Could you leave a couple of your people in case we need more manpower? This is a big place."

"Sure."

"We're hiking!" Gramm said to White and Milo with uncharacteristic excitement.

White shrugged. "I'm not the one who minds a hike."

"My hiking limit is three miles," Milo said. "If anybody cares." Nobody did.

The family was sitting on the back veranda, each in their own sitting area. As Gramm took his first step, Major Peters jumped up. "Lieutenant, you have to talk to me. I am in charge of family security."

"No, I don't! Sit down!" Gramm shouted. "We'll get to you later."

Peters set his jaw as he sat down.

Gramm addressed the group. "I'm Lieutenant Ernie Gramm of the Duluth Police Department. This is Sergeant Robin White, and Police Consultant Milo Rathkey. We would appreciate it if you all remained seated. We will get to all of you."

Clay Campbell stood up. "No need to investigate anything, Lieutenant. Peters is the thug who attacked my brother."

Peters jumped to his feet and advanced toward Clay. "That's a damn lie! I'm your brother's only friend here."

"Back off!" Clay shouted.

"Clay's right. Peters is the one I called about. He attacked me yesterday!" Mazy chimed in.

"Another lie!" Peters barked.

"You shut up! My wife doesn't lie!" Michael shouted, standing nose to nose with Peters. Deputy Blackburn edged in between the two men and ordered them to sit down and remain seated, or they would be handcuffed.

Michael sat down next to Mazy. "Clay's right. Peters is a thug. If you check his belly, you'll find a bruise where I had to kick him after he attacked me."

"I was the one being attacked!" Peters charged.

"Quiet! All of you!" Gramm demanded.

White walked over to the only non-shouting family member—Greer Campbell. "You're rather quiet."

"I have nothing to say."

"Who are you and what relation are you to Chip Campbell?" White asked.

Greer straightened her back and tossed her white hair back behind her shoulder. "I'm Greer Campbell. Chip and Clay are my nephews. Mazy is my great niece. Major Peters is no relation."

"When was the last time you saw your nephew, Chip?"

"I have the house next to Chip and Grace. I saw them both yesterday afternoon."

"What time?"

"I think about four or five. Grace was drinking wine and Chip was on the phone."

"Where were you last night?"

"Sleeping, I imagine."

"Did you hear anything?"

"Night sounds. We have a lot of creatures up here that call out in the night."

"Were any of those creatures human?"

"Not that I could tell."

"Who do *you* think attacked Chip Campbell?"

"Look how they act. Could be any of them," Greer said as she swept her bejeweled hand over the assembled group.

"Did you have a reason to attack your nephew?"

"I'm old. I don't attack anything."

"But did you have a reason to attack him—not saying you did."

"Chip's given name is Duncan Campbell—the fourth—and like all the Duncans in this family, he thinks he rules by divine right. I find that grating sometimes. My iced tea needs a refill. Are you finished?

"For now," White said.

Gramm waved White over to him. The two approached Major Peters. He puffed up and smiled at being interviewed first. For his part, Clay didn't seem to care. He was on his phone trying to reach McKenna.

§

247

Judge Olivia Murphy gaveled the hearing to order. Brandon Park's blog had alerted the puzzle hoard to the hearings, creating a packed courtroom. Judge Murphy's first order of business was to address that problem.

"I see we have a packed house today. I don't know why. This is a procedural hearing. When and if the court completes the puzzle, it will not be in open court."

There was a collective groan.

"And let that be the last outburst, or I will clear the court." Judge Murphy put on her glasses. The four attorneys—McKenna, Wautkin, Feinberg, and Wilson—stood. "After careful consideration of this matter, I feel that both sides have valid points."

"Bullshit!" Dutch Wilson, the District Attorney thought. *Gramm wants to see the completed puzzle. He won't be pleased with any 'both sides' crap.*

"Tomorrow at one o'clock, you four counselors will present your clients' puzzle pieces in my chambers. You will then leave. I will put the puzzle together and let the police inspect it for ten minutes. Photography will not be allowed. No one else will be permitted to see the completed puzzle. At the end of ten minutes, I will take the puzzle apart and return the pieces."

All four attorneys said at once, "Your honor!"

Murphy sighed. "One at a time. Ms. McKenna."

"I don't understand why Mr. Wautkin, Mr. Feinberg, and I cannot be in the room to make sure our client's pieces are not photographed."

Murphy bristled. "Do you not trust me, Ms. McKenna?"

"Of course, your honor. However, I have a fiduciary responsibility to my clients to insure the confidentiality of their property."

"I relieve you of that responsibility for the ten minutes the pieces are in my possession, Ms. McKenna."

"Your honor?" Wautkin rose.

"Mr. Wautkin?"

"I have a similar problem, your honor, but will defer to your solution."

"Thank you, Mr. Wautkin, so kind," the judge said sarcastically.

"Mr. Feinberg?"

"No objection, your honor."

"Mr. Wilson?"

"I feel that ten minutes may not be enough time for the police to…"

"Ten minutes or nothing, Mr. Wilson."

"We will take the ten minutes, your honor."

"Yes, you will," the judge quipped.

§

Peters led Gramm, White, and Milo to a table inside the lodge, leaving the deputy in the doorway. "Mazy Campbell is your person," he said bluntly as Gramm, White, and Milo sat. "Or it could be a person named Brandon Park, although I don't have a motive for him."

Gramm ignored the advice. "Sit down. When was the last time you saw Chip Campbell?"

Peters' nostrils flared as he reluctantly sat once again. "I'm helping you here, Lieutenant."

Gramm showed no sign of accepting the help. "Answer the question, Mr. Peters."

"That's Major Peters!"

"I do not see an oak leaf on your uniform, Elbert. In fact, I don't see a rank at all. So, *Mr.* Peters, answer the question—when was the last time you saw Chip Campbell?"

Peters expelled a good deal of air through his pursed lips. "About five in the afternoon in his backyard. He told me he was upset and might need me later in the evening."

"Upset about what?" White asked.

"He didn't say. He did tell me that a man named Brandon Park was coming to see him at six and that I was to escort him to the lodge."

"Did you?" Gramm asked.

"I did."

"Then what?"

"I expected Mr. Campbell to be there, in the lodge, but he wasn't. I went in search of him, but I couldn't find him. There was no answer when I called. When I went back to the lodge, Mr. Park was gone. I was upset. I accessed the lodge lobby camera and saw that he left the lodge on foot against my orders."

"Maybe he got tired of waiting and took off," Gramm suggested.

"Looking at the gate camera, his car did not drive out of the compound until twenty to thirty minutes later. He was on the grounds long enough to attack Mr. Campbell."

Milo jumped in. "You left Park, you didn't find Chip, you returned and didn't find Park."

"That's right."

"So, you don't have an alibi either."

Peters moved back in his seat as if he had been punched. "I...I don't need one."

"Yes, you do. People are accusing you of assault." Gramm said.

"Mr. Park wasn't the only outsider on the grounds last night. Michael Mason's motorcycle mechanic was wandering around." Peters laughed. "Mason fancies himself a racer."

"Fancies?" White asked.

"There was only onetime last year he didn't come in last...just next to last."

"Got a name for the mechanic?" Gramm asked.

"Not with me. I could look it up or you could ask Mason."

Gramm glanced at White, who nodded. "Mazy Campbell seems to think you attacked her. Why?"

"I didn't attack her. Mr. Campbell had been receiving notes..."

"What kind of notes?" Gramm asked.

"Vaguely threatening—sins of the father, old secrets new problems and time's up. Crap like that."

"How were they delivered?" Milo asked.

"Someone tacked them up on his porch post. Of course, we thought it had to be someone on the compound. Mr. Campbell was trying to remove Ms. Mason from the family. She is the likely suspect."

"Remove her from the family? What does that mean?" White asked.

"He wanted her off the board and out of the compound."

"Why?"

"She was disloyal and a liability."

"Did he succeed?" Gramm asked.

"At present, the move to oust her has stalled, but once Mr. Campbell's daughter, Mandy Campbell, joins the board, we will have enough votes."

We? White wondered. *Does Peters think he's a Campbell?*

"You seem to be close to Chip Campbell. What's your relationship?"

"Chip and I go back to Hartsborg Military Academy. It's a prep school."

18

Clay Campbell thought to use the slow progress of the police interviews to his advantage. Rising from his solitary table on the veranda, he advanced toward Mazy and Michael. Michael recognized a possible chess move. He nodded at Clay.

As he sat down, Clay said to Mazy, "I think we can help each other out."

"I'm listening," Mazy said, keeping her gaze straight ahead.

"Chip may be out of action for some time. I propose we move to replace him as the chairman."

Mazy whispered, "Replace him with whom?"

"Me, of course."

Mazy should have been surprised, but she wasn't. "You said we could help each other out. What's in it for me?"

"If Chip recovers and attempts to oust you again, I will vote no."

Mazy took a deep breath, stood, and attempted to leave.

Michael touched his wife's arm. "Don't be hasty, honey. That's not a bad deal."

Mazy shook off Michael's touch, joining Greer at the far end of the veranda.

With his wife gone, Michael made a chess move of his own. "Clay, I want a seat on the board."

Clay rolled his eyes. "Family only, Michael. You know that."

"Times change Clay. I convince my wife to put you in as chairman. I get your vote on the board. We're both happy."

Clay thought for a moment. "Possible."

Greer looked at her great niece. "You seem perturbed. Clay must have made his move to replace Chip."

Mazy tilted her head. "How did you know?"

"I was waiting for it. When you get to my age, you began to anticipate the moves people make based upon their character or lack of it." She looked over at Clay and Michael talking amicably at the far table. "To that point, I think your husband is cutting his own deal. Be careful."

White walked in and nodded to Mazy, who rose and followed her inside. Peters had left, saying he was going to the hospital to check on Chip. Mazy took his place at the table.

"Major Peters thinks you're the person who quashed your uncle," Gramm said.

"Major Peters is an idiot. For some reason Chip keeps him around."

"Is he right? Did you attack your uncle?"

"No."

"Your uncle wanted you removed from the family."

"He did." Mazy sat, hands folded, giving away nothing.

"How did that make you feel?" White asked.

Mazy laughed. "Is this a therapy session?"

"Answer the question, please," White admonished.

"I was angry."

"Angry enough to…"

"No."

"You found your uncle, correct?" Gramm asked.

"I did."

"Tell us how you came upon him?"

"Peters attacked me yesterday, accused me of leaving some notes on Chip's porch. I was angry about that and was coming to tell Chip I was filing charges against Peters."

"So, you were on the road…"

"No, we don't take the road. There are a series of paths between the houses that the generations of Campbell kids have worn down over the decades. I was on the path from my house to Chip's. I saw him sprawled on the ground. At first, I thought he was dead."

"What did you do?"

"I was frozen. I just stared. Then I saw his back rise and fall like he was breathing, so I called 911 and Aunt Grace, Chip's wife. I then alerted all the family members including my husband. I did not call Peters. I guess either Clay or Michael called him."

"Do you have any idea why someone would attack your uncle?" White asked.

"I would have thought he would be the one attacking other people. He's totally paranoid these days. He's crazed about this stupid contest. I think Peters winds him up. Chip needs to worry more about his own brother."

"Clay?"

Mazy smiled and lifted her eyebrows. "He just approached me about *his* becoming chairman of the board replacing Chip."

That's cold, White thought.

"Where were *you* last night?" Gramm asked.

"I was with my husband. We watched television."

§

"No! No! I don't want you here!" Grace Campbell shouted at Major Peters when he walked into the ER waiting room. Her visceral reaction to him shocked her.

Officer Preston, sitting in a nearby chair, thought about intervening but let it play out.

"Calm down, Mrs. Campbell," Peters admonished. "You're getting hysterical."

Grace jumped up and crossed to him, standing nose to nose. "Look, you toad, I said I don't want you here. Your job was to protect us."

"I'm doing my job," Peters said. "How do I know you didn't attack your husband?"

Grace flinched as if someone had punched her. "Just go!"

Peters grabbed her shoulder, which was enough for Preston to act. She leaped out of her chair, grabbed Peters' arm, and wrenched it behind his back. "The lady asked you to leave."

Two hospital security personnel charged through the emergency room doors. "Do you need help, officer?" one asked.

"Escort this man out of the hospital," Preston said, wrenching his arm another notch.

"I'm going, I'm going," Peters said. Preston let go of his arm and Peters stormed out of the building, followed by the security people.

"Thank you," Grace Campbell said, collapsing into the nearby chair. "I saw you sitting here. You never said why you are here. Is it because of Chip?"

"We think the person who attacked your husband may be the same person wanted in the suspicious death of a man—one of those treasure hunters."

"Oh, spare me from that stupid puzzle. Chip keeps harping on it over and over."

"Did you notice your husband was not with you last night?"

Grace looked up at Preston. "Chip has trouble sleeping. He often goes out for walks, says the fresh air helps him. That's the supposed beauty of where we live. We can go out at all hours and walk the grounds without anything happening. So much for gates, and walls, and security. The sooner Major Peters is out of our lives, the better."

§

Clay was called in for questioning, but rather than sitting down, he proceeded to the lodge's kitchen, leaving Lt. Gramm and company looking at each other. Sgt. White popped up and raced after him. Clay returned with bags of snacks.

"I don't know about you people, but it's getting late, and I'm hungry." Clay opened a bag of chips, laying the rest of the snacks on the table.

Milo grabbed a bag of peanuts. Gramm and White continued on without benefit of food.

"I understand you want to become chairman of the family board," Gramm said.

If Gramm thought the question would rattle the man, he was wrong. Campbell shrugged. "Well, of course. My brother's job now is to heal. Mine has become running the family business in his stead. It's all about the family and taking care of each other."

"When did you see your brother last?" Gramm asked.

"Yesterday. He was all put out about something, but he wouldn't tell me what. He kept saying we were in trouble, and he was going to fix it."

"What kind of trouble?"

"He wouldn't tell me. I asked him. He said he'd handle it. I had a business call, so I let it pass—circle back later."

"Who do you think attacked your brother?" White asked.

"That clown, Peters. Chip was all there was between Peters and the highway. I think Chip caught him at something."

"Something?" White questioned.

"Chip got three notes that weirded him out. They were tacked to his house. I think it was Peters winding him up."

"To what end?" Milo asked.

"Peters kept his job by feeding Chip's fears. We don't need some puffed-up puppet like Peters strutting around—never did."

"Where were you last night?"

"Bashing my brother in the head," Clay quipped, opening a second bag of chips.

"Is that a confession?" Gramm asked.

"It's a joke."

"We are not amused. Where were you?"

"At home with my kids. My wife's visiting her sister in Edina."

Milo leaned forward in his chair. "Why would someone kill Ham Gilbert..."

"Who's Ham Gilbert?"

"The floater in the St. Louis River. I'm wondering why someone would kill him but leave his puzzle piece on the dashboard of his car."

"Oh yeah. I don't know, but it seemed to bother my brother."

"When?"

"Our attorney told us about it yesterday. Chip had a coughing fit."

"Why did your brother want to meet with Brandon Park?" Gramm asked.

"Who's Brandon Park?"

Is he really this dumb or just playing at it? White wondered.

"A blogger who is buying puzzle pieces," White said.

"And you think Chip wanted to meet him?"

"We do. Park was on this compound last night," White added.

"Chip never told me that. I don't think that's true."

"You and your brother are also buying puzzle pieces, correct?" Milo asked.

"Chip was in charge of that."

"How does that work?" Gramm asked. "Who does the actual buying?"

"Didn't I just say Chip was in charge of that? I don't know how he did it. I'm sure he didn't hold a sign on Superior Street saying *We Buy Puzzle Pieces*. If I had to guess, Peters was probably buying the pieces."

§

Michael Mason was alone on the veranda by the time the police got to him. "Did you interview everyone in order of importance?" he sneered. "Don't you want to talk with the dog first?"

"There is no dog," Gramm noted. "Is there a reason we should have talked to you earlier?"

Mason shrugged. "Only that you talked to my wife an hour ago. I kinda thought I should have come next."

"When was the last time you saw Chip Campbell?" Gramm asked with no apology.

"I don't know, maybe a week ago. I'm not *family*, as Chip calls his little club, so we don't talk much."

"What do you mean, you're not family? Aren't you married to Mazy?"

"One must be born into that club."

"So, your wife is family, but not you."

Michael looked at Gramm with a sickly smile. "Yes."

"Did you see Chip at all yesterday?"

Mason shook his head. "I said I haven't seen him for a week."

"What do you know about this puzzle contest?" Milo asked.

"Not much. Lewis, my late father-in-law, started it about a month ago. I know Chip was upset about it. I congratulated Lewis for upsetting the family, especially Chip."

"Lewis wasn't family either?" White asked.

"Wasn't born into the clan."

"Why did the contest upset Chip so much?" Milo asked.

"I do not know. You should ask Clay. That dead guy's puzzle piece said Cooke on it, so the treasure must be somewhere in Jay Cooke State Park. Neither Mazy nor I could figure out why Chip cared so much."

"But he did," Milo stated.

"Oh yeah. He even had someone buying up puzzle pieces."

"Who?"

Mason laughed. "Like I said, I wasn't family. Chip wouldn't have told me even if I asked, which I didn't."

"How do you know that piece has the word *Cooke* printed on it?" Milo asked.

"It was mentioned on some blog. I think the little shit that died had the key piece."

Gramm leaned into White and whispered, "Was that info in the blog?"

White nodded and said, "I understand you and Major Peters got into a physical altercation."

"I overheard him yelling at Mazy. I went out to see what was going on and saw Peters grab her arm. That went too far. I stopped him. Peters parades around here in a uniform, but I think that's just for show. If he ever was in the military, he isn't in shape now."

"Why did he attack your wife?" White asked.

"He accused her of sending weird notes to Chip. Mazy has better things to do than play childish games. Chip scares himself all the time. No one needs to help."

"Peters told us you had your mechanic on the grounds last night."

"I did. I'm a racer. We're getting my bike in shape."

"Name?"

"What?"

"What's your mechanic's name?"

"Shane Bell."

"Small world," Milo mumbled under his breath.

"Where were you last night?" Gramm asked.

"I was with Mazy. We watched television."

"One last question," White said. "What kind of motor-cycle do you ride?"

"Ducati Panigale V2." Michael was impressed with himself.

Once clear of the family members, Gramm asked White why she wanted to know about Mason's motorcycle. "I wanted to find out for Preston. She rides. I figured she'd want to know about it. I'm pulling a Milo, getting useless information that we may need later."

19

Zeke was busy with his usual morning routine—stacking clean serving trays and wiping down tables—when he heard a knock on the front door. It wasn't the coded knock of a volunteer. He glanced at the security monitor and saw a portly man in a pinstriped suit and yellow bowtie pushing his glasses up the bridge of his nose. "What special hell is this?" Zeke muttered.

"What?" Gloria yelled from the kitchen.

"Talking to myself, Gloria."

"Do it quieter. I've got a lot to do back here."

Zeke went to the door and opened it a crack. "We serve at five."

"I'm not a customer," the portly man said. "May I come in? My name is Creedence…"

"No."

"My name isn't Creedence?"

"No, you can't come in."

"Ah, okay. Here's my card. I represent someone who wants to buy this building. I would like to talk to you."

Zeke knew this was coming. "We're busy. We feed people. Make it fast."

"It won't take long," Creedence said to a now empty doorway. Following Zeke, a tall man in jeans and a black t-shirt into the dining hall, Creedence closed the door behind him. When Zeke stopped and turned, Creedence introduced himself again and held out his hand.

Zeke ignored the gesture and went back to stacking trays. "How much time do we have?"

"Time?"

"Yeah, time, until we gotta get out of here. We need time to relocate."

"No, you don't," Creedence said, pushing his glasses up again, "provided you agree to one minor change."

Zeke stopped stacking, turned around, and stared at Creedence. "What?"

Knowing this should be welcome news to the gruff man, Creedence tried smiling again. The action just made his glasses slip down his nose—again. "My client wants you to stay. However, we will have to change the name of your establishment to Ellen's Kitchen. My client will pay for the new sign."

Zeke took this in for several moments. "How much will the rent go up?"

"Ah yes, that will change." Creedence smiled again. "Your rent will be one dollar a year, as long as we rename this place Ellen's Kitchen."

"Ellen's?" Gloria yelled from the kitchen. "My name is Gloria! This is my kitchen!"

"The guy who's buying this place is gonna charge us a dollar a year," Zeke yelled back.

"Good old Ellen!" Gloria yelled. "I always liked her."

"So, who is this guy?" Zeke asked, stepping closer to Creedence.

Zeke's height and close proximity unnerved Creedence, but he held his ground. "My client wishes to remain anonymous," He then tried to fill his unease with staccato details of all the updates that would have to be done to bring the building up to code. "New electrical, plumbing, that sort of thing—building appraisal and inspection, of course."

"Stop!" Zeke protested. "Some anonymous stranger wants to close us down while he supposedly fixes up the place to reopen at some later time. I'm not a fool. He wants to remodel the building and use it for something else."

Creedence held up his hand. "No, no, no. No fools here. My client informed me you feed people—families—like you told me a few minutes ago. The meals will not stop. We'll work around your schedule."

Gloria poked her head out of the kitchen pass through. "Hey, does this guy have enough money to get me a new stove? Only two burners work."

Creedence turned toward the kitchen, glad he remembered names. "Gloria, your input on remodeling will be most needed and appreciated."

"See, Zeke, some people value my input," Gloria said.

Zeke sat down on one of the benches with his back to Creedence, elbows on the table, hands folded. "So, you say the building has a new owner who wants us to stay rent free and has plans to improve the place? But he doesn't want us to know who he is."

"I didn't say my client was a he," Creedence countered, "but that is what my client wants, Mr. um…?"

"Zeke, just Zeke." Turning to Creedence, Zeke asked, "Is it you?"

Creedence laughed nervously and pushed up his glasses again. "Oh no, Mr. Zeke, not me. My client."

"Just Zeke. Not Mr. Zeke. Just Zeke."

"Okay, Zeke. My client is eager to begin. When can I schedule the appraisal?"

"What do I call you?"

"Creedence."

"Your mother like the band?" Zeke asked, smiling.

Creedence sighed, "Yes. She had every album Creedence Clearwater Revival ever made."

"Good choice in music. Come by anytime in the mornings after nine."

They exchanged phone numbers, and Creedence left.

"That's different," Zeke said as he and Gloria watched the front door close. "We have a new landlord, and the rent is a buck a year. Who the hell is Ellen?"

"I don't care. I'm tired of holding this kitchen together with rubber bands, duct tape, and good intentions," Gloria answered.

"It's a soup kitchen, Gloria! Soup kitchens always have second-hand equipment," Zeke insisted.

Gloria smiled. "Not anymore, Zeke! We seem to have a benefactor. We're going to be the Cadillac of soup kitchens."

"I wonder if we can name it Ellen's Soup Kitchen. I always liked soup in the name."

Gloria pointed a large spoon at him. "Don't push your luck."

Zeke sighed. "Ellen's No Soup Kitchen it is."

§

Gramm bellowed to Preston and White from his office. "Come in here! Tell me about the hospital," he ordered Preston.

"I just checked on Mr. Campbell about ten minutes ago. He's in an induced coma," Preston said. "Currently, he's stable. Can't say that about his family." She then detailed the scene between Major Peters and Grace Campbell.

"This Peters guy is unpopular," White observed.

In no rush, Milo socialized in the bullpen area, eventually making his way to Gramm's office. He leaned in the doorway. "Someone said something. Don't know what. It's bothering me."

Gramm looked up. "Sergeant White?"

"Yes?"

"Is Milo standing in the door talking about some unidentified person saying something...just something?"

"He is."

"Good. I just wanted to make sure I wasn't having a hallucination. Milo, grab a chair."

Milo wheeled a bullpen chair into the office. "You know, if you get a third chair in here, we wouldn't have to keep bringing one in."

"Sit down and let your mind lint percolate," Gramm said. "Preston was just telling us Major Peters was escorted out of the hospital waiting room yesterday at Grace Campbell's insistence."

"At some point, we have to interview her too," White said.

"Maybe later," Gramm groused. "I have invited Brandon Park to come up this morning and chat with us about being on the Campbell Compound yesterday afternoon. We need to grab lunch early because at one o'clock sharp, we, minus Milo, are expected in Judge Murphy's chambers to view the puzzle. We get ten minutes. Milo, while we're with the judge, maybe you can find Shane Bell."

"Only ten minutes? Not much time," White complained.

"I know, but I have a plan. First, look at it and see if you recognize the area. If we don't, I'll take the first row. White, you take the second, and Preston the third. Try to remember as much detail as possible," Gramm said.

"Pity I won't be there," Milo said. "I have a mind like a steel trap."

"Well, Mr. Someone-Said-Something, you can't even remember your mind lint," Gramm accused.

"That's a valid point," Milo conceded.

The Front Desk called Gramm to inform him that Park and his attorney were in the front lobby. He told the desk sergeant to escort them to interview room one.

"O'Dell is in one," the desk sergeant said.

"Then take them into two!" Gramm shouted, sure that O'Dell, Duluth's other homicide detective, was going to wrap up his case in *O'Dell time,* as the Deputy chief called it—meaning a lot faster than Gramm took with his cases.

Milo and Preston took up their usual position outside the interview room behind the one-way glass. "Anything to bet on here?" Preston asked.

"I bet Park insists he didn't try to kill Chip Campbell," Milo said.

Preston laughed. "You're so intuitive."

Gramm and White sat down. Gramm opened his fake folder and began. "Tell us about last night."

His attorney, Pat Wautkin, insisted that Gramm narrow the question.

"Okay, we have reason to believe that you were on the grounds of the Campbell Compound yesterday afternoon at the same time that Chip Campbell was attacked."

Park glanced at Wautkin, who nodded. "He called me. Asked me to come,"

"What did he want?"

"He said he had a deal to make me. He implied it would benefit me financially. I thought it rude to refuse the invitation." He wrapped on the table twice with his knuckles, as if he were knocking on a door. "Another layer in the game."

"Major Peters said he escorted you into the lodge and told you to wait. Is that accurate?"

Park nodded.

"We need a verbal response," White said.

"It's accurate," Park admitted.

"Where did you go after Major Peters left you in the lodge?" Gramm asked.

"I don't like to wait. I went for a walk. I wanted to see if anything on their grounds might match my puzzle pieces. Hiding the treasure on their own compound would be nasty gamesmanship, but not out of the question. If I knew my puzzle pieces were pointing to this compound, my price would go up substantially."

"All in the game?" White asked.

"Of course."

"However, the time you were checking the compound is the exact time Chip Campbell was attacked. It could be a coincidence, but then I hate coincidences."

"What's this young man's motive, Lieutenant?" Wautkin demanded. "There were a myriad of people on that compound with strong, compelling motives."

"How do you know they have motives?" White asked.

"They're an incredibly wealthy family. I thought you people always looked at family first. That's what you were doing the last time you and I discussed a murder."

"Did you find your pieces matched the compound?" White asked.

"Not going to say. For all I know, you people are hunting for the treasure," Park challenged.

"We're going to see all the pieces this afternoon," White said.

"I'll make you a deal. I'll tell you what I know this morning if you tell me what you see this afternoon."

Wautkin was about to consult with his client when Gramm said, "I'll make you a deal, Mr. Park. I'll make sure you have one of the better cells when I arrest you for obstruction."

Wautkin asked for a minute to talk to his client alone. Gramm and White stepped out. "What do you think?" Gramm asked, twisting his eyebrow.

"He plays games all the time. We don't really know where he went on the compound or why."

Wautkin indicated the powwow was over. Gramm and White sat down again. "My client would like to revise his statement," Wautkin said.

"I wanted to see if the compound matched my pieces, but I didn't go far," Park said.

"What were you doing?" White asked.

"My client wants a guarantee that no charges will be brought if he details a minor illegal activity."

"Was he running a dice game, counselor?" Gramm asked.

"I get anxiety attacks. I felt one coming on. Smoking a little something calms me down. I went into a bushy area at the back of the lodge. I did see that Major guy come back..."

"Back?"

"He was walking down a path in back of the lodge."

"Looking at the back of the lodge, was he coming from the right or the left?" White asked.

"Left. He went into the lodge building, stayed a minute or two, and then left again. I finished doing...ahh...what I was doing and returned to the building. I waited for five more minutes and then I left. Waste of my time."

Preston called up the compound in her mind. "Peters was returning from the direction of Chip Campbell's house," she said to Milo.

"Was he looking for Chip?" Milo mused. "Or coming back from trying to kill Chip?"

Gramm continued the interview. "Did you call Chip Campbell?"

"I called the number he used to call me. There was no answer."

§

"I told the police we were watching television last night," Mazy said to Michael.

"Good. So did I."

"Michael, where were you, really?"

"Like you told the police, I was inside, watching television," Michael smiled.

"No, you weren't."

"How do you know?"

"I was here. You weren't!" Mazy spat.

"Interesting." Michael dropped his smile. "When I returned from a walk by the lake, our house was empty."

§

"We don't have much time. Let's eat here in the office," Gramm said.

White reached for her phone. "I can order. What do you people fancy?"

"We could do the vending machine burritos," Milo suggested.

Gramm objected. "Delicious, but they play havoc with my stomach. The last time I ate one, I was up half the night."

"We could do sushi," Milo said.

White shook her head violently, as if a bee had flown into her ear. "I must be hallucinating. I could have sworn Milo suggested sushi."

"Mary Alice and I went to Fudos on First."

"And you had sushi?" Preston asked.

"No! But they had a rice bowl with all sorts of stuff. It was good. Oh yeah, rice cakes and heavily radiated peas. Those puppies were big."

"Edamame. They are good." White looked at Gramm for his order.

"I'll go with Milo's rice bowl and if it's terrible, I will complain about it for the rest of the week."

After a quick negotiation with Milo that included one text exchange with Mary Alice, White placed their orders at Fudos.

"Review of suspects time," Gramm said. "That always seems to work."

White looked at Preston, who was trying to keep from laughing. "How does that always work?" she asked Gramm.

"We go over suspects and Milo's mind lint kicks in and we spend the next week on paperwork."

"My mind lint is already vibrating," Milo said. "Somebody said something."

"You said that before. Who said something, and what did they say?" Gramm asked.

"Don't have a clue."

"Good, let's talk suspects. Contenders for who killed Harold 'Ham' Gilbert?"

"Jimmy Pleski," White offered. "He attacked Kayla Maki. He's violent, wants pieces, and we already have him in jail. Done."

"But he couldn't have attacked Chip Campbell," Gramm pointed out.

"Those two crimes might not be connected," Preston said.

Gramm raised his arms over his head and stretched his back. "True. Next suspect."

"Brandon Park," Preston offered. "He plays to win. He could have been trying to buy Gilbert's puzzle piece, and something went wrong during the deal. He was also in place to have assaulted Chip Campbell. He's a twofer."

"Anybody want to come to Park's defense?" Gramm asked.

No one raised their hand.

"Let's not forget the wannabe Major," Milo said.

"Why would he kill Gilbert?" Gramm asked.

"Someone is buying puzzle pieces for the family. Peters seems to work for Chip Campbell," White said. "Maybe Gilbert upset the Major's fragile ego during the deal. As for Chip, maybe he found out Peters killed Gilbert and threatened to come to us."

"That's three possible in one theory," Gramm complained.

"Clay Campbell," Preston called out.

Gramm took this one. "Bludgeon his brother, take over the family, but why attack Gilbert?"

"Maybe *he* was buying the pieces instead of the Major," Preston said.

Milo doubted that either Chip or Clay would get their hands that dirty as long as they had others to do it for them. "If we are going with family, what about Greer Campbell, Michael or Mazy Mason?"

"They all might have attacked Chip, but no connection to Gilbert," Gramm said. "Does anyone think the Consortium is involved?"

"That Charlotte Lane woman," Milo said. "I could read cold-blooded killer in her eyes."

"Be that as it may," White said, "I think we can pass on all three of them."

"Four of them," Milo corrected. "You forgot ten-year-old Darian has joined them. Maybe he has been the mastermind all along."

"Why don't you pass that theory on to the deputy chief," Gramm suggested. "He loves you—for now."

"Kayla can be explosive," Preston said.

"She likes sharp things," Milo laughed. "Not a blunt force trauma kind of gal. What about my buddy, Shane?"

"Oh crap, I forgot about him," Gramm said. "Gilbert and he may have had a falling out, and he was on the Campbell Compound the night before last. Zooms up in my book."

White's phone buzzed. "Food's here," she said.

"Good timing. Once again, we narrowed this down to everybody," Gramm sneered.

20

"Let's go over the ground rules," Judge Olivia Murphy told the group of lawyers and police assembled in her chambers. "I want you, one at a time, to hand your puzzle pieces face down to my court reporter, Ms. Kesha Abara."

Kesha nodded to the group as she sat at a dark wooden table with two chairs and one large white poster board.

"If it's acceptable with all the parties, Ms. Abara will color code the back of each piece to indicate ownership. So, let's begin."

Gramm placed his piece on the table first. Kesha labeled the back *G* in red. Kimberly McKenna handed over three pieces. They were labeled *C* in green. Pat Wautkin set down four pieces which received a *P* in blue.

Saul Feinberg was last. "I need to update the court. The consortium has added one more member, Darian Gibbson."

He added his four pieces, asking Ms. Abara to note the owner of each piece.

"I'll use orange and 'C' for consortium plus the first initial of the owner's last name. CM-Kala Maki, CH-Ben Heikkinen, CL-Charlotte Lane, and CG-Darian Gibbson."

The judge asked all parties, with the exception of the court reporter, to leave the room while she assembled the puzzle. She walked over to the table, took the pieces in hand, and placed them on the white piece of cardboard. Minutes went by.

Holding out the last piece, she asked her court reporter, "Do you see this?"

Kesha nodded.

The judge looked at the back. There was a bright red *G*.

The cops and lawyers were invited back in. The judge had placed another piece of cardboard over the puzzle. "I have completed the puzzle. In their filing to obtain warrants forcing puzzle piece holders to relinquish their pieces, the police indicated they held a piece that had the word *Cooke* on it. One of their reasons for needing to see the completed puzzle was to ascertain if the completed puzzle led to Jay Cooke State Park. I feel I have a fiduciary responsibility to inform all litigants in this matter that Lieutenant Gramm's piece does not fit in the puzzle."

Gramm was taken aback. "What?"

Feinberg, Wautkin, and McKenna talked over each other in their effort to be the first to declare the warrant invalid.

The judge held up her hand for silence. "Mr. Wilson?" the judge recognized the District Attorney.

"Your honor, the police have a murder which occurred in Jay Cooke State Park. Whether or not this piece fits the puzzle, the police found it in the murdered man's car. The key here, your honor, is that seeing this completed puzzle may help the police with no loss to the puzzle piece holders. I ask that your order stand, your honor."

The judge nodded. "I agree. Already this exercise has told the police that their puzzle piece does not fit. Where that leads, I do not know, but your point is well taken, Mr. Wilson. Letting the police see the completed puzzle may help the investigation and will not harm the piece holders."

At this point, the judge asked the lawyers to leave again. Gramm, White, and Preston crowded around the judge's desk preparing to see the completed puzzle.

"Ms. Abara has a timer," the judge said. "I will remove the top cardboard. You have ten minutes to look at the puzzle. Do not touch it, and, of course, no photography. Because your piece does not fit, Lieutenant Gramm, there is one missing piece at the center of the puzzle."

She removed the cardboard. Most of the map was green, with several blue lakes and rivers. Several of the green areas were darker. There were no labels. Gramm was trying to memorize the top row with four pieces. A large lake dominated the left corner. White trained her eye on the rivers, most of which went north and south. Her second tier had a yellow line running through it, which was probably a road leading to the now missing piece.

Preston's area was the least busy. She seemed to stop looking about halfway through.

The non-fitting piece had been placed alongside the completed puzzle. Gramm could see that not only did it not fit, but it was a different shade of green than the other pieces.

The court reporter's alarm sounded, and the judge took the puzzle apart, turned the pieces over, and put them into the labeled envelopes. The lawyers were invited back in and given their clients' puzzle pieces.

"Well, Lieutenant, I'm sure you now have your killer," Feinberg jabbed.

§

Milo had checked the booking file for Shane Bell to find his cell phone number. Bell answered on the fourth ring. "Yeah?"

"Shane, it's Milo. The cops want to talk to you again."

"No! I didn't do anything. I'm not going back there!"

Milo sighed. "Look, you can come in voluntarily, or they can haul you in again. Your choice. This is a courtesy call."

"Why?"

"Because I know you, and they're busy. Congratulations on your new job with Michael Mason, by the way."

"How the hell do you know about that? Are you following me?"

"You're not that important. If you want to know how I know, come up to the police station this afternoon."

"I'll think about it."

"Do that."

§

Gramm hurried White and Preston into his office. "While our memories are fresh, let's draw out each row of the puzzle as we remember it." He opened his printer, grabbed a handful of white printer paper, and threw it on his desk. "Let's get drawing."

Five minutes into the exercise, Milo walked in. "Not now, Milo!" Gramm held up his hand. "We've got to get this done."

"That's not where that river goes," White said to Gramm. "Your river has to line up with my river and I know my river was in my second piece."

"You're wrong!" Gramm charged. "The river goes straight down from my first piece to your first piece."

"Your first piece held the lake. The river flows south southeast past your second piece to my second piece."

Milo was standing behind Preston and looked down at her drawing. "Ah, Ernie…"

"Stop it, Milo! Whatever silliness you have, it can wait."

"I'm having trouble with the road," White said. "I think it goes through my pieces one and two before going up to your section."

"I don't remember a road," Gramm grumbled.

"Well, there was a road!" White insisted. "It was yellow and straight. The rivers are blue and squiggly."

"Ernie." Milo said again.

Gramm threw down his pen. "What?"

"Are you guys drawing a map of the puzzle?"

Gramm closed his eyes. "You can see that's what we're doing."

"The puzzle you saw in the judge's chambers?"

"Yes!" both Gramm and White shouted. "Go away!"

"Sure, no problem, but before I go, I would like to point out that Preston here seems to have drawn the whole thing. I'll be at the vending machines, should you need me."

Milo left.

White slowly turned to look at Preston. "Kate?"

"Ah, yeah, I sort of remember it this way." She slid her paper on the desk between Gramm and White.

They both looked down. Preston had drawn the puzzle as they had seen it, including the lines of the puzzle pieces themselves.

"I had trouble getting the border straight without a ruler," Preston said.

Gramm was silent for a few seconds before speaking. "I can see that. The borders. Pity. Because without those perfect borders, we can't see that you have memorized the entire damn puzzle!"

"Ernie, I told you that river cut through your second piece," White insisted, pointing to the river in Preston's drawing.

Gramm looked at her and blinked several times. "So, you did. However, I feel we are now all missing a big goddamn problem!"

"What's that?" White asked.

"Clearly, our colleague, Officer Preston, has a photographic memory, something we failed to disclose to the judge."

"I remember things. No one ever said I have a photographic memory," Preston defended herself. "I tried to tell you before, but Milo interrupted me."

Gramm picked up the phone and called Wilson. "Dutch, we have a minor complication. I don't think it's much. We did not know that Kate Preston could memorize the entire puzzle."

"She memorized the puzzle?"

"Yup. Just drew it out for us."

"If I were you, I would destroy it."

"What if we need to reference it?"

"She could redraw it or simply tell you what you need to know. The judge bought the argument that the existence of the completed puzzle in your hands could harm the puzzle piece holders. Make sure there is no completed puzzle."

"Got it," Gramm said, hanging up.

"You didn't even tell him that the borders are not totally straight," White complained.

Gramm leaned back, closed his eyes, and said, "Look at it one last time. Does it remind anybody of a place?"

"There's a lake," Preston said.

White laughed. "Lucky for us, we're in a state with only ten thousand lakes. Now I know how Preston takes those precise notes."

Gramm looked at Preston. "Do you have any other super-powers we should know about?"

"I compete in motorcycle motocross," Preston said. "I'm pretty good."

White smiled. "Oh, that reminds me, Michael Mason, Mazy's husband, races motorcycles, and knowing you ride, I got the brand of his machine."

"Great. What does he ride?"

"A...um...it's a..."

"Well, Robin, we can tell the judge that you do not have a photographic memory," Gramm joked. "Mason rides a Ducati."

"I'm impressed!" Preston exclaimed.

"Is it a good bike?" White asked.

"It is, but I was impressed with the Lieutenant's ability to remember the name Ducati."

Gramm shrugged. "I was young once."

White was left with the image of a young Ernie Gramm tearing through the Minnesota countryside on a motorcycle.

§

Kimberly McKenna's call to Chip Campbell reached his wife, Grace, who informed the lawyer that Chip had been attacked and was in a coma. McKenna questioned Grace for the details, hung up, and found Clay Campbell's number in her contacts.

There is never a shortage of excitement when I travel to Duluth, she thought. Clay answered on the second ring.

"Mr. Campbell, it's Kimberly McKenna. I was sorry to hear about your brother."

"Right, the police are still investigating."

"Any suspects?"

"All of us."

"I have just come from the judge's chambers where the police viewed the completed puzzle for ten minutes. There was one hiccup I wanted to make you aware of."

"Hiccup?"

"As in unexpected. The puzzle piece obtained by the police, the one with the word *Cooke* on it, does not fit in the puzzle."

"What does that mean?" Clay asked.

"That piece, which was found in the victim's car, is not part of the contest puzzle."

"What is it a part of?"

"Good question. You'd have to ask the police."

"Are you staying in town?"

"Only if you need me, otherwise I'll return to the cities this afternoon."

§

"Sit down, Milo," Gramm ordered when Rathkey returned from the snack room with a Diet Coke.

Milo's chair, which he had wheeled into Gramm's office earlier, was still there between White and Preston.

"Did you see the puzzle that Preston drew?"

"Sure, there was a round something, a couple of squiggly somethings, and a lot of green nothing."

"Did you recognize anything from it?" Gramm continued. "Did it bring any place to mind?"

A million comebacks flowed through Milo's brain, but, for once, he didn't speak to any of them. "Not a one."

"Okay, now forget you ever saw it."

"That's hard to do, because I saw it."

Gramm leaned back, stretching his neck again. "You weren't supposed to see it. I want you to clear it from your mind."

"That could be tricky. If I delete it, I could accidentally delete my grocery list for next week."

"Take the chance."

"I have the cat's hard food on that list. If they don't get it, I'm going to have to tell them and blame you."

"The price of leadership," Gramm quipped. "We can tell you that our puzzle piece…"

White held up the piece.

"Does not fit in the contest puzzle. It's a bogus piece," Gramm said.

"Remember, we found it on Ham Gilbert's dashboard," White said. "I think Gilbert was telling the truth to Shane Bell. He didn't find a piece in the hats, so he made his own piece to sell."

"Makes sense," Preston said. "He figures he could sell the fake piece, go back to North Dakota, and be long gone before the buyer figured out the scam."

"Are you thinking the buyer figured that out sooner than expected and killed Gilbert in a rage?" Milo asked.

"Exactly."

"It makes sense. That's why the piece was left on the dashboard. It was phony," Gramm added. "We need to find that buyer."

"Was it Brandon Park, or the Campbell family, or someone we haven't seen yet? There's one piece still not found or advertised," White asked.

"And who's buying the pieces for the Campbells?" Gramm asked.

"Clay Campbell says it's Peters," Milo said.

§

Mandy Campbell arrived at the family compound Wednesday evening only to find that her father was in the coma. This morning she had thrown on an old pair of running shorts and a t-shirt to join her mother at the hospital.

Grace Campbell and Mandy sat by Chip's hospital bed listening to the rhythmic beep of the heart monitor. Grace broke the silence. "The doctor said they've begun to reduce the drugs keeping him in a coma. He could wake up at any time."

"That good news," Mandy murmured.

"I suppose it is. His brain scans, or whatever they're using, show improvement—less swelling, a return to normal."

"Mom, his eyes," Mandy whispered and touched her mom's arm.

Chip blinked, looked at his wife and whispered, "Peters."

"Peters? What about him?" Grace asked.

Chip's eyes closed.

"Chip? Chip?" Grace tried to get another response.

Mandy pushed the call button. The duty nurse came in seconds later.

"He woke up," Grace said. "But now he's slid back into the coma."

The nurse busied herself, checking Chip's saline bag and blood pressure as she answered. "That will happen throughout the day. It's a good sign. I will let the doctors know." She accessed the computer in the room and logged something neither Grace nor Mandy was privy to and then left.

"Dad definitely said *Peters*," Mandy said.

"I never liked him or trusted him. I think your father was telling us who attacked him! I'm calling the police." Grace found Preston's card in her pocket and called the number.

Preston, Gramm, White, and Rathkey were still in Gramm's office when Preston's phone buzzed. She looked at the caller ID. "It's Grace Campbell, Chip's wife."

"Put it on speaker," Gramm ordered.

"Mrs. Campbell, how can I help you?" Preston asked.

"My husband came out of his coma briefly a few minutes ago. He said, 'Peters.' It was clear. Both my daughter and I heard him. Then he slipped back into his coma."

"That's all? Simply Peters?"

"Just that big thug's last name. He was telling us the identity of his attacker," Grace insisted.

"Will someone be with Mr. Campbell at all times in case he wakes up again?"

"I will be here, and my daughter, Mandy, will spell me. I expect my son this afternoon. Also, I hired private security to guard Chip. There is a man outside his room around the clock."

"That's a good idea. Thank you for calling, Mrs. Campbell. Please let me know when he wakes up again, day or night."

"I will." Grace hung up.

"Milo? What do you think?" Gramm asked.

Milo was staring at a blank space on the wall. "Major Peters is a big thug," he mumbled, "but the question is why?"

"Why is he a big thug?" Preston asked.

"Shh. Milo is having a mind lint moment," Gramm whispered.

Milo looked at Gramm. "If you've never seen Major Peters, would you say he was a big thug?"

"Grace Campbell has seen Major Peters," White said.

"And he is big," Preston added. "I know. I had to come between him and Mrs. Campbell in the hospital waiting room."

Milo was silent.

"Milo?" White asked.

Milo shook his head as if emptying it of cobwebs. "The question is why."

21

Agnes glanced around the empty gallery, then heard voices coming from the family room. As she followed the voices, she spotted Aunt Lana relaxing on the sectional. The conversation came from Milo and Sutherland, who were at the bar.

"Oh, good, we're all here," Agnes said. "I've been waiting to tell the details of our latest quest—a failed quest—but I'm hopeful Lakesong will reward us in the future."

"I was here last night," Milo complained. "Why couldn't I hear about it then?"

Agnes moved over to Sutherland and put her arm around his shoulder. "Because my husband was at the annual Twin Ports Commercial Real Estate Dinner."

"You weren't here last night?" Milo asked Sutherland.

"You didn't notice my absence?"

"I just thought you were being quiet."

Sutherland topped off Agnes' Martini with three olives and was rewarded with an Agnes look of joy. She toasted, "To Lakesong, her coyness is frustrating, but we love her anyway."

Glasses clinked to a chorus of "hear, hear.".

Martha entered with a tray of mini fried arancini balls. "I was not along on this adventure, which I was told occurred in the wine cellar."

"It did," Agnes agreed. "We missed your expertise."

"Being a world-renowned expert of hidden staircases is only one of my many talents. I also prepare food. No, really. So, before we learn of this failed adventure, please try the arancini balls," Martha said. "I have prepared them three ways: the marinara mozzarella for Mr. Rathkey, the pesto provolone, not for Mr. Rathkey because they are green, and the kimchi cheddar for those with an adventurous spirit."

To everyone's surprise, Milo reached for the kimchi cheddar. He looked around as he took his first bite. "What? Adventurous is my middle name."

Sutherland shook his head. "Milo Adventurous Rathkey?"

Lana tried one of each, as did Agnes and Sutherland. All agreed that the arancini balls deserved a place in the hors d'oeuvres rotation.

"If only Lakesong could have indulged in these appetizers, Martha, she would have placed signs to the hidden staircase," Agnes said.

"I am a bit worried about you roaming around in the wine cellar, but still patiently waiting for the details of the adventure." Sutherland mumbled around bites of the arancini.

"I like kimchi. Not that much of an adventure, really, and I only went into the wine cellar once," Milo said.

"Not you, Milo—Agnes' adventure."

"So cranky!" Agnes laughed.

Sutherland crossed over to the family room table. "I guess this is going to take some time. Just tell me the wine cellar is still in one piece."

"Of course, it is." Agnes held up her hand. "No wine bottles were injured in the making of this failed adventure."

"Glad we have nourishment," Milo added, joining Sutherland at the table.

"It was a dark and stormy night. Lana and I crept down the stairs," Agnes began.

"I don't remember rain," Milo offered.

"You don't remember Tuesday," Agnes countered.

"Forget the weather. It's a big house. Which stairs?" Sutherland asked. "Details matter."

"Good point. The main stairs in the kitchen hallway— the ones that lead past the vault to the wine cellar. We crept down the stairs…"

"Why were you creeping down the stairs?" Milo asked. "I assume you thought the staircase was hidden in the wine cellar. It seems to me a case of premature creeping."

Agnes gave Milo a look. "We are trying to solve a mystery, Milo. One always creeps when solving a mystery. It adds to the ambiance."

"I didn't know that," Milo said. "In the future, I will creep everywhere."

"That would be creepy," Sutherland joked, enjoying his play on words.

Martha delivered plates of roasted asparagus salad served on a bed of greens, feta cheese, and peppery radishes, dressed with a Dijon mustard vinegarette to everyone except Milo. He received his usual wedge of iceberg lettuce with blue cheese sprinkles lathered in blue cheese dressing.

"Is it that you love iceberg lettuce, or do you love blue cheese?" Lana asked.

"Both," Milo said.

As they began to eat the salads, Agnes continued her narrative. "Before I was so rudely interrupted, Aunt Lana and I *crept* into the wine cellar and surveyed the room, trying to decide on a course of action."

"I thought it must be in the red wine section," Lana said.

"We hoped a detailed search in that area would bear fruit," Agnes said.

"You found oranges and bananas?" Milo asked. "I would have thought grapes."

"Milo is banned from commenting for the next five minutes," Agnes ordered.

Milo turned to Sutherland. "I thought Agnes worked for me."

"That's a gray area," Sutherland said, dismissing Milo's objection with the wave of his hand.

"You used to be on my side."

"She's my wife. Perhaps you missed that announcement."

"I am going to continue, and I'm going to use hand gestures, which will delay the final denouement," Agnes teased.

Milo raised his hand. "We Rathkeys never, and I mean never, allow our denim raw to be delayed."

Agnes huffed and spread her arms out wide. "We searched the entire room—up and down, shelf upon shelf. The enormity of the task did not escape us."

"Enormity?" Sutherland asked. "Martha finds the wine she is looking for every day."

Agnes pointed a finger at him. "You've just joined Milo in the no comment jail."

"I thought you married her," Milo whispered.

"I did, but that was before I found out about her dramatic story telling talent with hand gestures. Now apparently, I am chained to a dungeon wall—with you."

Martha began to clear the empty salad plates, announcing the entrée was to be cedar plank salmon with mushroom pilaf...

"With the Martha's special seasoned salt blend on the salmon, I hope," Sutherland said.

"Of course. I have also included lemon dill sauce on the side."

"You were hunting high and low." Milo attempted to advance the story.

"And wide. High and low and wide," Agnes added with the appropriate hand gestures. "Eventually we came to a suspicious area of Portugal reds."

Sutherland began to speak, but Agnes waved her hands. "No, you're still in no comment jail."

"Milo got to talk," Sutherland complained.

Agnes ignored him. "We continued our detailed search. Flaunting all safety regulations, as we sometimes lost sight of each other."

"Is one of you missing?" Milo asked. "I understand there's quicksand down there."

Martha served the entrees.

"Our search continued." Agnes resumed her narrative. "Finally, we found it, the clue we had been looking for. You want to take it from here, Aunt Lana?"

"I am unable to pull away from this delicious salmon."

"What did you find, darling dear?" Sutherland smiled through gritted teeth. "I must know!"

"We found," Agnes paused for dramatic effect.

"A key? An old treasure map? Pieces of gold?" Sutherland demanded.

"A bottle of Italian wine in with the Portugal reds!" Agnes paused for the oohs and ahhs.

Silence.

Sutherland laughed. "That's not a clue. That's my joke with Martha. I bought that wine two years ago. My Italian section was full, so I placed it in the Portuguese section. Martha always chides me about that."

"Well, it looked suspicious to us, so we lifted it, expecting a magic door to open. It didn't. We then placed it in empty slots. Still nothing," Agnes said.

"It's not a secret anything," Sutherland said. "It was just an odd bottle of wine."

"We needed Martha with us. She held valuable knowledge," Agnes complained.

"At any rate, we drank it," Lana said. "Along with one of its cousins."

"So much for the missing staircase hunt," Sutherland laughed.

"After just one failed attempt? Goodness, no! I'm positive the staircase is there somewhere. Lana, tell them what you told me."

Aunt Lana put her fork down and folded her hands in front of her plate. "I think I mentioned this before. With these estates, it's not about what you see, it's about what the original owners didn't want you to see. The running of the house was supposed to appear to be magic."

"So, workers who didn't need to be inside the house would use this still-to-be-found south stairway down to the basement," Sutherland said. "I would guess there was a back-door out of the basement before the modern pool was built."

"Correct," Aunt Lana agreed.

"But why do we care?" Sutherland asked.

"Because it's one of Lakesong's secrets. We have to solve Lakesong's secrets," Agnes insisted. "It's like Milo solving a murder. It has to be done. Right, Milo?"

Milo was moving his pilaf around his plate.

"Milo?"

"I know why."

"Why? Why what?" Sutherland demanded.

Milo snapped to, as if coming out of a trance. "Stairs? Sure, I'm in favor of stairs. Always have been a pro-stairs guy."

"Is he okay?" Lana asked.

"We were talking stairs, and he just solved a murder," Sutherland said. "It's Milo's mind lint."

"Now this is fun!" Lana exclaimed.

§

Creedence Durant didn't realize when he agreed to work around the soup kitchen's schedule that it would mean early mornings and late evenings. At sundown, the wind had shifted and was now coming off the lake. Creedence Durant flipped up his jacket collar against the ever-dropping temperature while his contractor inspected the roof of the Lake Avenue Soup Kitchen. Creedence insisted on holding the ladder and staying until she came down safely. *At least I don't have to climb up on the roof myself.*

A half hour later, Durant's contractor, Tamara Busker, descended the ladder with good news. "The roof is in good shape, doesn't need any repairs." Tamara and her husband Bruce remodeled Creedence's house several years ago, and he trusted their work.

Creedence was shivering. He told Tamara he would wait inside while she put the ladder back on her truck. "Just come in when you are done," he shouted to her. She gave him a thumbs up.

Zeke was much friendlier this time, knowing that Creedence's client was helping, not hurting, his efforts to feed people. "What's up?" he asked as he let Creedence into the warm interior.

"My contractor is ready to inspect inside, and when she's finished, maybe we sit down and work out a preliminary plan for the remodel."

"This is fast. You've already gotten with the appraiser and the bank?" Zeke asked. "What interest rate are you getting?"

Creedence smiled. "It's an all cash deal."

"That must be one healthy income if your client needs this whole building as a tax write off," Zeke said. "Are municipal bonds tanking?"

Creedence didn't answer but thought, *interest rates, tax write offs, bonds tanking—you didn't always just feed people at a soup kitchen.*

Any further discussion was interrupted by Tamara coming through the front door. Creedence did the introductions. Zeke turned and shook her hand.

"Call me Tee," Tamara said, "everybody does. I'm gonna start upstairs. Is there anybody up there?"

Zeke shook his head. "We had a clothing consignment shop up there at one time, but that went bust during the recession—couldn't get a line of credit. It's empty now. The stairs are straight down the hall, through the serving area, by the back door."

"I'll find it."

Gloria offered Creedence a cup of coffee while he waited.

"Don't you want to go up there with her?" Zeke asked.

Creedence smiled. "I would be in the way. If you don't mind, I'll sit here and wait. I'm not in the way here, am I?" He pointed to one of the tables with only a few eaters.

"We'll work around you," Zeke said. "By the way, why are you here? I get the contractor, but why you?"

"I like the change of pace. I tire of crunching numbers and reading prospectuses all day."

"Gotcha." Someone began banging on the back door. "A delivery I gotta deal with," Zeke said and got up and left.

Creedence caught the eye of a fellow at the opposite end of the table. Not knowing what to do, Creedence nodded. The man glanced at Creedence who was not eating—only drinking coffee. He frowned and went back to his food.

§

Milo sat at his computer, scrolling through old legal documents. It was a laborious task. Campbell was too common a name. He deleted the name Campbell and replaced it with the name LaPointe. Several lawsuits came up, all old, all without specifics. In every lawsuit, the LaPointes were suing the Campbells for a share of the mining fortune. He wrote the details down to see if Saul Feinberg could find more information.

Saul usually had pastries from Ilene's Bakery in his van office parked behind the courthouse. The van would be Milo's first stop of the morning.

§

Tee joined Creedence at the long table, handing him several sheets of paper. "This absolutely needs to be done. We may run into more. You know how this goes. It's an old building."

"Can we make changes as we go along?" Creedence asked.

"That's up to you. Changes are expensive. You and Zeke need to decide on a timeline. I'm off for home—long day."

Tee left Creedence sitting at one end of a long table, still waiting for Zeke to finish serving the final customers. A tired-looking woman with three stairstep children had been quietly sitting at the opposite end of his table. One child, a boy, was sleeping in the woman's arms. A curly-headed-twirler was giggling as she dizzily reached for her mom to steady herself. The third came over to stare at Creedence, which made him uncomfortable. He never knew what to do with children. He didn't want to be rude, but, at the same time, he didn't want to talk to her because he didn't know what to say.

The girl spoke first. "You'd better get some food now, mister. Zeke is about to run out."

"I'm not here to eat," Credence said, immediately regretting the tone of his response.

The young girl was unfazed. "Are you waiting for a vulture?"

Confused, Creedence pushed his glasses up the bridge of his nose. "A vulture?"

"We already ate. My tummy is full." The girl rubbed her tummy. "My mom is waiting for a vulture. What are you here for?" The girl persisted.

"I have to talk to Zeke," Creedence said.

"Maddie! Come here! Leave the man alone!" her mother called.

"But he hasn't eaten, and he needs to talk to Zeke. I think he needs a vulture, too. We get it first, right Mommy?"

"Here, Maddie, finish my cookie."

"Don't you want it, Mommy?"

"No, I'm not hungry."

Zeke left the food serving area and gave Creedence a wave. "Be with you in a minute. I have one more thing to do."

"No problem," Creedence said, waving back.

Zeke walked over to the woman at the end of the table. Holding two slips of paper in his hand, he said, "Ma'am, I only have these for tonight and Saturday. Check with me again when you come in tomorrow. I hope to have at least one more."

The woman clutched the slips of paper while her younger daughter pulled on Zeke's jeans. "Zeke, I have a new twirl.

Watch!" The little girl held out her arms and twirled. Her arms held an imaginary skirt, which lifted as she spun faster.

Zeke applauded as the girl once again fell against her mother and steadied herself.

"Thank you, Zeke," the woman said as the baby sneezed. She wiped his face with a napkin from her pocket. "This will keep Tony out of the cold. Let's go, girls." The younger one twirled out the door while the older girl asked to hold on to 'the vultures.'

Her mother smiled. "I've already put them in my safe place." The family disappeared out the door.

Zeke came over to Creedence. "So, what's up?"

"I have the list of immediate improvements. You may want to look it over. What just went on with that lady and her kids?"

"They came to get fed like everyone else in here," Zeke said.

"What's a vulture?"

Zeke looked at him. "A big bird? Scavenger? Why do you ask?"

"No, no," Creedence laughed. "That little girl—not the dancing one, the serious one—said her mom was waiting for a vulture."

Zeke laughed. "Oh, that's Maddie. That's what she calls vouchers."

"Vouchers for what?"

"Rooms for the night. I get some from the Salvation Army, and a couple of the independent motels donate from time to time."

"What happens if you don't have any vouchers?"

"This family is lucky enough to have a car to stay in. Otherwise, they sleep in a shelter if they can find room and it's not too dangerous."

"Where's her husband, the children's father?"

"I don't know. I don't ask."

Creedence rolled up the construction schedule and stuffed it in his pocket. "You're not using the upstairs, right?"

"Like I told you, it's empty," Zeke said.

"Good. I need to talk to my client. I'm thinking our plan is not ambitious enough," Creedence said. "How much are those rooms if you don't have a voucher?"

"Sixty, seventy bucks. Some are a little higher."

"Where are they staying?"

"The Bayview. It's clean and they're generous in the off season."

22

Gramm didn't need the deputy chief to remind him that the murder of Ham Gilbert was now twelve days old, and the police were no closer to naming a murderer. Preston interrupted Gramm's morose thoughts. "I ran Elbert Peters through the database and got nothing."

Gramm gave her a pinched eyebrow look. This, she had learned, was not good.

"Wait, there's more. I thought Major or Majors was one of those names that could be a first name or a last name, so I tried Elbert Majors—bingo!"

Gramm looked at White, who had joined them. "Translate bingo."

"It's a game old people play," White said.

"I got a hit!" Preston boasted. "Elbert Majors, who is our Elbert Peters, is wanted in Faribault County for a DWI that resulted in the death of a pedestrian. The warrant is more than ten years old. I'm not sure if there is a statute of limitations."

The pinch in Gramm's eyebrows released. "Good work! I think everything is coming up Peters."

"What's the plan?" White asked.

"We arrest Elbert Majors, see if he talks. Even if he doesn't, we have the old warrant."

"We have to get into the compound."

Gramm smiled, "What's that saying about an enemy of my enemy?"

"Enemy?" White questioned.

"Okay, enemy is a little strong. The enemy of my suspect is my friend," Gramm backtracked.

"Still confused." White laughed.

Gramm picked up his phone. "Watch and listen, grasshopper." He punched in a number and waited. "Mr. Campbell, Lieutenant Gramm here. I have a favor to ask."

"I'm listening," Clay said.

"We are going to arrest Major Peters. We would appreciate it if you opened the gate for us. Oh, and of course, don't mention it to him."

"Lieutenant, I would be delighted. When you get to the intercom at the gate, key in 5536."

"Thank you." Gramm hung up and turned to White. "Let's bring a couple of uniforms with us, just in case."

White called the desk to get the backup.

"Where's Milo?" Gramm asked.

"He said he needed to talk with Saul Feinberg this morning," White said.

"Robin, get an arrest warrant. Kate check on Chip Campbell's condition. I'll alert Milo," Gramm said. "Finally! An arrest!"

§

How does Saul keep his van so clean? Milo thought to himself as he parked his Honda near the van in the court-house lot. Feinberg's Mercedes van never showed any signs of dirt or grime. *Does Saul have people to wash his car at night? Nah.* Milo laughed, then stopped, suddenly thinking of Mr. Anderson, the Lakesong mechanic, who washed his car at least once a week. Milo leaned his head down on the steering wheel. *Who am I?*

Feinberg pulled the sliding door back. "I saw you drive up. Come in Milo, Ilene's pastries are on the table."

"Pastries? Oh, you have pastries. From where? Did you say, Ingrid's?" Milo joked as he entered the van.

Feinberg laughed. "You know you are going to decimate my bakery box. I know you are going to decimate…"

Milo was already biting into a Bismarck with an éclair in his other hand. "What, no creampuffs?"

"They need refrigeration. What do you need?"

Milo sat down. "I was doing some research last night and uncovered two lawsuits, but I need more than my software can give me."

Feinberg smiled. "Tell me, when did I start working for you?"

"That's a good point, Saul. I'll just ignore it. A long time ago, a family named LaPointe sued a family named Campbell. I have the case numbers, but no details."

Feinberg wrote the two names down on a legal pad.

Milo picked up a napkin, wiped his hand, and fished a sticky note out of his jacket pocket. "Here are the particulars."

Feinberg picked up the yellow note with care. "There's jelly on here."

Milo looked at his other hand. "Oh, yeah, I didn't get it all." He picked up another napkin, scraping the rest of the jelly off his fingers.

Feinberg typed in the case numbers and pulled up both suits. "I know about this case. I studied it in law school. The LaPointes had a good argument. Hayden LaPointe died in a cave in—or so Duncan Campbell claimed—at the turn of the 19th century. The two partners had signed a succession agreement. If one died by accident or natural causes, the remaining partner became sole owner. Hayden LaPointe's heirs insisted it was no accident that Campbell murdered him. They sued for their share of the mine profits."

"Because there are two lawsuits, I assume they didn't win," Milo said. "Did anyone think of recovering the body to see if it was murder?"

Feinberg glanced up at Milo. "There were no champions of the poor and downtrodden back then."

"Such as yourself?"

"Well, now that you mention it, yes."

"So, the LaPointes are the downtrodden?" Milo asked.

"In this case, yes. The Campbell's had several judges in their pockets. They also had two mining engineers testify that the cave was dangerous—could cave in again. An attempt to recover Hayden LaPointe's body might lead to more loss of life. The LaPointes never had a chance."

"There are no lawsuits after the first two?"

Feinberg nodded. "The thought was they were paid off to go away—not as much money as they wanted, but enough to be comfortable."

"Where is this mine?" Milo asked.

Feinberg reached into the bookshelf behind his desk and produced an old-fashioned atlas. He thumbed through the pages until he came to a section of Carlton County. "Right there, just south of Round Lake."

"Really? An atlas. Paper with pages? How old are you?" Milo kidded.

"I'm a tactile kind of guy. I could do it on my computer, but then you'd have to get up and bring your jelly fingers over to this side of the desk."

"Always loved those atlases!" Milo exclaimed, taking a bite of the éclair. Setting the pastry down, he picked up his phone. "Don't be frightened. This is a phone, but it also takes pictures. If you lay your atlas flat, I will take a picture of the page. You won't be harmed."

"I thought you were the Luddite here," Feinberg charged.

Milo took the picture, grabbed the remains of the éclair, and stood up.

"On another topic, Joe is working out just fine. Thanks for asking," Feinberg said in reference to Joe Ripkowski, Milo's friend and fellow PI. Milo had recommended Joe to take Milo's place as Saul's investigator after Milo inherited millions. "He doesn't have your touch. If I come across a case that needs something other than a plodder, I will give you a call."

Milo affected a sloppy salute. "I am ready to serve."

"You got éclair cream on your jacket."

"A snack for later," Milo said, dabbing his jacket with the napkin.

§

Milo arrived at Gramm's office with time to spare. The arrest warrant for Major Peters had yet to be delivered. Gramm filled Milo in on Preston's discovery of Peters' real name.

A moment later, Preston walked back into Gramm's office. "The hospital says Chip Campbell is still in and out, but they think he will be fully conscious soon."

"Has he said anything more?" Gramm asked.

"He just keeps saying Peters," Preston said.

Gramm turned his attention to Milo. "We have this wrapped up. Where have you been?"

Milo took out his phone, pulled up the picture from Feinberg's atlas, and showed it to Preston. "Look familiar? Is this your map?"

Preston shook her head. "This isn't magic. I have a process. I have to draw it out first." Preston did a quick sketch of the puzzle map from memory. She held it up to Milo's phone. "What do you think?" she asked.

"Anything you want to share with the rest of the class, Milo?" Gramm grumbled.

"The Campbell family mine number two. That's where Lewis Rutledge was leading the treasure hunters," Milo said.

"Why?" White asked.

"I don't know. Maybe to get a rise out of the rest of the family, but I think it's the motive for murder. Sutherland's Aunt Lana…"

"Hold that thought, Milo!" Gramm said, looking at his phone. "Our arrest warrant is here. Let's roll."

The team formed up in the police parking lot. Gramm asked White about backup. "Hughes and Butler will meet us there."

"Are they together?" Gramm asked.

White laughed. "Hardly. Butler is part of the motorcycle unit. Hughes will be in her patrol car."

"Let's go in two cars," Milo suggested.

"Why?" Gramm asked.

"I hate riding in the backseat of anything. Preston can grab a regular patrol car."

"Make sure we are all armed. I've only seen Peters with a Taser, but let's be prepared. And be careful, there will be a number of innocent people around. If he's armed and runs, let him go. We'll catch him later."

"Vests?" White asked.

"Yes."

"Vests make me look bulky," Milo protested.

"Life has made you look bulky," Gramm countered.

On the way up to Island Lake, Gramm called Clay again. "We're on our way up."

"Good. I have called an impromptu meeting in front of the lodge. Board members will be there along with Major Peters."

"Very convenient," Gramm said.

"I thought you'd like it, Lieutenant."

Gramm hung up and said to White, "He's handing us Peters on a silver platter."

"He really doesn't like that guy," White said.

§

Milo was making idle chitchat with Preston when he received a call from Creedence.

"Creedence?"

"Milo, it has come to my attention that mothers and their children sometimes need a place to stay. Your personal project building has an empty second floor, which could house said women and children."

"You want to remodel the upstairs?"

"Yes. It would add to your tax deduction."

"Let's do it."

"Milo, you should ask me how much it will cost," Creedence advised.

"Don't care. My money guy handles all that. Oh wait, you're my money guy, and you seem to think this is a good idea. Let's do it."

§

"I'm back," Creedence said, walking over to Zeke. "Are you in touch with Maddie and her mother?"

"I see them when they come in, almost every day," Zeke said.

Creedence handed him an electronic key. "I've arranged a room at a nearby extended stay hotel. It's safe. I will get the bill."

Zeke looked at the key. "Nice. Too bad we can't do this for everyone."

Creedence smiled. "Maybe we can. I've talked to my client about expanding our idea."

The two sat down at the table nearest the kitchen and were joined by Gloria, who brought three cups of coffee.

"I was thinking," Creedence began, "we could put apartments upstairs, small ones, where families could stay for weeks or months. According to Tee, there is ample space up there."

"Is this guy made of money?" Zeke asked.

"Pretty much, and I never said it was a guy."

"A woman?"

"Never said it was a woman, either?"

Zeke raised his hands in mock surrender. "Okay. Let's talk about upstairs. It's not as simple as a bunch of apartments. If it's women and kids, they will require protection. Some of these ladies have nasty boyfriends or husbands who will come looking for them. We need someone to discourage such visits."

Gloria stood, hands on her wide hips. "I can," she declared.

Creedence weighed in. "Zeke seems to think some of these men are dangerous. Are you sure you want to do this?"

Gloria laughed and sat down next to Creedence. "Honey, I ran a home for battered women before it lost funding. I dealt with angry men."

Zeke mumbled, "I guess you dealt with 'em—put a couple in the hospital."

"I gave them a chance to calm the hell down. They didn't take it. I rent an apartment now. If I'm going to stay here, would I get an apartment as part of the job?"

"Certainly. How big do you want it?" Creedence asked.

"A bedroom, a kitchenette, a bathroom, and a sitting room," Gloria said.

"Like a living room?" Creedence asked.

"My grandmother called it a sitting room. It's where people sit."

"I'll add it to the plans," Creedence said, writing down Gloria's requests.

Gloria wasn't afraid to push. "And rent free?"

"Of course, it's included in the soup kitchen's dollar a year."

"That is one powerful dollar," Zeke said.

"My client would also pay you a stipend for your services," Creedence advised.

Zeke turned to Creedence. "What about benefits? Someone may get in a lucky punch."

"Hmmm, I think we can work out something in the way of health insurance and a 401K. Thinking about it, we will need to set up a nonprofit corporation." Creedence was talking to himself.

"We have work to do," Zeke said, getting up.

"No, I still need you. Just a few more minutes," Creedence said. "This is the plan. The first thing we'll build is a community kitchen for the apartments, except for Gloria's because she'll have her own. Once that's done, we can tear out this downstairs kitchen and rebuild it. We'll put a dumb waiter in so food from upstairs can be sent downstairs. It'll be a pain for a while, but I think it will work."

"If it won't interrupt our meals, it's a good plan," Zeke said. "I would like to thank whoever is paying for all this."

Creedence got up. "Thank everybody. Who knows, one of them might be him…or her."

§

Gramm pulled up to the now familiar gate at the Campbell compound. He keyed in the code given to him by Clay Campbell, and the gate swung open.

White was looking out the back window. "Great timing. Butler and Hughes are pulling up behind Preston's car."

The parade of cops entered the compound. No lights or sirens.

"The lodge is the fourth building on the right," White informed Gramm. "Big front porch."

"I've been there," Gramm snapped.

White had been with Gramm long enough to know the snappy tone was because of the fluid situation that could turn dangerous quickly—no cop's favorite.

Gramm pulled up in front of the lodge. As he and White exited the car, Gramm looked around. There was no family meeting that he could see or hear. "Already this isn't going right," Gramm said, stretching his neck.

"I hear voices around the back," White advised.

Gramm told Butler and Hughes to stay in front while he, White, Rathkey, and Preston walked toward the voices. Gramm motioned for Rathkey and Preston to circle one side of the lodge while he and White circled the other.

All the family members, plus Peters, were gathered on what Gramm considered the back lawn. Clay stopped talking when he saw the police entourage approaching from the sides of the lodge. "It looks like we have visitors."

"Good afternoon," Gramm said as he approached. "We would like to speak with Elbert Majors."

"Who?" Mazy asked. She didn't need an answer. The man she knew as Major Peters bolted, knocking Clay down and running on the path to Chip's house.

"Damn!" Gramm muttered. "Preston, stay here in case he doubles back!"

Gramm and White chased after the fleeing man.

White keyed her radio, telling Hughes they had a runner best chased on foot. Peters broke through the houses and headed for the dock, jumped into a canoe, and, before anyone could reach him, began paddling across the lake.

A frustrated White stood on the shore watching Peters paddling form recede into the distance. She was joined by Hughes, an out-of-breath Gramm, and a fuming Clay Campbell. "You're letting him get away!"

White turned to him. "What do you suggest? We didn't bring a boat."

"I did!" Clay shouted, tossing White his keys. "It's the little motorboat—yellow with a black stripe—tied to my dock."

White caught the keys and ran in the direction Clay was pointing. Hughes was with her.

Turning the corner to the dock, White laughed. "Two 90 horse Mercs?"

"Little motorboat?" Hughes questioned.

Milo and Preston stood with the rest of the family members on the back lawn, waiting for the outcome of the chase. "I wonder why he ran?" Milo asked Preston.

"Because he's the murderer, Milo."

"Nah, I think we've got the murderer right here." Milo said, pointing at Michael Mason.

Mason's face blanched. He looked around at the shocked faces and took off toward his house.

"Michael? Where are you going?" Mazy yelled after him.

"To get his Ducati?" Milo guessed.

"That's one fast bike," Preston offered.

"So, we're screwed?"

"No." Preston barked as she sprinted around the lodge, grabbing Butler by the arms. "I need your bike, now! Keys!"

Butler complied.

Preston swung her leg over the bike, squeezed the clutch, pushed the start button, and gunned the machine. The sound of a powerful motorcycle could be heard firing up in the distance. Preston spun the bike around. Milo ran to the side of the lodge just as Preston screeched to a stop and yelled at the family who were congregating at the front of the main building. "Where does he keep the Ducati?"

Mazy pointed to the house. "Out building behind my house, that way. What's going on?"

"You're never going to catch up with him," Milo yelled.

Milo heard her yell the word 'motocross,' as she gunned Butler's motorcycle and sprang off the road, through the trees, expertly weaving in and out like a giant slalom.

Milo began walking fast down the road. "In the future, I'm bringing my own car," he promised himself.

Gramm, having left Clay's dock, waited for Milo on the road. "I heard motorcycles. What's happening?"

Suddenly, in the distance, Preston popped up almost above the tree line and then disappeared again. Seconds later, the revving motorcycle sounds stopped with a crash—dead silence.

"Oh shit! I hope that crash was our killer and not Preston," Milo said, picking up his pace.

"The killer is in a canoe," Gramm yelled after him.

"No, he's not," Milo yelled back, rounding the curve by Greer's house. Preston was pulling a cuffed, scraped, limping Mason up the culvert on the side of the road. "You have the right to remain silent," she began. Her motorcycle was on its side. His was down the embankment, crushed into a tree.

"Move it!" Preston yelled at Mason, pushing him, causing him to fall. As she bent down to pick him up, a yellow ball of flame erupted from the crumpled Ducati, followed by the thunder of an explosion.

Preston hit the ground, throwing her hands over the back of her head.

Milo began running. Gramm followed, cursing old age. Milo dodged a few motorcycle pieces bouncing on the road as he came up to an unmoving Preston. "Preston?" Milo shouted. He bent down to check on her.

Preston looked up and smiled. "Wow! What a rush!"

Gramm caught up, looked at the police bike, and smiled at Preston. "You've got a lot of paperwork ahead of you."

She rose and jerked Mason to his feet. Blood trickled down his face, and as they began to walk, he fell, saying his ankle was broken. Gramm called for an ambulance before asking Officer Butler to come pick them up.

"I don't have a vehicle," Butler said. "Preston grabbed my bike."

"Oh yeah. Get Hughes' keys."

"The last I saw her, she was on a boat chasing the murderer."

Gramm shook his head. "Run down here and get my keys to the Interceptor. Make it fast."

"Where's here, sir?"

"Follow the road toward the entrance."

Mazy and Greer arrived at the commotion. "Michael?" Mazy asked.

Milo stepped in front of them. "Please stay back."

"Michael?" Mazy questioned. "Did you kill somebody?"

Mason was sitting in the road, bloody head in his hands. "No, I didn't! I don't know a Ham Gilbert."

"But Michael, Ham Gilbert was a very short man. You called him a little shit. How would you know that unless you'd seen him before?"

Clay came running, screaming at Michael. "What the hell did you do?"

Gramm pulled him back.

"Did you try to kill my brother, you stupid son of a bitch?"

Preston's phone buzzed. She answered it, handing a hand-cuffed, limping Mason to Officer Butler, who had raced to retrieve Gramm's vehicle and was now mourning the loss of his motorcycle. After several minutes on the phone, Preston said, "That was the hospital. Chip Campbell is out of the coma and has named Michael Mason as the man who attacked him, and he knows Mason murdered Ham Gilbert. Apparently, he was saying Peters in order to tell him about Mason."

Mason whispered, "I deserved to be a full member of this friggin family. I was not going to end up like Lewis!"

"Why kill Gilbert?" Gramm asked.

"So, he could plant the phony piece," Milo said. "It wasn't about what we saw, it was about what the family didn't want us to see. The mine."

Mason leered at Clay. "I was doing the family a favor, keeping people away from that mine. It worked! All those idiots were searching miles away in Jay Cooke park. You didn't even think of that."

Clay shook his head. "Geezus, Michael."

Mazy stood frozen. Greer put her arm around her niece.

23

Sunday was Martha's usual day off, but she was absent this Saturday as well—a rare trip to the cities to reunite with some old friends. She hadn't mentioned her companion for the trip was bestselling author Ron Bello because she didn't want people to gossip. Her oldest sib, Breana, recently returned from Chile, was riding herd on her brothers, Jamal and Darian.

Sutherland thought he would make breakfast smoothies for himself and Agnes but was surprised to find Milo already in the kitchen.

"What goes into your smoothie?" Milo asked.

"You're making breakfast?" a stunned Sutherland asked.

"I'm the son of a cook. If you don't want a smoothie, I can prepare a frittata or brioche French toast."

Agnes walked into the family room and said she would get the coffee urn cart. Before rolling it into the family room, she turned to Milo and said, "I'll take the French toast."

"Milo is making breakfast!" Sutherland declared, as Agnes sat down with her coffee. She walked over to Sutherland, rubbed his arm, and said softly, "Of course he is. You just keep thinking that."

Sutherland was confused. "I would like a piece of the frittata."

"Bacon cheddar or vegetarian?" Agnes asked.

"Bacon cheddar."

Agnes smirked. "Hey, Milo, you got orders here."

Milo emerged from the kitchen wearing an apron. "We chefs do not respond well to 'Hey, Milo!'"

"So sorry, chef. Sutherland would like a piece of the bacon cheddar frittata."

"Milo is the son of a cook," Sutherland said, defending his assertion that Milo was making breakfast.

Agnes took a sip of coffee. "Of course, he rose early, whipped together two frittatas, soaked the brioche, and gathered ingredients for smoothies. Sure, I believe that."

Sutherland stopped. Closed his eyes. "Martha did that, didn't she?"

"Aw, you look like I just told you the Easter Bunny isn't real," Agnes laughed.

"Hey, I am baking the frittatas and I have to grill the French toast," Milo complained. "I am also carefully heating the homemade maple butter in this saucepan. I had to it put on the stove myself."

Lana arrived at breakfast. "I'll have a slice of the vegetarian frittata," she said. "Don't bother claiming you made anything, Milo. I saw Martha make it all yesterday."

Agnes shook her head and whispered, "Sutherland still believes in the myth of 'Chef Milo and his Magic Kitchen,' where good boys and girls get freshly made frittatas and French toast."

"He's the son of a cook! It all made sense," Sutherland complained.

Lana laughed. "I don't think cooking skills are genetic."

The first piece of brioche went into the garbage. "Left it on a little long, but I'm getting the hang of it," Milo said.

Milo's phone *da dunked*. Sutherland picked it up off the table. "Milo's phone."

"Who's this?" Lieutenant Gramm asked.

"Mr. Rathkey's valet, sir," Sutherland mocked a British accent.

"Tell Mr. Rathkey Sergeant White, Officer Preston, and myself are on the way for a Martha breakfast and some answers."

"This Martha of whom you speak is not here this morning, but I have been informed that she had premade breakfast goodies which are now being finalized by Mr. Rathkey, who—I must point out—is the son of a cook."

"Really? Milo is making breakfast?" Sutherland could hear groans from the other passengers.

"Should we pick something up on the way?" White yelled.

"Oh, ye of little faith." Sutherland laughed.

"Too late. We're here. Open the gate," Gramm said.

Sutherland found the Lakesong app on Milo's phone and opened the gate. He rose from the table to greet them at the front door.

"Remind them I'm the son of a cook," Milo shouted.

Sutherland led the parade of visiting humans into the family room, where Agnes and Lana were already enjoying coffee. The two cats, Annie and Jet, were standing around Milo at the oven. They knew something was very wrong this morning but wanted to get their bacon before Milo ruined it.

"The morning room isn't big enough," Sutherland said to his guests. "We are breakfasting here in the family room."

"I don't know if I have ever done *breakfasting* as a verb anywhere," Preston said to White.

The aproned Milo appeared in the family room. "The breakfast menu is bacon, cheddar or vegetable frittatas, brioche French toast with maple butter, or crappy smoothies."

"A small slice of both frittatas, please," White requested.

"A large cheddar and the French toast. I'm healing," Preston said.

"What she said," Gramm agreed.

"Are you also healing?" Sutherland asked.

"I almost ran yesterday."

"I understand you caught the bad guy," Sutherland said.

"Preston caught the bad guy," Gramm corrected.

"I was on a boat in the middle of the lake apprehending a canoe," White complained.

"Why?" Agnes asked.

White shot Gramm a look. "We, that's the royal we, kinda missed the mark on exactly who the bad guy was. The guy we picked was bad, but old bad. Preston nailed the new bad."

"How exciting!" Lana said. "Did you wrestle him to the ground?"

Gramm laughed. "She plowed a motorcycle into him."

"Oh, my," Lana said.

"She made her motorcycle fly," Milo declared, as he entered the family room with a cart full of breakfast orders. He handed out the plates, getting each order wrong. A brief exchanging of plates began.

"I'm the cook, not the waiter." Milo poured himself a cup of coffee and flopped, seemingly exhausted, onto the sectional.

Agnes went into the kitchen and returned with two pitchers of orange liquid. Holding out the one in her left hand, she said, "Orange juice. The other is mimosas."

"Martha thinks of everything," Sutherland said.

"She squeezed the oranges, but I mixed the mimosas," Agnes said proudly.

White bit into her French toast. "Mmm. This is good."

"Thank you," Milo said. "I slaved over the stove for hours."

Gramm finished most of his frittata and took a coffee break before asking how Milo figured Mason to be the killer.

Milo joined the group at the table. "Aunt Lana gave me the answer."

"Me?"

"You said with old families it's not what you see, it's what they don't want you to see."

"I was talking about the staircase and how old families don't want their guests to see staff and workers," Lana explained.

"That misdirection also applied to the murder. We all thought that Ham Gilbert was selling a phony piece, but you made me realize that the purpose of the phony piece was to misdirect. Mason made the phony piece because the family didn't want treasure hunters near the mine. He thought it was his ticket into the inner circle."

"He murdered someone to impress his wife's family?" Sutherland asked. "That's crazy."

"Don't forget, being on the family board meant money for his passion, motorcycle racing."

"Who caused all this to begin with?" Agnes asked.

"Mazy Mason's father, Lewis Rutledge. According to her, he thought it was a joke," Milo explained.

"That's some disfunction," Preston said. "I mean, this Rutledge guy was part of the family."

"Are you sure Lewis Rutledge hid his treasure at the entrance to the mine?" Sutherland asked.

"Forensics found it early this morning. Sixty thousand dollars," White explained.

"You ruined the contest," Agnes said in mock outrage. "Darian might have found the treasure."

White laughed. "Darian is still a winner. The radio station is going to split the money among the puzzle piece holders. Make sure Martha knows."

"Okay, so the family doesn't want people digging around the old mine, but shouldn't that lead you to Peters?" Gramm asked.

"Majors," White corrected. "His name was really Majors, or Major."

Gramm held up his hand. "Let's end this game right now. We knew him as Peters. We're going to keep calling him Peters! Now, Milo, Clay Campbell told us *Peters*, was buying the puzzle pieces."

Milo shook his head. "Except for Gilbert's piece. Mason got to him first with his misdirection scheme."

"How did you figure that out?" Gramm demanded.

"Mason called Ham Gilbert a little shit. How did he know Ham was short? Mason and Gilbert should have never met. I was sure of my theory when Mason referred to Gilbert by his nickname, Ham. We never released that name."

"Kinda weak," Gramm said.

"Agreed. But then he ran," Milo laughed. "Lucky for us Preston is a motorcross champion."

"Motocross," Preston corrected, "and far from a champion." She rubbed her leg, the sore one that slid under the bike before she let it go, taking out Mason and his machine.

"All I know is she popped up over the trees, disappeared, and then there was a bang," Gramm said.

"So, Milo," White began. "Grace Campbell called Peters a big thug. You questioned that."

"Exactly. Grace Campbell knew Peters and correctly called him a *big* thug. Michael Mason supposedly did not know Ham Gilbert, yet correctly called him a little shit. Grace Campbell added the push I needed."

"Okay, we thought your mind lint was pointing to Peters." White said. "That's why we chased him. Why didn't you tell us it was about Mason? I wouldn't have had to get wet."

Milo sighed. "I can never be sure I'm right, and you guys were so sure it was Peters."

"Peters ran! Shouldn't that have indicated you were wrong?"

"It confused me, but when I confronted Mason and he ran too, I figured my theory was correct."

"Mason is talking like a songbird this morning, trying to get a deal with the DA," Gramm added. "He claimed he didn't mean to kill Gilbert. He admits hitting him, but says Gilbert fell into the river and Mason can't swim."

"Won't work," Milo countered. "He had to meet Gilbert with that phony piece already made. That's premeditation. If Gilbert survived the attack, he could have said that puzzle piece wasn't his and the entire ruse would have come apart. No, he had to kill Gilbert, and he did."

"Clever," White said, "but not as clever as Brandon Park."

"What do you mean?" Milo asked.

"When we arrived at the mine this morning, Park was already there. He figured out the misdirection, researched Lewis Rutledge and found his connection to the Campbells, and figured out what the family did not want anyone to see."

"I imagine he was upset about the police showing up," Milo said. "Back to Peters. How did you manage to catch him?"

White's face hardened. "The idiot jumped into the lake when we raced up to his canoe in the speedboat."

"I take it that was a bad move," Milo said.

"He can't swim. I had to jump in and pull him out. That's how I got wet, and that water is still cold!"

"Why did he run in the first place?" Milo asked. "That surprised me."

"Old warrant for vehicular homicide. We're transporting him to Faribault County," Gramm explained.

"Is Lakesong always this exciting—secret staircases, murders, chases?" Lana asked. Jet stood up, paws on Lana's leg, and squeaked.

"Jet thinks it's too much for a little cat to put up with," Sutherland laughed.

§

Clay Campbell called the meeting to order. "I would like to welcome my niece Amanda Campbell to the board."

Mandy nodded and smiled at the gathered family board members—minus Chip.

"I wish this wasn't the initial order of business on your first day, Amanda, but I think Mazy, given your husband's criminal activity, which has damaged this family's reputation, you should resign from this board."

Mazy gave him a deadly stare. "I refuse."

Clay sat up. "You're a smart young lady, Mazy, but I think you lack the skills to read the room. You're finished. I call for a vote on Mazy's removal from this board."

No one spoke.

"You need a second," Greer said.

"I know that. Why aren't you taking notes?" Clay demanded.

"I think, dear nephew, you lack the skills to read the room."

Clay turned to his niece. "Amanda? This is where you say, *I second the motion*."

"I know that, Uncle Clay. I just choose not to." She sat back, smiling.

Clay flicked his fingers at her. "The second, Amanda! Now!"

Amanda was silent.

"Given there is no second," Mazy said, "the motion fails. I would now like to move that, given Uncle Chip's expected long recovery, Aunt Greer take his place as chairman."

Amanda immediately chimed in with her own finger flick. "I second the motion."

Clay's face bloomed a crimson red. "What's going on here?"

"A coup," Mazy said.

"You can't do that!" Clay shouted.

"Read the room, Clay," Mazy sneered. "All those in favor of Greer Campbell becoming the new Campbell family chairman, say, aye."

"Aye."

"Aye."

"Aye."

"Nay!" Clay screamed. "And Nay! I have Chip's proxy."

"I doubt that," Mazy said. "The only thing he's giving right now are urine samples—no offense, Mandy. But even if you did have his proxy, the vote is three to two. Congratulations, Aunt Greer—long overdue."

"Amanda!" Clay drew a long, angry breath and tried to soften his tone. "Mandy, dear, you may not understand. This vote is double crossing your father."

"There is a lesson to be learned here, Uncle Clay," Mandy said. "Family members are on the board to further the family business. I've done well in school. I kept track of how poorly you and my father have handled our family's business. Did you think I wouldn't read what was sent to me?"

Clay's crimson color faded to a pale white. "Campbell men have headed this board since 1870."

"The *oldest* child has headed this board since 1870, until my sister Mackenzie was passed over and then banished," Greer challenged. "How does it feel?"

Clay laughed. "Is that what this is about? Chip and I were kids when that happened."

"But your father wasn't," Greer smiled. "The sins of the father."

Clay sat back, defeated. Staring at the anger in Greer's eyes, he realized that this coup had been long planned by Greer, right down to those notes tacked to Chip's porch. He also realized there was no new LaPointe lawsuit. Greer had made it up. He and Chip had been played.

§

White was zipping through her half of the preliminary paperwork. Gramm, who hated paperwork, was trudging through his part. She wondered out loud why Chip Campbell kept saying Peters as he was coming out of the coma.

"He wanted to tell Peters that Mason was the one who attacked him," Preston said. "Talked with his wife this morning." Preston had her own problems. She had to write an explanation detailing the need to destroy a perfectly good motorcycle, plus fill out a safety report. White told her to prepare for a stern lecture from the department's safety officer.

"What's the status of Jimmy Pleski?" White yelled out to Gramm.

He came out of his office, stretching out his neck and back. "He's charged with assault and robbery for the attack on Kayla. He's going to spend his summer in jail."

Preston looked up. "According to my calculations, Kayla should end up with about five grand for her puzzle piece. I wonder what she'll spend it on?"

"Maybe a new knife," White joked.

"Is that what everyone gets, five grand?" Gramm asked.

"Five grand per piece. We have assumed that was the going rate for buying pieces, so the Campbell family and Brandon basically get their money back," Preston said.

"Pity," White added.

"But Charlotte Lane, Ben Heikkinen, and Darian get five grand each. The one question is, what about Ham's piece? The real one."

"It should go to his heirs, if he has any," White said. "The Campbells thought they bought the piece, but Mason just pocketed the money. He took the genuine piece, killed Ham, and left the phony. It may be up to the courts, but I think the actual piece still belongs to Gilbert."

Gramm returned to his office. Preston followed. "This safety officer thing? Is that a big deal?"

Gramm sighed as he sat down. "I'm afraid it is. You took a motorcycle through trees, up over a mound, and into a suspect. That's a lot of risk."

"Do you know the safety officer?"

"I do," Gramm said, shaking his head. "I'm afraid it won't be pleasant."

Preston felt a chill go up her back. She turned around to see White standing in the doorway. "So, Officer Preston, do you want to do this safety lecture here or at your desk?"

"You're the safety officer?"

"I am," White smiled. "The job gives me a few extra bucks and I get to lecture people about acceptable risk. I have to admit, your case is something special. Only Milo playing chicken with an airplane tops it."

§

Zeke watched the construction crew put the finishing touches on his newly lighted sign. After some negotiation, Creedence had agreed to adding the word *soup,* so the sign now read, *Ellen's Soup Kitchen*. This was the first time the facility had a professionally lighted sign. Zeke was proud.

"Nice sign," said Mosley—a long time kitchen customer—as he walked by Zeke and entered the facility. Mosley liked to get there early before the crowds, so he could get his favorite spot. Gloria was directing the volunteers who were placing the enormous pans of food on a long table. Zeke came in and was pleased to see the progress.

"The sign's up. We have officially changed our name. We are now Ellen's Soup Kitchen," Zeke said.

Mosley perked up. "Is Ellen back?" he asked.

Zeke and Gloria stopped what they were doing and stared at him. "Ellen who?" Zeke asked.

"Whaddaya mean? It's your sign. I'm just wondering if Ellen is back. She could really cook! No offense, Gloria."

"None taken if you tell us who Ellen is," Gloria said.

Mosley ran a wrinkled hand through his long gray hair. "I get confused. It was a while ago. Ellen would come in once a month and cook. I just remember her lasagna—so cheesy." He laughed.

The line was beginning to form. Gloria left to help.

Mosley continued, "She had a son, little kid. He would come by with desserts. His name was…ahh, Marvin, Melvin, I don't remember." Mosley stopped talking.

Zeke got up and brought the broom and dustpan to the back room.

"Milo!" Mosley shouted. "That was it. The kid's name was Milo!"

The volunteers were serving, people were eating, Gloria and Zeke were busy—no one heard. Mosley began to eat his soup and thought no more about it.

CLUES, CASH, PIECES OF MURDER

If you wish to contact the authors, email us at authors@dbelrogg.com or leave a message at www.dbelrogg.com.

BOOKS BY D.B. ELROGG